W9-COG-899

FIC   TAL

RELEASED FROM CIRCULATION

WAYNE PUBLIC LIBRARY
3737 S. WAYNE ROAD
WAYNE, MI 48184-1697
734-721-7832
JUN   2010

Tales from Grace Chapel Inn

Something Old, Something New

Jane Orcutt

∞

Guideposts

NEW YORK, NEW YORK

Tales from Grace Chapel Inn is a registered trademark of Guideposts.

Copyright © 2004 by Guideposts. All rights reserved.

No part of this publication may be reproduced, stored in a
retrieval system or transmitted, in any form or by any means,
electronic, mechanical, photocopying, recording or otherwise
without the written permission of the publisher. Inquiries
should be addressed to the Rights & Permissions Department,
Guideposts, 16 E. 34th St., New York, NY 10016.

The characters and events in this book are fictional,
and any resemblance to actual persons or events is coincidental.

Acknowledgments

All Scripture quotations, unless otherwise noted, are
taken from *The King James Version of the Bible.*

Scripture quotations marked (NIV) are taken from
The Holy Bible, New International Version. Copyright © 1973,
1978, 1984 International Bible Society. Used by permission
of Zondervan Bible Publishers.

Published in association with the literary agency of Janet Kobobel
Grant, Books & Such, 4788 Carissa Avenue, Santa Rosa, CA 95405.

www.guideposts.com
(800) 932-2145
Guideposts Books & Inspirational Media
Series Editors: Regina Hersey and Leo Grant
Cover art by Edgar Jerins
Cover design by Wendy Bass
Interior design by Cindy LaBreacht
Typeset by Planet Patti Inc. & Nancy Tardi
Printed in the United States of America

WAYNE PUBLIC LIBRARY   3 9082 11598 5163
3737 S. WAYNE ROAD
WAYNE, MI 48184-1697
734-721-7832

Chapter One

"Whew!" Jane Howard flopped into a chair in Grace Chapel Inn's kitchen. She set a bucket of cleaning supplies beside her and then swiped at her forehead with the back of a hand. The red bandana she had wrapped around her long, brown hair was damp with perspiration, and her fair skin was flushed. "I'm glad that's the last bathroom I had to clean."

"I'm not too fond of the day after Labor Day myself," her sister Louise said, her tall frame filling another kitchen chair. Louise Howard Smith peeled off cleaning gloves and dropped a rag into her own bucket, which held wood soap and polish. "I love the holiday business, but it certainly makes for 'busyness' of our own." She ran a hand through her short silver hair.

"It looks like it will be another active fall season, too," Alice, the third Howard sister, said. "We have a lot of guests coming soon to see the autumn leaves. I'm afraid that we can look forward to many more of these cleaning sessions in the weeks ahead. Our weeks are free so far, but all the weekends are booked into winter."

Jane groaned. "Sometimes I wish we didn't get such good reviews." She tucked a strand of hair behind her ear. "Alice, did you pull the bed sheets from all the guest rooms?"

Her sister nodded. "They're already in the laundry room, with the first load in the washing machine."

Despite their fatigue, the Howard sisters were thankful that the inn they ran out of their Victorian home was flourishing.

Louise stifled a yawn. "Between your wonderful lunch, Jane, and the housework, I could use a nap."

"Maybe a short rest would be the best thing for all of us," Alice said, ever the practical nurse, "though I'm not sure how we're going to make it through this busy season if we have to take regular naps. I was lucky to switch shifts with someone else at the hospital, but I have to go back to my regular shift. I won't be here next Monday to help out after the weekend."

Jane sat up straight, and then smacked her forehead lightly. "Why didn't I think of it before?"

"What?" Louise stifled another yawn.

"Why don't we hire someone to help us with the cleaning? At least on Mondays."

"Do we really want to use our profits to do that?" Louise said, frowning. Since she and her sisters had opened Grace Chapel Inn, Louise handled most of the bed and breakfast's business affairs. She usually worried more about the bottom line than her younger sisters did.

"Do we really want to be tired all during autumn? Wouldn't it be nice to have a little more time to spend on pursuits other than cleaning bathrooms?"

"Or changing linens?" Alice grinned. "I'm certainly willing to look into it, Jane. What do you think, Louise?"

"Well . . ." Louise looked as though she were running an adding machine in her head. "I suppose it would be a time-saver."

"And save some aching bones," Jane said, rubbing her back with exaggeration. She winked at Alice, who smiled, not taken in by Jane's drama. At age fifty, Jane was the youngest and fittest of the three sisters, partially because she made it a point to jog regularly. Alice Howard found walking more to her liking, perhaps because she was twelve years older.

Jane popped up from her chair with new vigor after Louise's acquiescence. "I'm going to put some water on for tea, but then we need to discuss something."

"You don't want us to hire a new chef, too, do you?" Louise said. Jane, the inn's resident chef, had cooked at a famous restaurant in San Francisco before she returned home to Acorn Hill and opened the inn with her sisters.

"As if you could get rid of me." Jane laughed, setting the teakettle on the stove. She took out three mugs and a canister from the cupboard. "No, I wanted to talk about our next guest, Portia Keyes."

"She's due in Thursday, if I recall correctly." Louise slipped on her wire-rimmed glasses, fastened to a chain around her neck. She looked as though she was ready to consult their booking schedule, which was actually in its accustomed spot on the reception desk under the stairs.

"She should arrive around noon," Jane said.

"She requested a room with a private bath, so I scheduled her for the Garden Room," Louise said. Then turning to Alice, who had been at the hospital when the reservation was made, she explained, "Her secretary made the arrangements. She requested full board, and Jane agreed that we could provide it as a special service. She will be here throughout September and perhaps into October."

"Goodness," Alice said, "that will be unusual."

"She's coming here to work. She's a writer," Jane said.

"A *romance* writer," Louise added.

The kettle whistled, and Jane poured hot water into a

teapot. She placed the pot and three mugs on a tray and carried them to the table. Then she retrieved a plate of pumpkin muffins and joined her sisters.

Alice poured the tea and then sipped hers thoughtfully. "Are her books like those you see in the grocery stores? The ones with the covers of a man and a woman in a, ah, a . . ."

"Clinch, I believe they call it," Jane said, smiling.

Alice blushed. "I was going to say *hug*."

"I saw a national news program about a romance writer once," Jane said. "She'd written like, oh, fifty books. Everything she wore was pink and white. And I think she wore some feathery stuff, too."

"You mean a feather boa?" Louise said.

Jane laughed. "Yes. That always makes me think of a snake with feathers."

"I'm sure she's perfectly nice," Louise said.

"No doubt," Jane said, pushing back from the table. She put her mug on the table and reached for the bucket of cleaning supplies. "I'm going to put these away and then get out my new cookbook. I found an interesting recipe for pot roast, which is what I'm making for dinner tonight as a reward for all our hard work."

"And I think I'll take a walk," Alice said. "Maybe the fresh air will help me think of someone we can hire to clean for us."

"And I," Louise said, stifling a yawn with her lace-edged handkerchief, "will take a nap."

Alice decided to walk toward town. She left through the back door and walked a path to Acorn Avenue. Although summer still reigned, with grass, tree leaves and shrubs still green, soon, she knew, green would give way to the browns, golds and reds of autumn. As much as she loved the cooler weather, its coming always made her a trifle sad for a day or two. Winter was coming soon, and its harsher weather often limited the town's activities.

Right now, however, she felt snug and happy walking through Acorn Hill, her hometown. Passing Sylvia's Buttons, Alice waved at Sylvia Songer, the owner. She was reworking a window display for the fall season. She had draped an autumn-colored afghan over a rocking chair and was arranging a basket of polished, red apples and pots of yellow and rust mums amid lengths of her new fall fabrics. Alice thought about going inside for a chat but then decided against it. She did not want to disturb Sylvia's creativity.

Alice turned right onto Hill Street and passed Good Apple Bakery and the Acorn Antique Shop. After that was the Coffee Shop. Through the window, she could see Hope Collins chatting with a customer.

As she walked the streets of Acorn Hill, Alice thought about how they could find someone to do cleaning once a week at Grace Chapel Inn. A high school girl might be their best option.

Alice racked her brain. She worked with a group of middle-school girls, the ANGELs, who met on Wednesday evenings during midweek worship service. She used a theme-based lesson every week, and they often did crafts and helped with church events. Alice loved each one of her girls, but they were too young to help with the cleaning demands of Grace Chapel Inn. Perhaps one of them had an older sister who might want the job.

Crossing Chapel Road, Alice came upon Fred Humbert, the owner of Fred's Hardware, sweeping in front of his store. He paused at his work to give her a jaunty wave. "Hi,

Alice." He leaned on the broom and grinned. "Are you and your sisters taking a break today after your busy holiday weekend?"

Alice laughed. "It *was* a busy weekend. We were completely booked, and it seems like we spent a lot of time talking with our guests or pointing them toward various activities. We've just finished cleaning up, now that all the guests have gone home. Did you and Vera have a busy weekend?"

Fred shook his head. "I really didn't. The hardware store was quiet, and of course, I was closed yesterday. But Vera's been busy. School starts next Monday. She's over at her classroom right now. She's getting started on her bulletin board displays and organizing books."

"She has a full plate most of the time, but especially this time of year. Getting settled with a new class must be difficult."

"It is. I don't know how she does it, year after year. It was the perfect job when our girls were young. It allowed her to keep the same schedule as theirs. When they were off on school holidays, she was off, too. Now that Polly and Jean are in college, you'd think she'd slow down a bit."

"Does she ever talk about retiring?" Alice said.

Fred laughed. "Vera retire? You're more likely to get Mayor Tynan to leave office. That woman loves those students. She's a natural-born teacher. She keeps up with her kids well after they've moved on to middle school, then high school. Like you do with your ANGELs after they've outgrown your group, Alice."

Alice thought about this for a moment. "Jane and Louise and I were talking about hiring someone to do some cleaning for us once a week," Alice said. "Just to get us through the busy season. Do you think Vera would know a high school girl who might be interested?"

"I can certainly ask her. Or you might consider putting an ad in the *Acorn Nutshell*. If you talk to Carlene today, she might be able to put the notice in this Wednesday's issue."

"I suppose so." Alice furrowed her brow. "It would make sense for me to stop by Carlene's while I'm in town. I'm almost positive that Jane and Louise will agree, but I hate to act without consulting them first." She sighed. "Sometimes I wish I had the courage to join the modern age and get a cell phone, Fred."

He laughed. "I hear they do come in handy. Meanwhile, you're welcome to use the store's phone." He gestured toward the open door of his store.

Alice smiled gratefully and stepped inside.

Louise had already awakened from her nap before Alice phoned. She and Jane thought the ad was a wonderful idea and gave Alice their blessing to take out a small notice in the *Nutshell*. Jane helped to compose the wording over the phone, and Alice headed for the newspaper office, next to the post office.

The local newspaper was published in a small brown brick building that had been home to the *Acorn Nutshell* since its inception over ninety years before. Carlene Moss frequently talked about trying to get a Pennsylvania historical designation for the building, but never seemed to find the time to fill out the application. At one time, the building had used a letterpress printing press and Linotype, then later, offset printing equipment. With the advent of cold type, then desktop publishing, the outdated printing and typesetting equipment had been pushed to the back of the one-room building to collect dust.

Carlene now laid out the newspaper using a desktop

publishing program, then e-mailed it to a Potterston printer, who delivered each weekly edition to Carlene for distribution.

Alice opened the frosted glass front door, pausing to admire the gilt-edged black letters that spelled out *Acorn Nutshell* in old-style type. She remembered coming to the building for field trips as a child. She knew that Vera Humbert still brought her fifth-grade class here once a year to see not only how Carlene currently published the weekly paper but also how the aging press and Linotype machine had been used. Carlene still knew how to operate the old typesetting equipment. She had learned the job from her father, who had started at the *Nutshell* as a copy boy, then graduated to chief typesetter, a position he had held for sixty years until his death. For visitors, especially for school field trips, Carlene would set their names in metal type, called a slug, as a souvenir. Children loved to see their name backward in the raised metal. Alice still had the slug that she had received over fifty years ago.

When she heard the door open, Carlene peered around her large flat-screen computer monitor. Her ample L-shaped desk was covered with pages of printed copy, dictionaries, stylebooks, almanacs, a terra-cotta pot filled with English ivy, and a small aquarium that glittered with freshwater fish.

Carlene smiled, a dimple showing in each cheek. Her coarse, medium-brown hair, flecked with strands of gray, was pulled back in a short ponytail. Carlene was in her mid-fifties and, like Alice, had never married.

"Hi, Alice. What brings you here?"

"Business for the *Nutshell*." Alice smiled back. "My sisters and I want to take out an ad."

Carlene raised her eyebrows. "Not personal ads, I hope."

Alice laughed. "No, not today. We need to find a high school girl to help us out with cleaning at the inn. We thought that taking out an ad in the *Nutshell* would be the best way to find someone."

"Can't argue with you there," Carlene said, picking up a pen and pad of paper. "Tell me what you'd like to say, and I'll squeeze it into this week's issue. I was just getting ready to e-mail it over to the printer, but I had some white space that your ad should fill nicely."

Alice gave her the information, reading from a scrap of paper on which she had written the words Jane suggested. As Carlene typed them into her computer, Alice said a quick prayer.

Please bring us the girl who can best help us with our cleaning needs, but more importantly, whom we can somehow help in return.

After Carlene finished typing the ad, she showed it to Alice for approval. "It looks fine," Alice said.

"I'll run it tomorrow, then," Carlene said. "And remember, if you ever come across anything you think might make an interesting story, let me know."

Alice thought about the famous guest that Grace Chapel Inn was soon to host but decided to keep the information to herself for now.

After Alice's phone call, Louise decided to take a walk too. Even after resting, her joints felt a little creaky, and she hoped that a bit of gentle exercise would loosen them up. She decided to stop in at the Nine Lives Bookstore to see if Viola Reed knew anything about the romance writer Portia Keyes.

As she approached the small, red-roofed building, Louise saw Hope Collins' friend, Betsy Long. Betsy sat outside the bookstore on its wrought iron bench, engrossed in a copy of

Jane Austen's *Emma*. A Nine Lives plastic bag lay on the bench beside her. When Louise said hello, she glanced up briefly. "I watched the best movie last night, and Viola told me that it was based on this book."

Louise smiled. "I have not read that book in a long time, but it is wonderful. I always liked Jane Austen's novels."

"You mean she's written other books?" Betsy shook her head. "If I like this one, I'll have to check with Viola for more. I just had to stop right here and start the book, to see how close it is to the movie."

"I will leave you to your reading then," Louise said. "Good day, Betsy."

Betsy waved a short reply, already absorbed in the book.

Louise pushed open the beveled glass door and heard the familiar sound of the shop's bell. Portraits of famous authors, including Dickens, Shakespeare and Twain, lined the pale taupe walls above the pine bookcases. Viola was standing on a short stepladder, dusting the upper shelves in the biography section, and she smiled when she saw Louise.

"How nice to see you," Viola said. She set down her rag and descended the stepladder. Heavyset, she huffed a little as she reached the floor. The bookseller wore one of her trademark large, colorful scarves. Today it was a splashy lime-green, yellow and pink silk square draped around the neckline of an equally bright lime-green dress.

"It is good to see you too, Viola. Did you have a good holiday weekend?"

"Very nice," Viola said. "The store was busier than usual with the holiday traffic. Then I got in a shipment of new books and found one on contemporary European politics that kept me riveted all weekend. Each evening I left the shop and headed home, then found myself reading until nearly ten o'clock." She paused to adjust her bifocals. "I suppose you and your sisters were busy too."

"Very much so," Louise said. "In fact, we are looking into hiring some cleaning help. With the autumn tourist season already upon us, we thought perhaps a high school girl could help us with the extra work."

"If you find someone good, let me know. I could probably use some help myself." Viola glanced distastefully at the dusty upper bookshelves. "Are you here to check out my latest shipment of books? I received a new biography of C. S. Lewis. I'm afraid it's still in the shipping box, however. I just got it in this morning."

"I won't trouble you then," Louise said. "I can always come back another day. What I am really interested in is whether you have any books by the author Portia Keyes."

Viola furrowed her brow. "Portia Keyes. Portia Keyes. I'm not sure I'm familiar with that name. Let's check the computer."

Viola moved to the checkout stand, where she kept the cash register and her computer. She gently removed the orange marmalade cat, Harry, from a stack of papers, and started typing on the keyboard. Louise stood on the other side of the counter and waited patiently.

Viola stopped typing and waited, consulting the screen. "Portia Keyes. It says she's a romance novelist, author of more than fifty books."

"That's a lot of writing," Louise said.

Viola sniffed. "How hard can it be to write romance novels? Man meets woman, man loves woman, man loses woman, love conquers all, the end. After a generous sprinkling of intimate scenes, of course." She peered down her nose at Louise through her bifocals. "Why the interest in Portia Keyes?"

Louise paused, and then decided she couldn't be secretive with Viola. "She's booked at Grace Chapel Inn through September, and she arrives Thursday. I thought it would be nice to see one of her books in advance."

"Louise Howard Smith, don't tell me you're actually interested in *reading* that stuff?"

"Not really," Louise said. Louise was an avid reader of nonfiction, particularly esoteric material on religion, and Viola Reed knew it. "I only wondered if you knew anything about our soon-to-be guest."

Viola shook her head. "I've never heard of her, but then you know I don't keep much contemporary fiction in this store. Especially romance novels," she said, with a touch of pride in her voice.

"I know." Louise sighed. "Well, it was worth a try."

"Wait a minute," Viola said, tapping the keyboard again. "There. I knew it. Look."

She turned the monitor around so that Louise could see. There on the screen was a photo with *Portia Keyes* captioned underneath. To the side of the photo was a two-paragraph biography of the author.

Louise scanned the text, glanced at the photo, and then reread the text. "Oh my."

Viola folded her arms, looking smug. "I think you Howard sisters are going to have your hands full."

Jane squinted at the copy of the computer page that Louise had brought home with her. "I think that Portia Keyes looks like an interesting person. I like that royal-blue dress she's wearing."

"It seems well off the shoulder," Louise said, "and rather, *er*, low cut."

"Her hair looks nice," Alice offered, trying to find something positive to add to the conversation. "All those blond curls swept up on top of her head."

"I'll bet she had to use a whole canister of hair spray," Jane said, grinning.

Louise sighed. "Well, if looks were not enough to warn us, her author biography is. Did you read her comments? 'Love, in all forms, is the answer to life's problems.' And how about this one: 'A chocolate a day keeps a woman's depression away.'"

"What's wrong with that attitude?" Jane shrugged. "I like a good chocolate myself. Boy oh boy, if that's her attitude, wait till she tastes my truffles."

"Your truffles are lovely," Alice said, touching Jane's arm. "And I'm sure our guest will appreciate them. It's just that—"

"She sounds like that romance writer you saw on the news program," Louise cut in, "writing romance books and eating bonbons for breakfast."

"So what if she likes a little chocolate?" Jane asked. "As far as what she writes or believes, as long she doesn't make us read it or believe it too, I guess it's none of our business."

"I guess you're right," Alice said, shaking her head.

Chapter Two

On Wednesday, the ad for cleaning help ran in the *Acorn Nutshell*. At seven thirty on Thursday morning, the doorbell at Grace Chapel Inn sounded.

The sisters were eating breakfast in the kitchen. "You don't suppose that's Portia Keyes, do you?" Jane said, looking up from her scrambled eggs.

"She's not due in until noon," Louise said.

The doorbell chimed again.

"Whoever it is is in a hurry," Alice said, laying her napkin aside as she rose from the table to head for the front door.

Since she was scheduled to work that day at the Potterston Hospital, she was dressed in her nurse's uniform. She straightened the waistband and touched her hair briefly before opening the front door.

Standing on the porch was a young woman clutching the *Nutshell*. Her bright-blue eyes pleaded hopefully under a lengthy thatch of bleached blond bangs, which looked too long for her chin-length hair. She wore a short red T-shirt that didn't quite meet the band of a pair of hip-hugger blue jeans.

"Are you looking for a maid?" she asked, without preamble. She pointed at the ad in the newspaper.

"We're looking for someone to help us with cleaning," Alice said, smiling. She didn't know this girl's name, but her face looked vaguely familiar. "Are you interested in the position?"

"Oh yes, ma'am, Miss Howard," the girl said. "I just wanted to stop by and ask if you could please not fill the position until I've had a chance to talk to you about it. I have to catch a ride to school, and I'm already late as it is. Would it be all right if I came by this afternoon to talk to you? Maybe we can catch up on things a bit, too."

"That would be fine," Alice said, slightly confused. *Do I know this girl?* "I'm confident we won't fill the position before then, and now that I know you're interested, we'll definitely give you a chance to talk to us."

"Oh, thank you." The girl blew out a long breath, which sent her bleached bangs whirling.

A car parked at the curb honked, and she yelled over her shoulder, "I'm coming," before turning back to Alice. "Thanks again, Miss Howard. I'll dash over just as soon as I get finished with school."

Without waiting for an answer or allowing Alice to learn her name, the girl bounded down the path toward the car. Alice stared after her, long after the car had driven away, trying to place the girl's face. She was not one of Alice's former ANGELs. Alice remembered the former members of her church girls' club, even those who were now grown women.

"Who was at the door?" Louise said, when Alice returned to the kitchen.

"I'm not sure," Alice said.

"I'm guessing it wasn't Portia Keyes," Jane said. "There. That's my guess for twenty questions. Louise, do you want to take one?"

Alice smiled at her younger sister's teasing. "No, it wasn't Portia Keyes. It was a high-school girl who inquired about the cleaning position. She said that she was on her way to school, but she wanted to make sure we hadn't filled the position. I told her we hadn't, and she said she'd be by this afternoon to talk to us about it."

"Wonderful," Louise said, setting her cup down into its saucer, "but why do you look concerned, Alice?"

"The girl seemed to know me," Alice said, "but for the life of me, I couldn't place her face. I know she was not one of my ANGELs."

Jane put a loving arm around her older sister. "Maybe one of us will recognize her when she comes back this afternoon."

"Yoo hoo!" The back door opened, and the sisters' aunt, Ethel Buckley, entered the kitchen. Ethel lived in the carriage house across the way. "Well! I'm surprised to find you ladies still at your breakfast. It's already past seven-thirty."

"Is there something special we should be doing, Aunt Ethel?" Alice said.

"*Special?*" Ethel looked taken aback that Alice should even ask. "Of course you should be doing something special. It isn't every day that you have a famous writer in your inn."

"Sit down, Aunt Ethel," Jane said, waving the teapot. "I've got some tea left over, and some English muffins. Would you like one with jam? It's homemade."

"Well . . ." Ethel wavered, then sat down. "Don't mind if I do."

She smiled at Jane, who set a plate in front of her, with an English muffin, butter and a thick dollop of strawberry jam. "Thank you, dear."

After allowing her aunt a decent amount of time to chew and swallow, Louise leaned forward. "Tell us what you know about Portia Keyes, Aunt Ethel."

"*Mfff,*" Ethel said, gesticulating as she struggled to swallow the last of her muffin. She smiled in appreciation at Jane, who poured more tea for her aunt and then sat at the table.

The sisters waited expectantly. Ethel sipped her tea, returned the cup to the saucer, and then glanced up to find her nieces staring at her. "What? Is something wrong?" She brushed her napkin across her lips. "Do I have something on my face?"

"We're surprised that you know about Portia Keyes," Alice said.

"Viola Reed let the news of her visit slip out," Ethel said. "Don't blame her. It's a small town, and eventually one hears things. Though I'm hurt that you girls didn't share your big news with me first."

"What big news?" Louise said.

"Why, that Portia Keyes is staying here, of course."

Jane groaned. "Auntie, I feel like we're going in circles. I take it, then, that you've heard of Portia Keyes?"

"Of course I've heard of her. She's only the best romance writer of all time."

The sisters looked at each other. Jane had to cover her grin by sipping from her coffee cup. Louise turned to her aunt. "Have you read any of her novels, Aunt Ethel?"

"Every single one. Oh, I know that stubborn Viola Reed won't carry what she considers trashy novels in her bookstore, but I buy Portia's books over in Potterston. If I can't find them at the supermarket, I get them at the bookstore there. *They* don't have a problem stocking good books."

Jane set down her cup, her lips still twitching. "Do you like the romance parts?"

"Of course. That's the best part." Ethel smiled, then looked from each one of her nieces to the other. "What's wrong with you girls? Portia Keyes is a wonderful author, my favorite. I came over here hoping to meet her, and you act as if I'm talking about a serial killer."

Alice touched her aunt's arm. "Portia Keyes hasn't arrived yet. She won't be here until at least noon. Perhaps we can arrange a meeting between you and her ... if she's agreeable, that is."

"Why wouldn't she be? I'm probably her biggest fan."

"Yes, well, but her secretary said that she was coming here specifically for the peace and quiet of our small town, so that she can get some writing done," Louise said. "We wouldn't want to disturb her creativity. She has come here to get away from the distractions of home."

"Yes, Auntie. She does have all those love scenes to write," Jane said, with as near a straight face as she could muster.

Louise glanced at her youngest sister sharply. "Perhaps you could give our guest a day to settle in, Aunt Ethel. Maybe tomorrow would be a better time."

Ethel looked crestfallen. "I suppose that would be best," she said, and then brightened. "I had hoped to get her some sunflowers, anyway. They're her favorite flowers, the romance reader magazine says." She rose and headed for the back door. "I guess I'll head out to Wild Things and see if Craig has any in stock. Thanks for the breakfast, Jane. Toodle-oo, girls."

When they heard the door close behind her, the sisters looked at each other, and then burst into laughter. Jane had tears running from her eyes, and even Louise, the most sedate sister, could not stop laughing. She pulled a handkerchief from her skirt pocket and wiped her eyes.

"Wh-what was *that* all about?" Jane said, finally recovering. "Who knew that Aunt Ethel was a closet romance reader?"

"I don't think there's any closet involved," Alice said. "She doesn't seem to hide what she reads. It just never came up in conversation."

"It is not the sort of discussion you have at a church board meeting," Louise said. "Do you suppose Florence Simpson reads such books too?"

"I suppose a lot of women read these books," Jane said. She thought for a moment, then added, "I can't say I'd blame them. I've read a romance novel or two in my life, and they're quite fun."

"Jane!" Louise and Alice said in unison.

"What's so bad about love stories?" Jane said. "Everybody likes a book with a happy ending."

"But are they not called *bodice rippers*?" Louise said. "With good reason, I understand."

Jane shrugged. "Maybe you can ask Portia Keyes about that when she arrives."

"Or Aunt Ethel," Alice said, smiling.

The three sisters burst into laughter again.

Alice headed off to her shift at Potterston Hospital, and soon Jane was bustling in the kitchen, preparing Parmesan pork chops for dinner and a strawberry cheesecake for dessert.

It was eleven thirty, still thirty minutes from the time Portia said she would arrive, so Louise settled herself at the piano in the parlor. She liked to practice particularly difficult pieces, which required her utmost concentration, when the house was quiet. She had plunged into a Rachmaninoff concerto and was totally immersed in the music when she had the strangest sensation that someone was in the parlor with her.

Unnerved, she pulled her hands from the keyboard, mid-arpeggio, and turned. Standing in the doorway was a small, elderly, white-haired woman wearing a light denim skirt, matching vest and red shirt. Her smile was warm and engaging. "Please don't let me stop you. That was lovely."

Louise rose from the piano bench, confused. "May I help you?" She wondered if the stranger was a saleswoman of some sort.

The woman moved forward, extending her hand. "I'm Ada Murdoch. It's so nice to meet you. You must be one of the Howard sisters."

Louise automatically shook her hand. "I am Louise Howard Smith." She paused, cocking her head. "Is there something I can help you with?"

"Oh dear." The woman frowned. "My secretary is usually so efficient about these things. I'm supposed to have a reservation for today."

Louise felt a twinge of panic. Had one of the sisters neglected to write down this guest's name? Never before had they run into any reservation snags at Grace Chapel Inn. Then she calmed herself. Except for the Garden Room, all the other guest rooms were available—at least until the weekend. "There is no problem for now. We have room for you, but I am afraid only until the weekend. I am so sorry. Perhaps the scheduling problem is at our end. Let me check the book. Please follow me."

She bustled out of the room and to the desk area under the stairs, where she withdrew the schedule.

"My secretary's been in a bit of a muddle with a family illness lately," Ada said. "Perhaps she didn't confirm my reservation."

Louise sighed, pointing at the day's date. "As you can see, we only have one person scheduled to arrive today."

Ada looked at the paper and smiled. "But there I am. I'm so relieved there wasn't a mix-up. I'd be crushed if I couldn't stay at your inn. I've heard so many charming things about it."

Louise did a double take, first looking at the schedule, and then at the woman. "Are *you* Portia Keyes?"

"Guilty," Ada said, laughing. "I'm a bit early. It's a bad habit of mine, being too early. And I had hoped that Julie scheduled me under my real name. I wanted to keep this trip low-key, without a lot of fuss, so that I could get some writing done."

Louise glanced at the famous author. Portia Keyes, or rather, Ada Murdoch, certainly did not look anything like the Howard sisters had imagined. Instead of a designer dress, or even a sophisticated business suit, the woman's grandmotherly denim outfit looked rather like it might have come from a discount store.

"You don't recognize me from my book jacket photo," Ada said with a twinkle in her eye.

"Well . . ."

Ada laughed. "That glamour photo is at least twenty years old, and didn't look much like me even then, but it still helps to sell books."

"Well, despite this lapse, I assure you that we will do our best to accommodate you, and I welcome you to our home," Louise said, recovering long enough to remember her hostess duties. "Here is a registration paper," she said, pulling out the customary form for guests. "If you will just fill it out . . . name address, that sort of vital information. And I assume you drove here."

"Yes, I did." Portia smiled. "I parked in the lot just over there beyond the house. Is that the correct location?"

Louise nodded, poising a pen over one of the registration

papers. "I will need the year, make, and model of your auto. License plate number, as well, if you know it. For insurance purposes, of course."

"Of course," Portia said, and then rattled off the make and model of a five-year-old American sport utility vehicle.

"A rental car?" Louise asked.

"Nope. The old girl's mine."

Louise filled in the car data, then turned the registration card around so that Portia could add the rest of the necessary information.

A five-year-old SUV? How odd. Louise would have expected someone famous, particularly a romance writer, to drive something more luxurious.

"What I've seen so far of your inn is lovely," Ada said, handing over the completed forms. "Your brochure said that this was your family home, correct?

"Yes, it was built in the late nineteenth century. Our mother died some fifty years ago, and we turned it into a bed and breakfast after our father passed on recently. My sister Alice is at work, and she is a nurse at a nearby hospital, but my sister Jane is in the kitchen. I am sure that you would like to get settled in your room. Then I would be delighted to introduce you, Portia, er—"

"Please call me Ada." She smiled. "Yes, I'd like to get my bag and laptop upstairs and freshen up a bit. After that I'd love to meet your sister and have a look around your inn."

Louise helped Ada upstairs, ushering her into the Garden Room. Ada oohed and ahhed over the soothing green paint and floral border and the rosewood furniture. "I'll feel quite at home here, I'm sure," she said.

Louise also showed her the private bath and pointed out the Do Not Disturb sign. "Feel free to use this when you are at work," Louise said. "That is, if you plan to work in your room, of course. You are also welcome to use the library."

Ada said that she was not sure where she would work, but that she was certain she would enjoy her surroundings.

Louise left her to settle in, then headed for the kitchen. Jane was just setting a springform pan into a rectangular pan of water and popping it into the oven.

"Whew, now I can concentrate on the main course," she said, shutting the door. "I heard you playing the piano, Louise. It was good background music for my cooking. Did something happen? You stopped quite a while ago."

"Our guest arrived."

"Portia Keyes? I thought she wasn't supposed to get here until noon."

"She was early." Louise said, shrugging. "She is upstairs getting settled in and then she would like to take a quick tour of our inn. And meet you, of course."

Jane dusted her hands on her apron. "Is she wearing a slinky dress? Does she have on a ton of makeup and expensive jewelry?" She squinted. "She doesn't have one of those little froufrou dogs with her, does she? She knows we don't allow pets, right?"

Louise held up her hands. "My goodness, Jane. No, she did not bring a dog. Truthfully, she is not at all the woman we imagined. I don't think we will have to resort to such measures," Louise said. "She is rather . . . normal."

Louise started to tell Jane that Portia Keyes was really Ada Murdoch, and then decided that perhaps their famous guest might want to reveal the truth about her *nom de plume* herself. Fortunately, Jane commented that it was nearly time for lunch and that she had better get it started. An hour passed, and still Ada had not descended. Louise went upstairs to invite her to dine with them, but the DO NOT DISTURB sign was hanging on the doorknob. She heard the distinct *tap-tap-tap* of computer keys and decided that Ada had plunged into her work.

Much to her disappointment, Jane learned that she would have to meet their mysterious guest later.

⚭

Alice had almost forgotten about the other visitor at the inn that day, until shortly after she arrived home from the hospital and the high-school girl with the bleached-blond hair and exposed waistline showed up at the door.

"You haven't filled the cleaning position yet, have you?" she asked, breathless and looking hopeful.

"No, dear. No one's even inquired about the position." Alice stepped back from the door. "Please come inside and let me call my sisters. I'm sure they'd like to talk to you."

"Thank you, Miss Howard."

Alice ushered her to the parlor and rounded up Louise and Jane. "The high-school girl is back," she said.

"Did you figure out where you knew her from?" Jane said.

Alice shook her head. "How could I tactfully ask?"

The girl was seated on one of the Victorian Eastlake chairs, reaching for a mint in one of the silver hospitality dishes. When she saw the sisters, she guiltily pulled her hand away. "I'm sorry. I didn't get any lunch today, and these looked so good."

"No lunch?" Jane clucked her tongue. "We have lots of leftovers in the kitchen. We can talk as well in there as in this formal room."

Alice and Louise readily trailed after Jane, who already had her arm around the girl and was leading her toward the kitchen.

The girl took one look at the black-and-white checkerboard floor tiles, warm red cabinets, butcher block counters and smiled. "It looks so cozy here."

"It is," Jane agreed. "I can't cook well if my surroundings don't feel right. We redecorated the entire house once we decided to open it as a bed and breakfast."

"What I've seen so far is fantastic," the girl said.

Jane bustled to the refrigerator to find a suitable lunch. Alice gestured at the table, and the girl seated herself on the edge of a chair. She blew at her bangs, and Alice saw that her eyes were heavily made up with black eyeliner and mascara.

For some reason, she reminded Alice of a lost lamb. Gentle honesty seemed to be the best way to converse with this girl, so Alice plunged ahead with her admission. "I'm sure we've met somewhere, but I can't remember. What is your name?"

"Oh, I shouldn't have expected you to remember me, Miss Howard. My name's Martina Beckett. A year ago my mother was a patient of yours at Potterston Hospital. We lived in Potterston until a few weeks ago. My dad couldn't take living in the house there anymore. He said it reminded him too much of Mom, so we moved to Acorn Hill."

"Your mother was Sandra Beckett, wasn't she?" Alice laid her hand over Martina's. "She had ovarian cancer."

Martina nodded, her eyes filling briefly with tears. She sniffled, and then smiled faintly. "You remember."

"Of course I do." Alice squeezed her hand. "She was a brave woman, and she spoke about you often. I only met you a time or two, as I came into the room. I'm sorry that I didn't stop to chat, but I didn't want to intrude on your time with her."

"You probably don't recognize me because I hadn't dyed my hair then. It was brown. Daddy raved about your care for Mom. That's why when I saw your ad in the *Nutshell*, I figured it was an answer to prayer."

Alice was taken aback. "Then you are interested in applying for the cleaning position?" Louise said, covering for Alice's silence.

"Yes ma'am." Martina turned to her. "Your ad says it would be once a week, on Monday, which would be just fine. I'm in high school, so one day a week is all I would want to work anyway." She glanced at Alice, then back at Louise. "Of course, I could work extra if you needed help on other days."

"We think one day a week would be sufficient," Alice said, "but we appreciate your offer."

"You haven't asked about the pay," Louise said. She named an hourly figure that the sisters had agreed upon.

Martina nodded. "That sounds fair. You'll be happy with my work, I promise. I take care of the house for Daddy and me, and anyone will tell you that it looks good. I can run a washer, dryer and vacuum cleaner like nobody's business. I'm not afraid of washing windows or floors or anything you need. I like to work. And," she added, "I need the money."

Louise smiled. "I am glad to hear you are not afraid of hard work. We have four guest rooms that will need taking care of. Let my sisters and me talk this over and let another day or two go by, in case there are any other applicants. Then we'll get back to you."

Jane set a heated bowl of homemade vegetable soup and a cold roast beef sandwich beside Martina, and then poured a glass of cold milk. "Meanwhile, you'd better eat this lunch."

Martina thanked Jane, and then bowed her head briefly in prayer. Alice was struck by the seeming incongruity between the girl's looks and her actions, but she felt strangely warmed by Martina's presence. She had a feeling that the girl was the answer to her own prayers about Grace Chapel Inn's cleaning person.

After showing Martina the rest of the house and describing her expected duties in more detail, the sisters saw her to the door. Martina thanked them for the lunch, and then bounded out the door and down the steps toward a waiting vehicle. Alice mentioned to her sisters that it was the same car that had waited for Martina at the curb that morning.

Jane shrugged. "It's probably a boyfriend who's giving her a ride."

"But will she have a dependable way to get here every week?" Louise said.

"Maybe she's earning the money for a car for herself."

"Or maybe auto repairs on that one," Jane said, grinning, watching out the window as the car drove down Chapel Road, backfiring most of the way.

Alice sighed. "I'd like to give her a chance, if possible. It's hard for a young girl to lose her mother at such an important time in her life."

"But she would only be working for us," Louise said. "Maybe we should just try to do something more."

"Sometimes the best thing you can do for people who are grieving is to give them a sense of usefulness," Jane said. "When I was going through my divorce, cooking became more of a passion to me than ever before. I felt better, knowing that I was contributing to the restaurant's success."

Alice nodded. "I think Father would approve of such a sentiment. Besides, she said she needed the money. It would be helping her to provide her a safe place to earn it."

"Are we agreed?" Louise said. "Shall we hire her?"

Alice thought. "Let's give it until Saturday. If we don't hear from anyone else, we'll know she's meant to work here."

"Remember in the Bible how Gideon asked for a sign from God by laying a fleece on the ground and asking Him to cause it to rain only on the wool? It sounds to me like you're putting out a fleece," Jane said.

Alice thought about Martina's T-shirt and hip-huggers. *It's more like I'm trying to keep the fleece on the lamb.*

Chapter Three

The Do Not Disturb sign stayed on Ada's doorknob into the evening. Jane's Parmesan pork chops sat on the counter, alongside a fruit salad, homemade bread and fresh asparagus. The dining room was set with the sisters' second-best tablecloth and the Wedgwood Wildflower china.

"If I serve it now, do you think she will come downstairs for dinner?" Jane asked.

"Oh dear," Louise said. "I just assumed she would be hungry by now and that we could all eat together and get to know one another. But she *will* be here for the entire month."

"It seems like our famous romance novelist is a bit of a recluse," Alice said. "I was upstairs earlier, hoping to catch a glimpse of her, and all I heard was the sound of computer keys."

"I was upstairs earlier too," Jane admitted, "but I didn't hear any typing."

"Maybe she was resting," Louise offered.

"Maybe she's dead," Jane said, with a gleam in her eye.

"Jane Howard!" Louise said. "You have been reading too many mystery novels."

Jane sighed and lifted the plate of pork chops. "We can eat here in the kitchen, as usual, and if she comes downstairs, we can take everything out to the dining room. Or reheat it later."

"I think that's best." Louise moved to help Jane carry the meal to the table. "We don't want to disturb her, especially when she was so emphatic about needing time to write."

"I was looking forward to meeting her," Alice said, removing everyday plates and silverware from the cabinet and drawers, "particularly since you gave us that description of her, Louise."

"Yes, I want to see if she's as normal as you described," Jane said.

Louise glanced upstairs. "I'm beginning to wonder if I really met her myself."

The sisters ate their dinner, cleaned up, packaged all the leftover food and stored it carefully in the refrigerator, but still the writer did not appear. When they finally headed for bed several hours later, the sisters each tiptoed past her door, but didn't hear a peep.

Jane nudged Louise with her elbow. "Maybe she's too shy to come down. Maybe we should check on her."

"We must respect our guest's privacy, Jane." Louise glanced worriedly at the door, but set her mouth in a firm line.

Just the same, after Jane and Alice had said good night and headed to their rooms on the third floor, Louise scribbled a short note that said Ada was welcome to help herself to anything in the refrigerator and that the sisters' bedrooms were on the third floor if she needed them for anything. She slipped the paper under Ada's door and headed upstairs to her own room.

After breakfast the next morning, the elusive writer had still not put in an appearance. Jane was clearing the last of the breakfast dishes when she heard a familiar "Yoo hoo!" and saw Ethel enter from the back door into the kitchen. She was holding a handful of sunflowers wrapped in green floral paper.

"Where's Portia Keyes?" Ethel said, pushing through the swinging doors to the dining room, as though determined to search the house.

Jane followed her, amused. "We hope she's still up in her room."

Ethel turned to her niece. "Is she nice? Is she as sophisticated as the romance reader magazines say? Is she beautiful and charming, just like all her heroines?"

Jane laughed. "We don't know, Auntie. Louise is the only one of us who's met her, and that was only when Portia checked in. She never came downstairs."

"Never?" Disappointment echoed in Ethel's voice. "But she had to come down to eat, didn't she?"

"Apparently not. I slipped a note under her door last night, inviting her to wake me if she wanted something to eat."

"I slipped a note under her door too," Louise said, entering the dining area from the sisters' office.

"So did I," Alice said with a laugh, following Louise into the room.

The sisters looked at each other. Ethel grinned. "At least I know you're trying to take care of my favorite author. It seems to me, though, that you could have persuaded her to join you for dinner last night. Or breakfast this morning."

"We don't want to disturb her," Jane said. "She scheduled this time here to do a lot of writing. She left the Do Not Disturb sign on her door all night."

"Well, I don't care what you say, a body has to eat." Ethel headed toward the stairs, sunflowers wagging their yellow heads with her purposeful steps. "I'm just going to march up there and—"

"Oh, Aunt Ethel, please, no," the sisters cried, nearly in unison, trailing after her.

Ethel refused to be persuaded, taking the stairs as quickly as she could. "Do you think we should tackle her?" Jane whispered to Louise. "I'll grab one arm, you grab the other and—"

"We have an obligation to our guests, but we have an obligation to family too," Louise whispered back. "Besides, I must admit I am a little curious about our guest's health at this point."

No sound could be heard behind the Garden Room's door. Ethel rapped smartly on it, calling out, "Portia? Portia Keyes? I'm Ethel Buckley, your greatest fan. I've brought a small gift to welcome you to Acorn Hill."

No answer.

Ethel rapped again. "Ms. Keyes?"

No answer.

"Maybe she's in the shower," Alice said. "Really, Aunt Ethel, I—"

Ethel turned the knob and opened the door. Jane was horrified, but curiosity got the better of her. Suppose their guest needed medical attention?

The three slips of paper that the sisters had slipped under the door now sat on the rosewood dresser. The bed had been slept in. A half-empty bottle of water sat beside the bed.

Ada Murdoch, also known as Portia Keyes, sat cross-legged on a small Oriental carpet beside the window, in a meditative pose.

The sisters crowded around the doorway, shocked into silence. A wide, multicolored scarf held back Ada's white hair. She wore a black leotard and matching stirrup tights over her thin frame. She opened one eye, then the other, and smiled. "What took you so long?"

Ethel, Portia Keyes's self-avowed number one fan, stood stock still, her mouth hanging wide open. The sunflowers seemed to droop in her hand.

"You've been waiting for us?" Jane was the first to speak. Louise and Alice seemed shocked into silence as much as Aunt Ethel.

The writer laughed, and then rose slowly. She whipped off her scarf and wiped the perspiration from her neck. "I suppose you think I'm daft."

"Why, no," Jane said, thinking just the opposite. The woman had to be in her mid-seventies, but seemed as spry as Jane. "I lived in San Francisco for a long time, and many older people do yoga there."

"Older people? *Bah.* I refuse to think of myself as a senior citizen. As for yoga, I don't practice it. I just do a few stretching positions daily for my arthritis. It's also my prayer time."

Jane was even more impressed. "We didn't mean to interrupt you, Ms. Keyes."

"We were concerned since we hadn't seen you for almost a full day," Alice said.

"Yes, and I wanted to give you these flowers and welcome you properly to Grace Chapel Inn, Portia," Ethel said, thrusting the bouquet in the author's direction. Ethel then glared at her nieces as though they did not know how to treat such an important person.

"Why, thank you," the writer said, accepting the bouquet.

"But you mustn't call me Ms. Keyes or Portia. I prefer to go by Ada Murdoch."

"Why on earth should we call you by that?" Ethel said.

Ada turned to Louise. "Didn't you tell them about my real name?"

"It seemed too personal," Louise said. "And when we met yesterday at lunchtime, I assumed you would be meeting my sisters soon and that you could tell them then."

Ada smiled warmly. "That was sweet of you." She turned to the others. "My pen name is Portia Keyes, but my real name is Ada Murdoch."

"Ada Murdoch, Ada Murdoch," Ethel said, rolling it around on her tongue. "It just doesn't have the same ring as Portia Keyes."

"Exactly." Ada laughed. "And that's why years ago I chose Portia as my pen name."

Ethel looked pensive for a moment. "I don't believe I can remember to call you anything but Portia Keyes," she said.

"That's quite all right," Ada said.

"Ada, these are my sisters, Alice and Jane," Louise said. "And this is our Aunt Ethel."

"How nice to meet you all," Ada said.

Alice and Jane murmured their own acknowledgments. Ethel seemed struck speechless again, Jane noticed with amusement, which was a rare situation for their ordinarily vocal aunt.

Ada handed the flowers to Louise. "If one of you would be so kind as to put these sunflowers in a vase, I'd love to set them on my dresser here. I can look at them while I'm writing. But now, if you'll excuse me, I need to shower and get back to writing."

"Would you like some breakfast?" Louise said. "You must be starving, having done without dinner last night."

Ada smiled. "I didn't mean to be rude, but you'll have to forgive me if I don't show up for all meals. The reason you didn't hear from me yesterday was because I got into the groove, as writers say when their work is going well. And when that happens, it's easy for me to cut myself off from reality. I don't think about food, I don't think about seeing other people. I'm in my own world, creating a story for my readers."

"Those love scenes must be pretty engrossing," Jane said mildly.

"Love scenes? Oh heavens. I hate writing those. Kisses here, hugs there . . . . It's all the same."

"What about the other stuff?" Jane could not help but ask.

"Other stuff?" Ada looked perplexed.

"The more intimate scenes," Jane said.

Ada laughed. "I don't write explicit love scenes, if that's what you're after."

Ethel put her hands on her hips, finding her voice to admonish her nieces. "Is that what you girls thought? That Portia is a writer of smutty books?"

Louise and Alice glanced at each other. Jane suddenly felt ashamed of her earlier teasing. "We just assumed that being a romance writer, you would include certain, er, intimate scenes in your books."

"Oh heavens, no!" Ada laughed. "How my dear departed Alfred would hoot at that. When I started writing my novels thirty years ago, romance novels were just beginning to be labeled as such and were tending toward those highly evocative scenes. My publisher wanted me to write a book with some of that, but I told Alfred I just couldn't do it. He advised me to stick to my principles, so I prayed about it, then told my editor that if it meant I never published again, I still wouldn't write any such scenes."

"And what happened?" Jane said.

Ada shrugged. "God honored my prayer, and my books started hitting the best-seller list. Apparently there's still an audience of old-fashioned readers like me," she said, winking.

"If you've been writing thirty years, you must have written a lot of books," Alice observed.

"This book I'm writing here at the inn will be my one hundredth."

"Wow!" Jane responded.

"What an honor it is to have you staying with us," Louise said. "Especially on such a momentous occasion."

"We'll give you all the privacy you need," Alice added. "So that you can work in peace."

"I could fix a basket of wrapped cheese and crackers for you to keep here. So that you'd have something to eat when you're too busy to come downstairs for a full meal," Jane said.

"Would you, dear? That would be lovely. I'm afraid I become a bit of a recluse when I'm in full writing mode. Please don't take offense. And now—" She gestured at the door.

"Of course," Ethel said, with an air of authority. "Girls, let's let Ms. Keyes get to work. She's got a one hundredth book to write. And I can't wait to read it."

True to her words, Ada stayed in her room and wrote most of the day. The sisters often heard her typing, even when they were heading upstairs for bed.

"You would think she would have finished that book by now, the way she whacks away at that keyboard," Louise said.

"Aunt Ethel said she read in one of her romance reader magazines that before Portia starts her actual writing, she types up a lot of her research in advance."

"Does anyone know why she picked our inn to do her writing?" Louise said. "Do you suppose she saw that glowing review in the *Innkeeper's Journal?* "

"Who knows?" Jane shrugged. "At the rate she's staying in her room, we may never see her again until it's time for her to check out next month."

By Saturday morning, it was apparent that no one else was going to apply for the job of cleaning person. The sisters were busy all weekend, with the inn full of guests who required their attention. Alice found time, however, to call Martina Beckett and tell her that the job was hers. Martina was overjoyed and promised to be at the inn right after school on Monday. Since her classes were over at twelve-thirty, she said she would be there by one o'clock.

At the appointed time, she appeared on the doorstep, with her school backpack and plastic grocery sack, which she held up for inspection. "Cleaning clothes to change into," she said.

Jane smiled, wondering what Martina's idea of grubby clothes looked like. She was already wearing faded blue jeans and a gray T-shirt. Nevertheless, Jane knew how important clothes were to teenagers, no matter how raggedy they might look to adults. She ushered Martina into the house and showed her upstairs to her own room so that the girl could change clothes.

"We had a busy weekend," she said, when Martina reappeared. "So there'll be plenty for you to do."

"I'm ready to work," Martina said. "Just point me in the right direction."

Jane handed her a list that she, Louise and Alice had

made up, so that Martina could check off the chores that needed to be accomplished. She took her through a tour of each guest room, pointing out what had to be done. She showed her the washing machine and dryer in the laundry room, and then handed her a bucket of cleaning supplies. She told her to ignore the Garden Room if the Do Not Disturb sign was on the door handle.

"If you have any questions, just give me a call," Jane said. "I'll be in the kitchen working on dinner. Louise is giving piano lessons, so avoid the parlor."

"Where's Miss Howard? I mean, Miss Alice?" Martina said.

"She works at the hospital on Mondays until five o'clock so you probably won't see her much."

"Oh." Martina looked crestfallen. "Well, I guess I'd better get to work." She grabbed the cleaning bucket and headed for the stairs.

"Martina?"

"Yes?" She turned back.

"Stop by the kitchen when you're done. I'm making some ginger cookies, and I'll need a taste tester."

Martina smiled. "Sure thing."

At Potterston Hospital, Alice wondered how Martina was doing on her first day at Grace Chapel Inn. Ever since the girl had reminded her of young Mrs. Beckett's untimely death, Alice had remembered many things about the woman and how she had left behind a husband and a grieving teen. She wished she could do more for Martina, but Martina was too old for Alice to invite to join the ANGELs. She wondered if and where Martina and her father went to church and if the girl was involved in youth activities. She was still trying to decide how to broach the subject with Martina, when she spotted Rev. Kenneth Thompson, the pastor of Grace Chapel, sitting alone at a table in the hospital cafeteria.

"Pastor Ken," she said, "how nice to see you."

"Alice," he said, rising. "I'm glad to see you too. Do you have time to sit with me for a moment?"

"Actually, I'm on a lunch break, and I'd love to join you, if you'd like some company."

"I'd be delighted." He pulled out a chair for her. "I was about to get some coffee. What kind of tea can I bring you?" he said, knowing that Alice did not drink coffee.

"They have a nice Earl Grey here," she said.

"I'll have it for you in a moment."

Rev. Thompson retrieved the beverages and returned to the table, handing Alice a Styrofoam cup of tea. "Thank you," she said, accepting the cup. "I have to admit that it feels good to sit for a moment. We've been unusually busy today. What brings you to the hospital, Pastor Ken?"

"Visiting a sick church member."

"Nothing serious, I hope."

"The Dolans' toddler had tubes put in his ears this morning, but he's out of surgery and doing fine." He shook his head, and then sipped his decaf. "When I spoke with Louise outside of church yesterday, she mentioned that you and your sisters were hiring a high school girl to do some cleaning around the inn."

Alice nodded. "In fact, I was just thinking about her when I ran into you. Her name is Martina Beckett, and her mother died here at the hospital last year. She and her father have just moved to Acorn Hill from Potterston. Do you know them?"

The pastor shook his head. "No. I don't believe I've ever met them."

Alice nodded. "I'm concerned about their support system," she said. "It's often the case that friends rush to help a grieving family right after a loved one's death, but in a few months, everyone goes about his and her business. I know it would have been difficult for me after Father's death if Louise and Jane hadn't so quickly decided to stay in Acorn Hill."

She cradled her cup between her hands, sipping thoughtfully. "I hope we can be more to Martina than just employers."

The pastor smiled. "More than once Grace Chapel Inn has been 'a place of hope and healing,'" he said, quoting from the plaque hanging on the inn's front door. "If Martina needs help of any kind, I'm sure she'll know she can turn to you and your sisters."

When Alice returned home early that evening, she met Martina as the girl was on her way out the front door. "Hi, Miss Howard," Martina said. She was wearing cut-off shorts and an oversized blue T-shirt with huge bleach spots. Her bangs were damp with perspiration, and she looked tired.

"Hi, Martina," Alice said. "I was hoping I'd get to see you, to say hello. Did everything go well?"

"Oh yes," she said, gesturing toward the kitchen. "Ms. Howard is fixing me a bag of cookies to take home."

Alice smiled inwardly. Here she had been worried about Martina, and of course, Jane was already helping her, even in a small way.

Martina gestured at the porch swing. "Do you mind if I sit here while I wait for my ride?"

"Not at all. May I sit with you?"

Martina sat down. "I'd like that." She set down her backpack. "School's hardly started and we're already loaded down with work."

"What sort of homework do you have to do?"

"Besides the usual math and English papers, my history teacher, Mrs. Butorac, has assigned a genealogy project. We're going to be studying the American Revolution this year, so she wants us to try to find out where our ancestors were during that time. She said it would be really cool to find out if any of them lived in this area."

"That's an interesting idea," Alice said. "Lots of people in Acorn Hill would probably like to know the same information. I know my sisters and I would."

Suddenly she remembered Carlene's words about interesting articles. "Do you mind if I tell Carlene Moss at the *Acorn Nutshell* about your class project? She might want to write it up in the newspaper."

"I don't mind," Martina said. "And I'm sure Mrs. Butorac wouldn't. She loves history and makes it fun for us. She'd probably love finding out if somebody in town knew a lot about this area during the Revolutionary War." She jumped up, grabbing her backpack. "Oops! There's my ride. Gotta go, Miss Howard."

The front door opened, and Jane thrust a bag into Martina's hands. "Don't forget your cookies."

"Thanks, Ms. Howard, Miss Howard," Martina said, waving to them both as she bounded down the steps toward the waiting car. "See you next Monday."

"Bye." Jane waved back.

Alice chimed in with her own farewell, and then she and Jane sat side by side on the porch swing. Once again, Alice had not been able to get a good look at the car's driver. "I wonder who's picking her up every day."

"It's Ingrid Nilsen. Wasn't she one of your ANGELs?"

Alice smiled. Ingrid had been a sweet-tempered girl with long blonde hair, a beautiful smile and a giving heart. She had grown into a lovely young woman, and her family still attended Grace Chapel. "I've never seen her with Martina."

"Martina and her father only recently moved to Acorn Hill from Potterston," Jane reminded her. "We'll probably be seeing those two girls together more often. Martina told me that they have the same class schedule."

"It's nice that she found a friend so quickly." Jane pushed the swing into gentle motion with her heels.

"Martina told me about an interesting project that her history teacher assigned the class," Alice said. "The students are supposed to research their family trees back to Revolutionary times, if possible, since that's what they're studying. I thought that Carlene Moss might want to write an article about their research. She's always looking for interesting ideas for articles, particularly about things going on in town."

"You don't think she'll want to interview our star guest, Ada Murdoch, do you?" Jane said.

Alice laughed softly. "Nobody's heard of Ada Murdoch and apparently hardly anyone here has heard of Portia Keyes, either. If Ada sticks to her room as much as she says she will, she should be able to escape any publicity in Acorn Hill."

"What about Aunt Ethel?" Jane sighed. "As Portia Keyes's number one fan, she might try to push her into the spotlight."

"She heard what Ada said. Surely she'll let the poor woman have the peace and quiet she needs to write."

Jane looked at Alice. Alice looked at Jane. "Oh dear," Alice said.

"Yes, 'oh dear.'" Jane laughed. "Maybe we can send Aunt Ethel on a European tour for the month of September."

Chapter Four

Alice had to work much of that week, so it was Friday before she could make time to get in touch with Carlene at the *Nutshell* office. She decided to phone, rather than bother Carlene at work, and the editor suggested they meet at the Coffee Shop for lunch.

Once there, Carlene got right down to business. "If you have a story idea for me, I can write off the price of lunch as an income tax expense," Carlene said, as she slid across the red faux-leather booth seat.

"Is that legal, Carlene?" Alice sat on the other side of the table. "I don't want to get you into trouble."

"Of course it's legal. This is a business lunch."

Hope Collins approached the table, order pad in hand. Her short hair, naturally dark but with light highlights this month, was tucked behind her ears. "Hello, ladies."

"Hi, Hope," Carlene said. "Love the new hair color. Very stylish."

"Thanks," Hope said. "I hate my natural color, but I got tired of being a blonde. I figured this was a good compromise for a while." She held up the order pad and a pencil. "What would you like? The special today is taco salad."

Carlene's brow furrowed. "It's not too spicy, is it? I don't like food that burns my tongue."

"It's mild, Carlene," Hope assured her. "We serve it with a side dish of hot sauce for those who like their food spicy."

"I'll try it," Alice said.

Carlene shrugged. "Why not?"

Hope wrote down their order, along with their beverage choices, and then tucked the pencil behind her ear. "I'll bring your drinks in a jiff," she said, and then headed toward the kitchen.

Carlene pulled out a legal pad from the brown leather tote bag beside her on the seat. "All right, Alice. What's this great story idea?"

"I don't know how great it is." Alice felt embarrassed that she had dragged Carlene down to the Coffee Shop just to tell her about a high school assignment. "It sounded interesting when I heard about it."

"What is it?"

"Mrs. Butorac, a history teacher at the high school, has assigned her class to research their family trees back to American Revolution times, if the students can. Who knows what they might find out? Especially kids with families that have lived in this area for a long time."

Carlene furrowed her brow again, deep in concentration. "That's not a bad idea, Alice. It would make a nice brite for now and perhaps a longer feature story later."

"What's a brite?"

"Sorry. Journalist lingo. It's a small, happy story. Not too newsy, but still of interest. Where'd you hear about this?"

"Martina Beckett, the girl who answered the ad we placed in the *Nutshell*."

"So someone responded? Good. When does she start working for you?"

"Her first day was Monday. She'll help us get through the autumn season, anyway."

Carlene's pencil was still poised over the paper. "Are you expecting lots of business in the next few months, then?"

Alice thought about Ada Murdoch, aka Portia Keyes. She had barely shown her face during the past week. Evidently, she was getting lots of work done. Alice certainly did not want to disrupt that by saying anything to Carlene. "We get lots of folks during the autumn months who use our inn as a jumping-off point for their leaf-peeping jaunts."

Carlene twirled the pencil, impatiently, it seemed to Alice. "Anybody of interest staying at Grace Chapel Inn? Any out-of-towners I might want to interview?"

"Here's your salads," Hope said, setting large plates in front of them. "And a bowl of hot sauce in case you're feeling adventurous." She winked at Carlene.

The editor visibly shuddered. "Not me, Hope. I get enough stomach troubles just trying to get the *Nutshell* out every week."

"Thank you, Hope," Alice said, breathing a sigh of relief that she had not had to answer Carlene's question.

The two women chatted about inconsequential things while they ate their lunches. Carlene pronounced the taco salad tasty and mild enough for her palate. She made it a point to compliment June Carter, the Coffee Shop's owner, on the way out. Alice had a feeling that the Coffee Shop would be serving taco salad on a regular basis, since Carlene sometimes wrote short reviews about items on the shop's menu in the *Nutshell*.

Carlene promised to get in touch with Dee Butorac, the high-school history teacher, for details for the article. She thanked Alice for her help and told her to share any other news that she thought might be interesting to the newspaper's readers. Grateful that she had not let slip anything about

Grace Chapel Inn's distinguished guest, Alice said good-bye to Carlene and lingered in town for some shopping.

She thought about popping into Nine Lives Bookstore for a new read, and then decided against it. She doubted that Viola Reed had any interest in discussing Portia Keyes since she did not like the type of books she wrote, but Alice still did not want to run the risk that the sisters' guest might be a topic of conversation. She remembered that she needed to pick up some craft material for the ANGELs meeting the following week, so she headed to Sylvia's Buttons.

On sudden inspiration, she made a quick stop at the Acorn Hill Library. The elderly librarian who had worked there for the past fifty years had passed on, and the town had only recently hired a new one. Nia Komonos, a tall young woman of Greek descent, met Alice at the door.

"Hello, Alice," she said, her dark eyes flashing with pleasure. "It's so nice to see you."

Alice smiled. Nia always wore conservative suits, but her staid attire could not camouflage her outgoing, sunny nature. She was a Pittsburgh native who had recently graduated from the University of Pittsburgh with a degree in library science and wanted to work in a small town. She was enthusiastic about Acorn Hill and even more enthusiastic about reading.

"It's nice to see you too, Nia. I see that you're busy, so I'll just browse."

"Help yourself." Nia smiled and then waved at the stacks of books. "I have plenty of shelving to keep me busy."

Alice walked slowly in front of the books, pretending to peruse the titles, but she already knew what she wanted to check out. Sure enough, in the fiction section, under K, she found several books by Portia Keyes. She selected one called *Time Will Tell*, and then browsed the shelves again to pick up a few other books. She wanted to have some decoys when she checked out.

Nia accepted her library card and scanned the books into the computer system. "What made you choose these books?" she said.

Could everyone in town today see what she was trying to hide? "I wanted to see if that old saying is true."

"Which one is that?" Nia continued scanning.

"The one about judging a book by its cover." Alice smiled. "Actually, I'm hoping it's wrong because these covers looked interesting."

Nia held up *Time Will Tell*, which was the last book to scan. The cover showed an old-fashioned pocket watch, a magnolia and crossed swords. "I've heard of this author before," she said. "She wins lots of book awards."

"Really?" Alice said, in what she hoped was an offhand tone.

"I've never read any of her books myself, but I should. People often ask me for recommendations."

"Yes, I find recommendations from people whose judgment I trust very helpful," Alice said.

"Maybe you could tell me what you think about it, after you read it," Nia said. She stacked the books for Alice and smiled.

"I will," Alice said, gathering the stack. "Thank you, Nia."

"Good-bye, Alice. Don't forget about that review."

Once outside, Alice sighed with relief. *I better head home before I manage to spill the beans about Portia Keyes's presence at the inn.*

Bustling up Chapel Road, she passed Fred's Hardware on Hill Street. Vera Humbert, Fred's wife and Alice's best friend, was just entering the store. Despite her plan to hurry home, Alice veered off the path to talk to Vera, who had already rushed inside. Alice was about to follow when she heard Fred call his wife's name.

"Vera! What's wrong?"

Vera broke into sobs. Alice saw her run to Fred's embrace. She apparently could not stop crying, despite Fred's comforting reassurance. "Come on, now. It can't be that bad."

Alice was torn between leaving and wanting to comfort Vera, but she knew that her friend's place was with her husband. She backed out of the store's entrance, unnoticed, and turned away.

On the walk up Chapel Road, all the spring seemed to have disappeared from Alice's step. What could be wrong with Vera? Had something happened at school? It was 3:15 PM, which meant that Vera had only had enough time to walk from the elementary school to Fred's store.

Father, whatever is wrong with my dear friend, please comfort her. Please let her know that You are with her and that You love her. Give her and Fred strength to overcome this problem. Guide me and all of their friends to help in any way we can. Amen.

By the time she had finished praying, Alice was back at Grace Chapel Inn. As always, she felt better for taking her concerns to God, and she vowed to continue in prayer for her friend. If Vera wanted to talk to her about her problems, Alice would be there to listen.

Alice had hardly a spare moment to read Ada's book, since the sisters were busy with their latest weekend guests. In addition to the reclusive Ada, guests filled the other three rooms, and all but Ada checked out on Sunday. On Monday, Martina showed up for her second week of work. Again, Jane had a snack for her in the kitchen after she was finished and a bag of extras to take home. This time Jane had made doughnuts, and they were eating some in the kitchen when Louise wandered in.

"That was my last piano lesson of the day," she announced,

taking a seat at the table. "Monday is one of my busier days. It seems that all my students want to get their lessons over with early in the week."

"Have some apple cider," Jane said, pouring a glass from a pitcher on the table. She slid a plate of doughnuts across the table to her sister. "One of these ought to perk you up too."

"*Mmm*," Louise said, biting into the powdered-sugar-covered confection. "Delicious."

"It must be nice to have such a wonderful cook in the family," Martina said to Louise. "And you . . . you're so talented with music. I heard you playing the piano during the lessons today. Were you showing your students how it should be done?"

"I think she was just showing off," Jane said, winking at Martina.

Louise looked cross for a moment, and then relaxed. "Martina is right, Jane. I was simply showing my students how selected passages should be played."

"It was beautiful," Martina said.

Louise wondered what Martina's interest in music might be, but did not pursue the subject. Most young people today were not interested in classical music. "Thank you," she said, without elaboration.

"How's your genealogy project coming?" Jane asked.

Martina licked the last of the powdered sugar from her fingers, and then guiltily wiped them on a paper napkin. "Pretty good. Ingrid—she's my best friend—she and I were working together on the project, looking up information, first about her family, then mine. My dad and her parents found out about the assignment, and now they're interested too. I'm sure Mrs. Butorac wanted us to do the work ourselves, but honestly, our folks have started spending a lot of time on the computer, tracing our family trees."

"Genealogy is a popular hobby," Jane said.

"I hope I find out something interesting. So far my dad and I have only been able to trace our family back to the early twentieth century. It's even harder for Ingrid. Her family immigrated to the United States in 1912, so they don't have many records. They're writing to relatives back in Norway, though, to get more information."

"Did Mrs. Butorac say whether or not you students should trace one particular side of your family?" Jane said.

"She said that we could choose either our father or mother's side," Martina said, and then cocked her head to one side. "If you'll excuse me, I think I hear Ingrid's car out front now."

Jane handed her a paper bag. "Here's some doughnuts for the road," she said. "Save a few for your dad, all right?"

"I will." Martina took the bag, smiled, and gave a little wave. "Bye, Ms. Howard. Bye, Mrs. Smith. See you next week."

They heard her clatter through the foyer then out the front door. Ingrid's old car once again backfired noisily down Chapel Road.

The sisters looked at each other, each thinking about the boisterous energy of youth.

"Was I that noisy when I was young?" Jane said.

"Absolutely," Louise said, smiling over her cup of cider.

That evening the sisters sat down to dinner in the kitchen. Jane had decided on comforting home cooking: meatloaf with marinara sauce, mashed potatoes and fresh green beans. The sisters talked companionably about their day, and they shared notes.

"I don't suppose Ada Murdoch will be joining us for dinner," Alice said.

Jane shook her head. "If she doesn't let me know in advance that she plans to dine with us, I serve dinner in here."

"It's a shame," Alice said thoughtfully, scooping mashed potatoes onto her plate. "I finally got a chance to start one of Ada's books on my lunch break today."

"Did Aunt Ethel lend you one of her copies?" Louise asked.

Alice shook her head. "I checked it out of the library on Friday. I was afraid that I would inadvertently let on that Ada was a guest at our inn, so I had to be careful around Nia. I want to protect Ada's privacy. And her writing time."

"Viola already knows that Ada is here," Louise pointed out.

"Yes, but Viola doesn't think much of Ada's writing, so she won't seek her out. However, I'm thoroughly enjoying the book," Alice said. "It's set during the Civil War and, from what I can tell, seems historically accurate. I feel like I'm right in the middle of battle. The characters are so real too. I feel as if I know them."

"Maybe you'd let me borrow it when you're finished," Jane said. "How about you, Louise? Are you interested in reading it?"

"I'm reading the new C. S. Lewis biography that I bought at Nine Lives the other day."

Alice knew that Louise seldom read fiction, but she was sorry to hear her sister summarily dismiss the idea of reading one of their guest's novels. *I suppose life would be fairly boring if we sisters all had the same tastes, though.*

"How is Nia doing?" Jane asked Alice.

"She seems to be doing well," Alice said. She remembered her walk home from the library and what she had seen at Fred's Hardware. The weekend had been so busy that she had not had a chance to call Vera or even tell Jane and Louise. "I wish I could say the same for Vera Humbert."

Louise set down her fork. "What is the matter?"

"I'm not sure," Alice said, "but when I passed by Fred's store on Friday, Vera was just rushing in, and she was crying."

"Oh dear," Louise said.

"Did you find out what was wrong?" Jane said.

Alice shook her head. "I wanted to stay and find out, but Fred was consoling her, and I didn't feel that it was my business."

"I am sure that if it is something important, she will tell you in due time," Louise said.

The sisters heard a throat clear. "Do you mind if I join you?"

They looked up to see Ada Murdoch standing in the doorway, eyeing their meal with a mixture of hunger and reticence. "I don't mean to intrude," she said.

"Nonsense. We would love to have your company," Louise said, rising to make room for Ada at the extra seat.

"We're glad you could join us," Jane said, retrieving an extra place setting from the cabinet. Alice quietly poured an extra cup of hot tea, which she set before Ada. Louise passed the food down to Ada, who loaded her plate with generous helpings.

"Well!" She beamed at Louise, Jane and Alice. "You ladies certainly know how to make a boarder feel at home."

"I would have served the meal in the dining room if I'd known you'd be hungry for dinner," Jane said.

"Your kitchen is just fine," she said. "I don't want to interrupt your private family time, but I reached a good stopping point in my research and realized I needed a good, solid meal."

She turned to Jane. "The goody baskets of crackers and cheese and fruit that you've left at my door have been wonderful. I appreciate your going the extra mile to make my stay productive."

"We're glad to help," Jane said. "We do whatever we can for all our guests to make their stay with us as pleasant as possible."

"We want to be more than an impersonal accommodation and restaurant service," Louise said. "We want each guest to feel at home."

"You must have had a lot of guests this weekend," Ada said. "The place was jumping with activity."

"I hope no one disturbed you," Louise said.

"Not at all." Ada dug into the meatloaf with gusto. "Jane, this is *wonderful*. Where did you learn to cook so well?"

"I used to be a chef in San Francisco. The Blue Fish Grille."

"That's one of my favorite places to eat when I'm there," Ada said. "I'm sorry I'm missing so many of your meals while I'm here."

"You are welcome to join us any time," Louise said. "Just pop down to the kitchen."

"And there's usually leftovers in the refrigerator," Jane added. "Feel free to put some in the microwave if you feel like eating at an odd hour."

"I just may do that," Ada said. "Sometimes I find myself at a writing lull at the strangest hours."

"I am reading one of your books, Ada," Alice said. "*Time Will Tell*. It's very engrossing."

"Thank you." Ada waved her fork, and then lifted another piece of meatloaf. "I wrote that book about seven years ago. I did lots of research in Vicksburg for that one. Lovely part of the country, if you don't mind the humidity and heat in the summer."

"What are you working on now?" Jane asked.

Ada swallowed a bite, and then smiled. "I'm sorry, dear, but I don't talk about what I'm writing until I'm near completion. I don't want to jinx my train of thought or my work in progress."

Alice thought that was peculiar, and a bit superstitious, but she had often found that the artistic types who stayed at Grace Chapel Inn had their quirks.

Ada ate the last bite on her plate, a green bean, then sighed with satisfaction. "Well, ladies, I'd better head back upstairs. Thank you for giving me a much-needed break."

"You're welcome," Jane said.

"I guess we will see you . . . whenever we see you," Louise said.

Ada winked. "You betcha."

The phone rang as the sisters were relaxing in the parlor. Alice hoped that it might be Vera. It had been three days since she had seen her friend so upset, but she had not heard a word. She had called the Humberts', hoping to coax Vera on a walk, but Fred had answered and had acted mysterious on the phone and said that Vera was busy.

When she answered the phone, however, Alice was surprised to hear Nia Komonos' voice. "This is Nia. I can't believe you didn't tell me," the librarian said.

Alice froze. Had Nia discovered Ada Murdoch's presence? "Hello, Nia. Tell you what?"

"About the high school genealogy project. I heard about it from Carlene Moss. She was in the library this morning and mentioned something about writing an article on it for the newspaper. She said the article was your idea."

"I didn't know you would be interested," Alice said, confused.

"Genealogy is my passion," Nia said. "I was thinking about starting up a special genealogy section here at the library. Maybe even conduct classes. There are a lot of senior citizens in Acorn Hill, and genealogy is popular with that age group."

"I think that would be wonderful," Alice said. "And I'm sure the high school students would especially appreciate your help while they work on this project."

"That's a marvelous idea," Nia said. "I'll get in touch with Dee Butorac and see if we can coordinate some special lessons with the students. Maybe their parents too."

Alice wondered if it was a good idea to get parents involved in a student project. She had learned from working with her middle schoolers that the best way to get them to learn something was to give them just enough information to get started, and then let them complete the project themselves—with a little supervision, of course.

"I'm so excited about this, Alice," Nia said. "It can be hard, getting accepted in a small town. Maybe this will help show that I'm really concerned about the people living here. Thanks, Alice. See you later."

Alice hung up the receiver, feeling more sympathetic. She knew that others had had struggles being accepted by town members. She still wondered about the wisdom of the librarian and town members taking over the students' project. *It's not my place to say anything. Nia and the teacher can work this out.*

Alice smiled. At least Nia Komonos had not discovered that Portia Keyes was staying at Grace Chapel Inn. Apparently small town talk did not reach that far. Yet.

Chapter Five

Wednesday afternoon, Louise had a cancellation from one of her piano students. Since that gave her some extra time before dinner, she decided to head for Fred's Hardware. Her metronome had not been working correctly for a while, and she needed it for piano lessons. Perhaps it simply needed a new battery. If so, Fred was the only retailer in town who carried the size she would require.

"Hello, Louise," Fred said when she entered. "What can I do for you today?"

"My metronome does not keep an accurate rhythm anymore," she said. "Can you look at it?" She pulled the musical timekeeper from a canvas tote.

"*Hmm.*" Fred took up a screwdriver and pried the back of the metronome. "The wires look good. Maybe it just needs a new battery."

"That is what I was hoping," she said. "I can never remember where to find the size on it, so I just brought the whole thing along."

Fred consulted a shelf neatly stacked with batteries and found the right size. He carefully removed the old battery and replaced it with the new one. When he turned the switch, the metronome *click-clacked* with perfect precision.

"That's all it needed," Fred said. "Want me to dispose of this old battery for you?"

"Thank you. I would appreciate it."

Fred replaced the back on the metronome, and then rang up the purchase. Louise set her purse on the counter and counted out her cash. After he handed her the bag and receipt, she paused for a moment. "Fred, I don't mean to pry, but is everything all right with Vera? Alice saw her crying the other day."

Fred looked uncomfortable. "She asked me not to tell anyone, Louise. She has a few things to sort out first."

"Well, if there is anything we can do to help, you know where we are," she said. "Alice is particularly concerned about her dear friend."

"I'll tell her, Louise," Fred said. "I'm sure she'll want to speak to you all very soon."

More puzzled than ever, Louise headed home.

"Now what do you suppose he meant?" Jane said, after Louise reported the conversation.

Louise sighed. "I'm not sure. But I hope that we can help with whatever is wrong."

Alice had just returned home from working her shift and was walking up to the house when she heard a car park at the curb. She turned and saw Vera exiting the driver's side. Her friend's face looked blotchy, and Alice wondered if she had been in tears all day and if she had managed to teach school.

"Hello, Alice." Vera produced a weak smile.

"It's good to see you," Alice said, waiting for her friend to catch up with her on the sidewalk. "Have you come for a visit?"

Vera nodded. "I wanted to talk to you about a matter of concern, but I was hoping I could talk to all of you sisters at one time. I haven't spoken about it to anyone else in town yet. You're the first."

Alice's heart sank as she and Vera entered the house. When Louise and Jane saw Vera, they sprang into action to make their friend feel more comfortable. "I'll fix a pot of tea," Jane said, heading for the kitchen.

"Perhaps we should sit in the library," Louise offered.

Vera swiped at her wet eyes. "You don't have to go to any trouble on my account."

"Nonsense," Alice said. She was happy that Louise had suggested the library. With its tweed-patterned wallpaper, mahogany bookshelves and autumn-colored upholstery, it always made her feel as if her father were present. And that reminded her to send up a quick prayer to her heavenly Father, asking for guidance and help.

Vera perched on a russet-colored chair and set a tapestry throw pillow in her lap, as if for protection. She smoothed her finger over and over the pillow's thread. "I'm really at a loss," she finally said.

"Here's tea." Jane bustled into the room with a tray laden with the inn's Wedgwood teapot, cups and saucers. She poured and handed Vera a cup.

Alice settled in the other russet chair and moved it closer to Vera. "Please tell us what is wrong, Vera. We've been worried about you."

Vera absently lifted her cup as if to drink, and then lowered it again. Her eyes filled with water. "My baby . . . Polly . . . is going to be married." She burst into tears.

The sisters let the words sink in. Louise was the first to respond, perhaps because she was the only sister who had a daughter of her own. "But, Vera, that's wonderful news. You should be happy, not sad."

"I ... I ... am," Vera managed to choke out between sobs. "I couldn't be happier."

Louise and Jane laughed gently. "You have a funny way of showing it," Jane said.

Alice had not joined in with Louise and Jane's laughter, knowing that something more was troubling her friend. "Then why are you crying, Vera?"

Vera sniffled and managed to stop her tears. Alice passed her a tissue box from Daniel Howard's desk, and Vera pulled out a tissue and blew her nose. When she was composed, she smiled at the Howards. "Fred says I'm just being silly. But part of me is sad at losing my first-born daughter."

"That's natural," Jane said. "It's always difficult to deal with change regarding your loved ones. Especially when it shakes up the family dynamics."

"What about her young man?" Louise said. "Have you met him?"

"Oh yes. Alex is a wonderful man. He and Polly have known each other for three years. He visited here last summer, do you remember?"

Alice had a vague memory of meeting him. He was tall, clean-cut and exceedingly polite. He had attended Grace Chapel with Polly and her family too. "Yes, I remember," Alice said.

"He graduated this summer from Penn State's nursing school, and he proposed to Polly this past Friday. She called me at school to tell me. She said she just couldn't wait to share the news."

"Is that why I saw you crying at the hardware store?" Alice said.

Vera nodded. "She told me about their engagement, but she also told me that Alex wants to be married as soon as possible. He's joined the Army and will have to report for basic training for medical officers in six weeks."

Alice thought that she understood Vera's tears better. After completing basic training, many young men and women were shipped overseas and saw action.

"So it will be a rush wedding," Vera said. "She wants to have it in the chapel, of course, but there will hardly be time for me to absorb all this . . . this . . . change." She burst into tears again.

Louise took the cup and saucer from her hands and set them on the desk, and then she embraced the distraught woman.

"Polly and Alex are in love," Jane said. "Think about how happy they are."

"Yes, and what a fine young man Alex is, wanting to marry your daughter before he goes into the Army," Louise added.

"I . . . I know," Vera said. Alice handed her another tissue, and Vera composed herself again.

"I know what we should do," Jane said. "We should hold a bridal shower for Polly. Do you think she could come home on a weekend for us to give her one?"

"She'll be home every weekend until the wedding, which is less than four weeks away," Vera said. "I imagine she'd be available for a shower. After . . . after they get married, she'll still live in State College, to finish her studies at Penn State. She's supposed to graduate in May."

"So they'll probably be getting an apartment together," Jane said, "and I'm sure they could use all sorts of new things. Let Louise, Alice and me give her a shower, Vera. Ask her to jot down what they most need, kitchen, bath or whatever, and we'll plan a shower accordingly."

"Oh, Vera, I envy you," Louise said. "I'm not sure that Cynthia will ever get married. You will have such fun helping Polly to plan the wedding, but more importantly, after that, you will have a son in your family."

Vera seemed to brighten at that. "I suppose Fred will enjoy having a man to talk hardware and football with."

"There, you see?" Louise smiled.

"Yes, Vera. Just keep your chin up and think thoughts of love," Alice said.

"I'm sure that's what Polly and Alex are doing," Jane said, winking.

Vera smiled more broadly, looking in turn from one sister to the next. "I'm so lucky to have such friends. I think I can tell the rest of the town about our . . . our news."

"And it's *good* news," Alice reminded her. "Love is always good news."

Alice thought about love as she continued to read Ada Murdoch's book. It was hard to believe that the down-to-earth woman ensconced in the Garden Room was the same one who wrote tender love scenes. Alice did not usually care for romance in her novels, but Ada's scenes were heartfelt and not silly at all. She could see why Ethel liked the books, and she was sorry that they had teased her about being a romance reader.

One night while she was reading in bed, she set aside the book and thought about Mark Graves, the college beau who had reentered her life not too long ago. A chief veterinarian for the Philadelphia zoo, he often traveled outside the country. He came to Acorn Hill occasionally to visit Alice, but it had been a while since she had seen him.

Alice kept in touch with his sister, Susan Newby, who had given her a standing invitation to visit Philadelphia. Alice didn't see how she could take time away from her nursing duties, as well as the inn, for a vacation, but maybe one day she would consider it.

In the meantime she had *Time Will Tell* to provide for her escapist needs.

During the week, autumn had officially arrived, and the maple leaves were beginning to turn color. Saturday morning, Ethel sauntered into the kitchen, where Jane was cleaning. The inn's weekend guests had all left for their day's adventures, and Louise and Alice were occupied upstairs.

Ethel was dressed in her nicest suit and pumps, which she usually reserved for Sunday services. Smacking her handbag on the kitchen table, she announced to Jane, "This has gone on long enough."

Jane took one look at her aunt's outfit, but did not bat an eye. "Hello to you too, Auntie," she said.

Ethel crossed her arms. "I'm talking about Portia Keyes. I mean, Ada Murdoch, or whatever she wants to call herself."

"What's wrong with Ada?" Jane said.

"What's wrong? She's holed up in that upstairs room, letting the beauty and friendliness of Acorn Hill pass her by. That's what's wrong."

"Oh, Aunt Ethel, you know she needs time to write."

"Fiddlesticks. She can't be writing nonstop. I'm here to take her to lunch, and I'll only take no for an answer from her own lips."

Alarmed, Jane tried to reason with her aunt. "But she doesn't want to be disturbed. You heard her say that."

"I won't be disturbing her. I'll be feeding her. You girls *have* been doing that, haven't you?"

"Of course," Jane said, miffed that Ethel would think otherwise. "But she's only been asking for cheese and crackers and finger foods. I leave them in a basket outside her door every day."

Ethel looked aghast. "Is that any way to treat a famous author?"

"But, Auntie . . ."

"I'm marching right up there and inviting that woman to lunch," Ethel said, heading for the stairs. "If she doesn't want to go, she can tell me so herself."

"But, Aunt Ethel, she needs quiet so that she can work."

"Nonsense!" Ethel charged up the stairs and rapped firmly on Ada's door, ignoring the Do Not Disturb sign. "Ada? It's Ethel Buckley. It's a beautiful day and a Saturday to boot. I'm here to invite you out to lunch."

The door opened, and Ada, clad in a thick terry bathrobe, stood there smiling. "Can you wait thirty minutes for me to freshen up? I'd love to have lunch with my number one fan. Perhaps you'd also consider showing me your town."

Ethel smiled smugly down at Jane, who stood at the foot of the staircase. "I'd love to. Meet me downstairs whenever you're ready."

Ada appeared in the foyer a short time later. She was dressed in a sensible black knit pantsuit with a blue shirt. "I *am* tired of being cooped in that room," Ada said to Ethel and Jane. "I had just taken a shower, hoping to get my energy flowing for work. But I believe a day off would do me some good."

"Aren't you worried about being discovered by people in town? Aren't you afraid that they'll impose on your time?" Jane asked.

Ada smiled. "Do you know why I selected Acorn Hill and your inn to do my writing?"

"Well . . . no," Jane admitted.

"One of the main reasons is that according to my research, few people in this town read my books."

Jane stared at her blankly. "How do you know that?"

"I had my assistant do a check on all the bookstores in this area of Pennsylvania. There's only one bookstore in town, Nine Lives, am I correct?"

Jane nodded.

"According to my assistant, Nine Lives doesn't even stock my books. By choice."

"The owner isn't a fan of popular fiction," Jane said.

"Yes, well, believe me, I've run into that type before. 'It's popular, so it can't be relevant,' am I right?"

"That's pretty much what Viola Reed thinks all right," Ethel said. "I have to buy your books in Potterston."

"Alice had to get *Time Will Tell* at the library," Jane said.

"Which was one of my donations," Ethel said. "Otherwise, it probably wouldn't be *there* either."

Ada smiled tolerantly. "Don't worry. I've heard all this before. It doesn't faze me. In fact, it's a good thing now because I can write here and not worry about being bothered too much."

Jane wondered if Ada Murdoch considered Ethel a bother, but Ada turned to her and said, "I'm glad you're here to encourage me, though, Ethel. A writer likes to meet her fans and appreciates their support."

Ethel beamed. "Shall we go to lunch then?"

"I'd love to. Jane, will you join us?"

"Thanks, but I have some gardening to do." She was tempted to accept the offer, but decided that it would be more fun for Ethel to have some private time with Ada Murdoch. The two were closer in age and probably shared many interests.

"Off we go then," Ethel said gaily, opening the front door. "Oh, I can't wait to introduce you to Lloyd Tynan. He's the mayor of this town and a gentleman friend of mine, as well."

Jane closed the door behind them, smiling to herself. Ethel would no doubt fill in Ada Murdoch on the town's gossip before they even got to the Coffee Shop.

After all of Alice's talk about Nia Komonos and the library, Louise was reminded that she wanted to see if there were any new classical CDs available for borrowing. One of Nia's first projects when she became the librarian was to establish a lending CD, video and DVD collection. The library had a small budget, but she stretched it for all that it was worth by collecting books and other media from garage sales and used-book-and-record stores when she visited Philadelphia and Pittsburgh.

Nia was tapping away at the keys on the computer at her desk, but she looked up when Louise entered and smiled. "Good morning," she said softly, in order not to disturb the other patrons.

Louise approached the librarian's desk so that she could speak softly too. "Hello, Nia."

The librarian smiled. "The genealogy project is getting underway. I have several students here today, researching."

"And several parents too, I see," Louise observed, noticing the adults sitting with the young people.

"Yes, they've taken quite an interest as well. I've started them by suggesting some general Web sites. Lots of them have dug out records already in their possession, like family Bibles, that hold valuable information."

"Genealogy can be an obsession, I am told," Louise said. "My sisters and I certainly enjoy learning about our family tree."

"But have you ever researched it thoroughly?" Nia said. "You can start with the information you already know, then work backward. How far back have you traced your family?"

"Not too far," Alice said.

"Maybe you'd like to attend the seminar this afternoon that Dee Butorac and I are having here at the library," Nia said, her eyes shining. "Many of her students will be here, along with anyone else who's interested. Would you and your sisters like to attend?"

"Well . . ." Louise didn't know if Alice or Jane would be interested, and she was not sure, herself.

"It won't take too long, and I promise not to drone on," Nia said, laughing. "We're just going to suggest some more places to look for family information. Web sites, public records, information like that."

Digging for more family information did sound interesting, and Louise *had* wondered about her family history. "I will check with Alice and Jane," she said, "but I will be back here."

"Oh good," Nia said. "I know how fun and lively things are when you sisters are involved."

"That is nice to hear . . . I think," Louise said.

"Be here at three o'clock," Nia said.

"All right," Louise said. "And now I will leave you to your work while I browse the CDs."

"I got a new Mozart CD on my last trip to Philly," Nia said. "The London Symphony Orchestra. I thought of you when I bought it for our collection."

"Thank you, Nia. I am sure I will enjoy it."

Louise told Alice and Jane about the lecture at the library. Alice thought that it sounded interesting, but Jane begged off. After Ethel and Ada had left, she put on her overalls, and her plan for the day was to clear out all the dead plants. She secretly didn't want to hear all the finer details of genealogical research, but she diplomatically asked Louise and Alice to take notes for her.

"Maybe I can help later," she said. "But right now, I've got to get this gardening started. Then I have to start on my soufflé for dinner."

"I think it sounds like fun," Alice said. "I've often wondered about our other ancestors. And Jane will be here if any of our guests return to the inn and need anything."

"Maybe Ethel and Ada will be at the lecture," Jane said, winking. "Ethel said she was going to show Ada the town."

When Louise and Alice arrived at the library, they did not find Ethel and Ada, but every seat was taken. Lloyd Tynan was helping to set up extra chairs.

"Afternoon, ladies," he said. "I haven't seen this kind of a turnout at the library since its renovation years ago."

"It *is* nice to see so many people around so many books," Louise said.

She and Alice took seats at the back of the gathering. They waved at Martina Beckett, who was seated up front with her father. Ingrid and her parents were right beside them. Nia and Dee Butorac had arranged all the chairs in front of the librarian's desk and set up a projection screen behind it. Nia fiddled with a projector, which was linked to her computer.

Dee Butorac was passing out packets of papers stapled together. A slim, fortyish woman with short hair and an easy smile, she emanated the enthusiasm that made some teachers great. Louise remembered that she had won several teaching awards, one of them on the national level. She lived outside Acorn Hill on several acres with her husband, Brad, and their daughter, Janice, who was in Vera Humbert's fifth-grade class at Acorn Hill's elementary school.

"My class has already received this information," Dee was saying, "so this is mostly for you newcomers. It tells you the first steps in genealogical research, how to organize your data, and how to use the computer. Ms. Komonos and I will give you some general Web sites to check, as well as more specific sites, such as those for a census and other public records. We'll tell you about forms you can download to keep track of your research and show you how to fill them out using a PowerPoint presentation we've prepared. Finally, we have a list of books that we recommend, some of which can be found in this library and some of which Viola Reed has stocked at Nine Lives."

"This sounds like a lot of work," Alice murmured to Louise.

"I agree," she whispered back, wondering if researching the family tree was such a good idea after all. It was not as if she and her sisters had a lot of free time. "It also sounds as if it could easily become a time-consuming hobby."

"I've heard some of the nurses at the hospital refer to themselves as genealogy widows because their husbands are so wrapped up in their research."

"There's nothing quite like getting dragged from one cemetery to another, researching old tombstones, is there?" Louise said.

Despite their reservations, the sisters listened attentively to Nia and Dee's lecture. The librarian and the teacher were thorough in their presentation and spent a long time answering questions afterward.

During their walk home, Louise and Alice agreed that most of the people present had been swept up with Nia's and Dee's enthusiasm. Many townspeople had been at the library. Louise and Alice agreed that the adults seemed more eager to do this work than the students. They had spoken with Martina and her father, and Mr. Beckett seemed more animated about the subject than Martina. He had plenty to say about the ways and methods he would use to find out more about his ancestors. Martina spoke politely when Louise tried to engage her in conversation, but did not seem to have much to say on her own.

"I hope the parents don't wind up doing the work for their children," Alice said. "The project was intended for the students."

"I agree," Louise said. "Mr. Beckett seemed a little too engrossed in the subject for my tastes. I am a little skeptical that some of these parents, er, children will actually be able to trace their ancestors back to Revolutionary times. Mrs. Butorac has only given them a few weeks, and she admitted that the work will be done primarily outside of class."

"It will have to be done outside of *our* normal schedule too," Alice said. "We may not be able to meet the students' deadline."

"Still," Louise said, considering, "it would be fun to try. How about if you research Mother's branch of the family, and I take Father's? We can help each other if need be, and this way we will be covering more of the family tree."

"I think that's a splendid idea," Alice said. "If Jane has time, she can help both of us."

Louise smiled. "I have a feeling this is going to be very interesting."

Chapter Six

When Alice and Louise returned home, they found Ada and Ethel sitting at the kitchen table with Jane, laughing uproariously. Ada was finishing a story about one of her many overseas travels and the difficulties she had had in language translation.

"So I kept insisting on *jabón*," she said, struggling to hold in the giggles, "thinking that I was ordering ham. I thought the waiter looked a little amused, but I never dreamed that I was ordering anything different."

"Oh no. I think I know what's coming." Jane laughed.

Ada nodded. "He brought me some fine Spanish soap, served on a bed of parsley. I was saying *jabón*, the Spanish word for *soap*, rather than *jamón*, which means *ham*. I don't know if he was just trying to be accommodating or having some fun at the expense of an American tourist."

"Either way, it makes for a great story," Ethel said, chuckling.

"Oh, honey, I have lots of great stories," Ada said. "Book signings alone make for interesting conversation. You wouldn't believe the comments that authors get at those events."

"Why, that's a great idea," Ethel said. "We should have a book signing for you here at Acorn Hill."

Ada laughed. "This is my one day off, Ethel. I have to get back to work. Besides, if Viola Reed doesn't stock my books, I don't think she'd be too interested in having a book signing for me."

Louise, who feared that Ada had steered too close to the truth, hurried to change the subject. "How did you enjoy your tour of Acorn Hill?" she asked. She hoped that Ada had not been bothered by anyone in town.

"It was wonderful," Ada said. "I love small towns, and yours has moved to the top of my list. I won't say that I get *mobbed* when I go to bigger places. Most people don't recognize me in person since my author photo is so different from what I look like in real life. But in a small town, people generally don't keep track of who's on the best-seller list."

"*Hmmph.* I do," Ethel said. "I like romance novels, even if *some* people consider them trashy."

The sisters glanced at each other, remembering how they had laughed not too long ago at Ethel's taste in literature. Now that they knew Ada, and Alice had read some of her work, they all looked a little embarrassed.

"Yes, Acorn Hill is a nice place," Ada said. "We had lunch at the Coffee Shop, and then we strolled up and down the streets, browsing in the shops. I bought some fresh sunflowers from that nice Mr. Tracy at . . . what was the name of his store, Ethel?"

"Wild Things," she said.

"Yes, that's it. Oh, and we met the mayor. Very nice man. He and your aunt make a nice couple, don't you think?" She nudged Ethel companionably. "Maybe I could model my next hero and heroine after you two."

"Oh, go on," Ethel said, laughing, but her expression said she was pleased.

"Speaking of Lloyd," Louise said, "we saw him at the library. He was setting up chairs for a seminar that Nia and Dee gave on genealogy research."

"There were quite a few people there," Alice said.

"Lloyd mentioned something about having to help with that," Ethel said. "In fact, he gave that as a reason he couldn't have lunch with us."

Ada turned to Ethel. "I enjoyed your tour so much. It did these old bones of mine good to get out and walk around. It is really lovely with the leaves starting to change. I wish I could stay longer."

"I see your license plate is from Michigan. Is that where you're originally from?" Alice asked.

Ada laughed. "I live in Michigan most of the year. During the winter, though, I try to visit my daughter and her family in Florida. It keeps me away from the cold and gives me a chance to take care of my grandson. My daughter's a teacher, so I help her out during a lot of school months by taking care of her little Bobby."

Louise thought about Vera Humbert and her daughter's impending marriage. She wondered if Vera had considered the fact that one day she might have grandchildren. Maybe the thought would cheer her up.

Ada gathered up shopping bags, filled with purchases from town. "I'd better get back upstairs and hit the keyboard for a bit. Tomorrow I have to get back to work with a vengeance if I want to have lots of free time in Florida. Winter will be here before you know it."

"Tomorrow is Sunday," Louise said. "You are welcome to join us in the morning for services at the chapel."

Ada looked pleased. "Well, now, I think I'd like that. I'd forgotten that your brochure said you owners were daughters of a preacher. I would love to have an inside look at that old chapel. I might want to use it as a setting in one of my novels sometime."

Louise told her the time of the services, and then Jane mentioned that she was serving Belgian waffles for breakfast in the dining room for all of their guests. Ada admitted that she had a weakness for homemade waffles and would be downstairs in time to eat and then attend church with the sisters. At the mention of Jane's waffles, Ethel allowed that she might be persuaded to join them for breakfast too.

The sisters glanced covertly at each other and smiled.

Well before the church service started the next morning, Louise took her seat at the old pipe organ. She loved to run her fingers over the keys before actually making any music. She closed her eyes and remembered being young, back to when she first played the organ at the chapel. She said a prayer that she would play to the best of the talent that God had given her and that through the music every member of the congregation would be uplifted.

She opened her eyes and began playing. The organ was so old and wheezing, desperately in need of repair. Every week she told herself that she would speak to the church board, but she hated the thought of straining the budget.

As the music swelled from the old instrument, it became a special prayer for the family and friends she saw entering the chapel: Alice and Jane, of course, and Ethel, but also Ada Murdoch. Martina Beckett entered with her father, alongside Ingrid Nilsen and her family. To the best of her recollection, Louise thought that it was the first time she had seen the Becketts at Grace Chapel.

Other town members entered, and then Louise saw Fred

and Vera Humbert. Today Vera was smiling, and close beside her sat her eldest daughter, Polly. On Polly's right side sat her fiancé, Alex Neal. Jean, Vera's other daughter, was also there, home for the weekend from Penn State with Polly.

Louise smiled. Henry Ley, the associate pastor, brought her playing to an end, then invited everyone to join in the first hymn, "We Shall Gather in the House of the Lord."

How fitting, Louise thought. Here were so many of her friends and loved ones, worshiping together in this old chapel. She sounded the first notes and played with all her heart.

Jane made her way toward Polly Humbert after the service. Because she and her sisters had been busy with guests all weekend, she had not had a chance to visit the Humberts and chat.

She did not imagine that Polly *or* Vera had much time to talk, however, as weddings took a lot of effort to plan. Especially one on such short notice.

"Hello, Polly," she said, giving the young woman a peck on the cheek. "I was so happy when I heard your good news."

"Thank you, Ms. Howard." Polly blushed, a becoming compliment to her long sandy-blonde hair. "I don't know if you've met my fiancé."

A tall, dark-haired man was talking to Vera, and he had his back turned. Polly gently tapped him on the back, and Jane noticed the tender expression on his face when he looked at Polly.

If Portia Keyes could capture a look like that in words, Jane would forever call her the world's best romance writer.

"Alex, this is Jane Howard," Polly said. "She's one of the sisters who own Grace Chapel Inn."

"How do you do, Ms. Howard." Alex held out his hand.

His green eyes seemed to look straight into Jane's, with respect and admiration for what he had evidently heard about her.

"I'm so glad to meet you, Alex," Jane said, shaking his hand. "Congratulations to you. The Humberts are wonderful people. You couldn't marry into a nicer family."

Alex smiled at his future in-laws, who were accepting congratulations. Then he put his arm around his bride-to-be and smiled down at her. "I think they're all pretty special."

"Oh, Alex." Polly smiled, and then nestled against him, looking up at him adoringly.

Jane's heart twisted. She had forgotten what it was like to be so deeply in love. Once upon a time, she had felt the same way about Justin Hinton, her ex-husband, even though she had been forty when she married him. She had once had a romantic heart like that of young Polly Humbert.

She shook her head. That was behind her, and Polly and Alex would not follow that rocky path. "Do you have an engagement ring?" she heard herself ask.

Polly held out her left hand to reveal an emerald stone. "I didn't want a diamond," she said quietly. "I wanted green, to match the color of Alex's eyes."

Be still my heart. Jane smiled. "I'm sure you have many wedding plans to make."

Polly nodded. "Since it's on such short notice, we're just having a small wedding. Nothing fancy. But it does take a lot of planning. I'm sure I'll be in Acorn Hill every weekend until the big day. I wish I hadn't already started school for this semester, but Mom's going to help me plan. She's already gathering a lot of information for me."

"Let me know if I can do anything to help," Jane said. "Every girl wants a lovely wedding."

"I wish we had more time for you to have exactly the kind of wedding you want," Alex said, his face clouding.

Polly reassured him by touching his hand. "It *will* be exactly what I want."

Alex beamed.

"Well, hello there, lovebirds." Florence Simpson, one of the church's board members, insinuated herself between Polly and Jane. She grabbed Alex's hand and started pumping. "And this must be your fellow. I'm so glad to meet the man who's marrying our little Polly."

Alex looked bewildered. Polly glanced apologetically at Jane, who signaled that she understood. She turned to look for Alice, who was introducing Ada to Vera and Fred. Louise touched Jane's elbow and whispered in her ear. "Looks like Florence is going to monopolize Polly and Alex's time."

"At least I got to meet Alex," Jane said. "He's a nice young man. I think he and Polly will be very happy."

"Do you think Vera looks happier than she did the other day?"

Jane studied their friend's face. Vera smiled at something Ada Murdoch said, then smiled again at Alice. "I believe she does look happier, now that you mention it, Louise."

"Did Polly talk about her wedding plans at all?"

"She just said that she would probably be in Acorn Hill every weekend to help her mother. Vera's taken over a lot of the planning."

Louise nodded at the front of the church. "Poor Martina looks lonely over there by herself. I was on my way to speak with her."

Jane glanced in the direction of Louise's gaze and saw that Martina stood alone, staring at one of the sconces at the end of the altar. Her father was deep in conversation with the Nilsens, still seated in the pews.

"I'm not sure what's going on with her," Jane said, "but I have a hunch that you can find out."

"Hello, Martina," Louise said. She kept her voice deliberately low, as she did when she was speaking to her younger piano students. Something in Martina's demeanor at the moment made Louise cautious about intruding on the girl's tender emotions.

Martina turned. "Oh, hi, Mrs. Smith. You played the organ beautifully."

"Thank you," Louise said.

"This is my first time to visit this church. It's lovely, and I really liked Pastor Thompson's sermon."

Louise smiled warmly. "I am delighted that you and your father chose to worship with us today. Did you come with the Nilsens?"

Martina nodded. "Daddy's getting to be good friends with them, especially since we started this genealogy stuff at school."

The girl's tone was slightly bitter, Louise noticed. "How is your research coming along?"

"It's all right, I guess." Martina wrapped her arms around herself and seemed to close up about the subject. "Would you have a few minutes to show me the organ?"

"Why ... certainly," Louise said, surprised. She could not remember the last time anyone had asked to look at it. Most of the congregation seemed to take the wonderful old instrument for granted.

She led the way to the back of the church, where the organ sat, close to the main entrance. "Have a seat," she said to Martina, who sat gingerly on the bench.

"Is it all right if I touch the keys?" Martina said. "I don't want to play or anything, I just want to see what it feels like to put my hands on different levels."

"Of course," Louise said.

Martina put her hands on two of the rows of keys. Louise

showed her the stops and how she made different tones and sounds.

Martina smiled. "It must be wonderful to play this. Especially in front of so many people."

"I would let you tap out a few notes, but there are still people in the church," Louise said. "Would you like to come here some other day and see what it can do?"

"I'd love it, Mrs. Smith." Martina's eyes shone. "You see, I'm a big fan of *Phantom of the Opera*, and I'm really excited about organ music lately."

"I would be happy to teach you more about it. Organs have a long, colorful history." Louise glanced up and looked toward the front of the chapel. "Your father seems to be looking for you, Martina. He's probably wondering where you are."

The girl sighed and slid off the bench. "I guess I'd better go, then. I'm sure we'll have lots to talk about. We always do after he spends time with the Nilsens. And now today we'll have church to talk about as well."

Louise smiled warmly. "I'm glad you came today, Martina. We don't get much time to talk when you're at the inn. If you are ever in our end of town, even if it's not a Monday, feel free to stop by. I can't guarantee that I will be free, since I am often giving piano lessons. But if I'm available, I would be delighted to chat. Jane and Alice feel the same way."

"Really?"

Louise nodded. "Now go meet your father. I'll see you tomorrow."

Martina looked happier than she had earlier. "Bye, Mrs. Smith. Say hello to Ms. Howard and Miss Howard for me. You guys are the best."

Louise was not sure what she and her sisters were the

best at, and she was not sure how she felt about being referred to as a guy, but she liked Martina Beckett. Unlike many other young people, she was considerate and seemingly interested in the affairs of her elders. *Who is taking whom under her wing?*

The sisters talked Ada Murdoch into eating Sunday dinner with them. She did not need much prompting, once she smelled the heavenly aroma of the shrimp-and-crab au gratin that Jane had popped into the oven just after church. Ethel looked disappointed that she could not join them, but she had promised Lloyd Tynan earlier in the week that she would have Sunday dinner with him.

"I think he just wants to drive over to Potterston to eat at a cafeteria. Why he likes that food, I'll never know. But what can you expect from a man who used to bowl?" Ethel sniffed.

"I like bowling," Ada said.

Ethel looked horror stricken. "Oh. Well. I guess it *is* a good form of exercise."

Ada winked at Jane, who struggled to keep her composure.

After the sisters had said good-bye to the last of their weekend guests and they and Ada had finished Jane's delicious dinner, Ada announced that she was going upstairs to rest. "Just for a bit," she said. "Just long enough for a kitty wink."

Louise looked puzzled. "I beg your pardon?"

"A kitty wink. A really short catnap, you know." She nodded toward the inn's snoozing cat. "I'm sure your Wendell knows exactly what I'm talking about." She headed for the stairs. "Have a good afternoon and evening, girls. I probably won't see you until tomorrow. I slacked off so much yesterday that I'll probably work well into the night without surfacing."

"Happy writing," Jane said. "As for me, I'm off to see

Wilhelm at Time for Tea. He's planning a trip to the California wine country, and we wanted to compare notes. You two behave yourselves."

Alice and Louise looked at one another. The house seemed quiet after a weekend of guests. "It appears as though we are the only ones left. I suppose we could play canasta," Louise said with a smile.

Alice laughed, and then mused, "Mother used to play that with her friends. I remember playing it with you and her, but I can't remember if only two people can play."

"Actually, I was thinking that now might be a good time to begin some family research. If you have nothing else to do, I thought we could start out together by using the computer to check a few genealogy sites."

"That's a good idea," Alice said. "Jane's the real whiz with the computer. I'd feel better with a little help. Just to get started anyway."

Louise smiled. "I feel the same way. Besides the computer, which is not exactly my forte, I feel overwhelmed with the forms that Nia and Dee gave us to fill out."

"Why don't we go into the library and fill out what we already have? We know our parents and their parents."

"That will at least take us back over one hundred years, into the nineteenth century," Louise said. "Just one more century to get to the American Revolution."

They retrieved the papers they had received at the genealogy seminar, and each pulled up a chair to Daniel Howard's desk. Looking at the blank ancestral charts made Alice feel sad somehow. All the unfilled lines intended for family names reminded her of all the deaths that had occurred and of all the ancestors they would never know.

Each sister wrote in her own name at the left of the chart. The family "tree" grew sideways, from the left, until the branches ended at the edge of the right side.

Louise caught Alice staring at the paper. "It does seem like a daunting task."

Alice smiled, smoothing the page with her hand. "Yes, but it also makes me wonder what we'll find. Maybe there's a Revolutionary War traitor in our background."

"Like Benedict Arnold?" Louise smiled thinly. "Perhaps there is a hero, Alice."

"Perhaps," she said. "Well, I suppose we'll never know unless we get started."

"If the job seems formidable, remember what Mother used to say: 'You eat an elephant one bite at a time.'"

Alice smiled. "You're absolutely right. And that's just where I'll start—with Mother's name. And Father's, of course. Our research will diverge from there, but we start with that in common."

To the right of their own names, Louise and Alice wrote in the relevant dates for their parents: birth, marriage and death. "Let's each write as much as we know beyond that, you for Mother's side and I for Father's. Then we can check each other's charts, to make sure we have the correct information. After that we will have to consult the computer or some other resource, I'm afraid," Louise said.

They worked silently for a while, the only sound that of pencils scratching on paper. Louise finished first, and she waited until Alice was finished too. "What do you have?"

"Mother, then her mother and father, Sarah and Matthias Berry, then his father's mother and father, Elizabeth and William Berry. His mother and father were Emily Charters Berry—"

Alice nodded. "And her husband, Benjamin Berry. He was the only son of Ethan Berry, and that's where my family tree stops. At least I got to a second page of the chart."

"Yes, all the way to our great-great-great-grandfather. Do you know what year Ethan was born?"

"In 1795. That is close to the American Revolution." Alice smiled. "We're almost finished with Mother's side of the tree. Perhaps we can trace Ethan Berry's parents to the Revolution. Do you suppose they will be easy to find?"

"If they are," Louise said, "I will enlist you to help me with Father's side of the family."

"How far did you get?"

Louise lifted the glasses hanging from a chain around her neck and perched them on her nose. "After Mother and Father, I have our grandfather and grandmother, Rose and George Howard." She glanced up at Alice. "And that's all I know."

Alice smiled. "It looks like we have a bit of detective work ahead of us, wouldn't you say?"

Louise lowered her glasses and smiled back at her sister. "Indeed."

"Speaking of detective work, I didn't get a chance to speak with Martina at church today, but she looked rather . . ." Alice fumbled for the right word.

"Sad?" Louise supplied.

Alice nodded. "That's how I would describe her. I saw you talking to her and showing her the chapel organ. Did she seem unhappy to you?"

Louise thought for a moment. "At first she did. For some reason I got the impression she was sad about her father. He was involved in talking with the Nilsens."

"Maybe she was ready to go home, and he was holding her up."

"I don't think so. I believe she likes the Nilsens, since they are Ingrid's parents." Louise paused. "I got the impression that perhaps she didn't like the conversation itself between her father and the Nilsens."

"Whatever could she object to?" Alice said. "I can't imagine that they would be discussing anything controversial, especially since they were in church."

Louise shrugged. "He seems to have gotten chummier with the Nilsens since the students started their genealogical research."

"Maybe Martina is simply tired of the homework."

"Or maybe she and Ingrid are tired of their parents trying to do it for them," Louise suggested.

"And maybe," Alice said, smiling slyly, "a certain Howard sister, who will be home tomorrow when Martina comes to clean, can have an innocent chat with her and see if there is anything amiss. Anything that we can help with."

Louise shook her head. "I'll have piano lessons the entire time she is here."

"Maybe Jane isn't doing anything. She seems to have a special rapport with Martina, don't you think?"

"I do. Jane also has a special way of finding out people's needs."

"I'll talk to her later today," Alice said.

Louise shuffled together all the papers, sighing. "If nothing else, maybe she can ask Martina to show us how to do research on the computer so that we can fill out all these ancestor forms."

Chapter Seven

The next day when Martina showed up for work, Ada came downstairs just long enough for Martina to clean the Garden Room and adjoining bathroom, and then the writer went upstairs and back to work.

As usual, Jane had a snack waiting for Martina in the kitchen when she was finished cleaning all the guest rooms and bathrooms. Martina sat at the table, eating warm brownies straight from the pan. "These are delicious, Ms. Howard. Do you give out recipes? Or is it a family secret?"

"It's a secret all right." Jane leaned forward and whispered conspiratorially. "I made them from a mix today because I was in a hurry. But don't tell anyone, all right?" She winked.

Martina laughed. "Why is it that my brownies from a mix don't taste as good as this, then?"

"Oh, I might have added a little something here and there," Jane said. "A little extra cocoa. A bit of melted chocolate . . ."

"Awesome!" Martina said, reaching for another square.

"I made an extra pan for you and your father to eat at home. Once they're cooled, I'll slice them up and put them in a container for you."

Martina set down her brownie. "That's really nice of you,

Ms. Howard. You don't have to give me and Daddy some-thing to eat every time I'm here."

"I like to feed people," Jane said. "It's a way of using God's gift to help others."

Martina resumed eating her brownie, chewing thought-fully. She swallowed, and then said, "I think that's how your sister, Mrs. Smith, feels about playing the organ too."

Jane nodded. "That's how my sister Alice feels too. God gave her the gift of service and nurturing, and she enjoys helping people that way. Those gifts help her to be a wonder-ful nurse."

Martina's eyes filled with tears. She tried to keep eating, but she finally had to set down the brownie and dab at her eyes with a napkin.

Jane leaned in close and put her arm around the girl. "Can I help with anything, Martina?" she said softly.

"Y-you and your sisters have already helped so much," Martina said, trying to stop crying. "I started cleaning your inn because I needed the money, but now I would come here just to be around you three."

"We're glad to have you here, Martina," Jane said. "And not just because you clean our rooms. You're welcome to visit any time. What can I do for you now?"

Martina dabbed another napkin at her eyes. "Talking about Miss Howard being a nurse reminded me of when she helped take care of Mom. I've been missing her lately and feeling kind of lonely."

Jane hugged her tighter. "That's natural, Martina. Have you told your father how you feel?"

Martina shook her head. "He's so wrapped up in this stupid genealogy project. He spends so much time research-ing with the Nilsens that none of them seems to pay any attention to Ingrid or me anymore."

So that *was the problem.*

"I have so much going on in my life right now. This is my senior year, and I have lots of activities and plans for college and stuff. But he doesn't seem to have time to listen."

"Have you tried talking to him about it?"

"Yes, but he always says that this project will be over soon and then we'll have time together. And besides," she said, her lip quivering, "I wanted to trace Mom's side of the family for this project, to feel closer to her, but he's only doing his side."

Jane's heart went out to the young woman. She had seen Jeff Beckett around his daughter and knew that he was not completely ignoring her, but Martina needed extra attention at this time of her life. "Have you told him that you want to research your mother's family?"

Martina twisted the napkin between her hands. "I don't have the heart. See, I know he's using this research to keep his own mind occupied. I know he misses Mom too."

Jane smiled, wiping away a stray tear on Martina's face. "You're a very smart young lady, Martina. Your father's probably throwing himself into this project to keep busy. But do you want my advice?"

Martina nodded.

"Tell him that you want to research your mother's history. Tell him that you need to feel close to her. If he wants to go on researching his family, fine. You can still work together and share information. My sisters are each taking a side of the family tree, but they've promised to help each other and work together."

Martina smiled, sniffling away the last tear. "That's not a bad idea, Ms. Howard. I guess Daddy won't know how I feel if I don't tell him."

"That's right," Jane said. "And I know that he wants you to come to him with any problem. That's what dads are for."

A car honked outside. "That must be Ingrid," Martina said, rising. "I've gotta get going."

Jane quickly packed the extra pan of brownies in a plastic container and handed it to Martina. "You and your father enjoy these tonight after dinner, and you tell him what's on your mind."

"I'll think about it," she said, heading for the door. She stopped, and then turned back. "And thank you for caring, Ms. Howard," she whispered.

On her way home from work, Alice stopped at Nine Lives Bookstore. She was nearly finished with *Time Will Tell* and wanted to see if Viola had any new mystery novels in stock. The bell rang overhead as she stepped over Harry, the orange cat, at the entrance, and she saw Viola and Ethel in deep conversation by the second row of shelves, where Viola was shelving some books. Alice could not hear what the women were discussing, but every time Viola moved away, Ethel matched her step for step.

Alice finally drew close enough to catch their conversation.

"—not fair to the town," Ethel said. "If it was some stuck-up nobody that wrote a hoity-toity biography . . ."

Viola pursed her lips. "That's a matter of opinion, Ethel," she said.

"Yes, it is, and it's mine." Ethel leaned close to Viola. "It's about time somebody told you how the cow ate the cabbage regarding books."

Viola gasped, straightening in response. Alice hurried forward and stepped between the two women. "It looks like you need an impartial mediator. Can I help?"

Viola sniffed. "Your aunt is trying to tell me how to run my business. If you can physically remove her from my bookstore, that would go a long way toward helping."

"I *am trying* to help," Ethel said, turning to Alice to plead her case. "I only asked Viola to host a book signing for Ada, I mean, Portia Keyes. It would be a lovely way for the town to honor her and allow her to sell some books. I've read in the romance reader magazines that that's what is done for authors."

Viola drew herself up even straighter, measuring each word. "I don't do book signings."

"You mean you *won't*, and it's only because Portia is a romance writer."

Viola narrowed her eyes. "Now look here, Ethel Buckley . . ."

Alice held up her hands. "Ladies, please. Aunt Ethel, it is Viola's store. She knows her customers better than we do, for starters."

Viola smiled triumphantly.

"But Viola," Alice said, turning to the retailer. "I do wish you would consider hosting a book signing. I'm almost finished with Portia's *Time Will Tell*, and it's a marvelous book. Full of history and suspense and, yes, love."

Viola sniffed. "*That's* what I object to." She flipped the end of a bright blue scarf over her shoulder, as if to say the discussion was closed.

Alice knew she should probably let the matter drop, but Ethel looked so earnest about honoring Portia Keyes. And the truth was that Alice thought a book signing might be fun. She decided to try a different tack. "But Viola, you often like to give readings of books. Would it be any different to let Portia read a passage or two from one of her own books?"

"I can well imagine how they would go over with this town," Viola said. "She'd flounce in here with a big feather boa around her neck and a tiara on her head and read one of those smutty passages."

Alice and Ethel looked at each other, and then broke into laughter. Viola's face went red. "What's so amusing?"

"Portia Keyes . . . Ada Murdoch . . . is nothing like that, Viola," Alice said. "She's older than you are, and she's the sweetest lady. She doesn't write love scenes like you're describing at all. They're full of tenderness and passion, yes, but there's not one sentence you'd be ashamed to read to a twelve-year-old girl."

"And they're full of history," Ethel added. "Tell Viola about the book you're reading, Alice. It's been a long time since I've read it."

"It's about the Civil War and is set in Vicksburg. The story is about a Union soldier who's stationed there, and about a young widow who's forced to live in a cave with her family because of the siege."

Viola made a face. "It sounds dreadfully boring."

"But it isn't," Alice insisted. "The cave family is running out of food. Shells drop nearby. The Union soldier is wounded in battle. There's a lot of action and suspense."

"Oh, never mind, Alice," Ethel said sharply. "It's plain that Viola's so stuck in her highfalutin literary ways that she won't consider honoring my favorite author. There's just one thing I want to ask you, Viola."

"What?" Viola looked cross.

"How many books have *you* written? Do you know how difficult it is to get a book published and to keep publishing year after year?" Ethel said. "You're always harping on this town to read more. It seems to me that if you really wanted that, you'd want to honor those who take the time to write for the rest of us." Ethel turned and left, the doorbell jangling behind her.

Viola looked stunned.

"I'm sorry, Viola," Alice said. "Aunt Ethel loves Portia's work, and she's only trying to help her. I'm sure she'll cool off and apologize. She knows it's your store."

Viola glanced through the glass door at the retreating figure of Ethel Buckley. "She certainly doesn't act like it."

Before she drove her blue Toyota home, Alice decided to check on Vera Humbert. She had spoken with her only briefly at church the day before and knew that Polly would have gone back to Penn State. Alice wanted to see if there were any new developments in the wedding plans.

Fred answered the door, his normally cheerful face drawn. "Hi, Alice. If you've come to see Vera, I'm afraid she's resting."

"Is she not feeling well?"

Fred sighed. "She came home from school exhausted. The principal has latched on to this crazy genealogy kick and decided that if the high-school students were studying it, the grade-school kids might as well do something similar. Vera's had to adjust her lesson plans."

"Oh dear," Alice said. "And with school having just started, I know that makes things extra hectic."

Fred nodded. "Polly dragged home all these wedding planner books and made Vera look over them too. She says that this semester is going to be so busy for her in school that she wants Vera to do most of the planning."

"Have they considered just having a simple wedding at the church and maybe some sort of party later?"

"Vera won't even ask Polly. She said that every girl should have a beautiful wedding. Oh, I don't think it'll be anything elaborate, but she still needs to plan on a dress, food, wedding vows, music . . . not to mention a reception."

"Poor Vera." Alice shook her head.

"Polly will come home on the weekends, but that doesn't give them much time to plan."

"No, it doesn't. Would you tell Vera that I stopped by and that I'm thinking about her? And please tell her that if there's anything I can do for her, I'd be glad to help."

"I sure will, Alice. By the way, I don't know if you should count on Vera for your walks. I have a feeling she's going to be too exhausted to keep up with any exercise."

"But that's precisely what she should be doing, Fred," Alice said. "Exercise will keep her fit and, in the long run, help her relax mentally."

"I'll tell her, but I don't think she'll do it."

"All right, Fred. Give her my regards."

On the way home, Alice was deeply concerned over Vera's stress, as well as Ethel's attitude toward Viola Reed. Ada Murdoch probably would not care one whit for a Portia Keyes book signing, especially in the small town of Acorn Hill. The issue was not worth a disagreement, and she hoped that Ethel would patch things up with Viola soon.

As for Vera, Alice did not know what she could do to help her friend, except pray. She took up the issue with her heavenly Father right there in her Toyota, and by the time she had parked the car and entered the house, she was feeling better.

The house was filled with a wonderful aroma wafting from the kitchen. Brownies, Alice decided, her stomach rumbling already with anticipation of dessert that evening. The foyer also looked exceptionally inviting, with gleaming woodwork and the faint smell of lemon polish. Everything looked neat and tidy since Jane now usually did major housework on Monday while Martina cleaned the guest rooms.

Alice loved coming home to the cozy house, where the people she loved most on earth lived. She hoped that their guests always felt just as much at home too.

"Nia Komonos called for you," Jane said. "And I have something to report about Martina."

"Oh, please tell me it's good news," Alice said. "This has already been quite a day."

"Let me tell you when Louise finishes her last piano lesson," Jane said. "That way I'll only have to tell it once, and we can discuss it together."

"That sounds good. And I have some things to report to you and Louise too."

When Alice phoned Nia, she reached her on the first ring. "Alice," the librarian said after exchanging greetings, "I have good news. What are you and your sisters doing on Friday?"

"Other than registering the weekend guests, nothing special, I think. Why?"

"Because so many of our high-school students were born in this area, the class is taking a field trip. Since Potterston is the county seat, the courthouse there should have many valuable records like births, deaths, marriages and wills. Any interested town members are invited too."

"Goodness," was all Alice could say. Everyone was certainly getting involved in this project.

"You don't work on Friday, do you?" Nia said.

"No," Alice said. "But we have guests checking in that day. I don't know if I'd have time to go to Potterston this week."

"I just wanted to let you know so that you can make arrangements to come along if you'd like."

"Thank you, Nia. Louise and I will discuss the idea."

Alice hung up the phone, wondering if anything else surprising could happen that day.

Jane could not stop laughing. "So Aunt Ethel let Viola Reed have it?" She leaned back in her chair at the kitchen table and laughed some more.

"I don't see anything funny about this," Louise said. "Viola is my friend."

"Yes, and Ethel is our aunt," Alice said. "I appreciate what she's trying to do for Ada, but I don't like to see a quarrel over a book signing. I hope Aunt Ethel apologizes soon."

"I think it serves Viola Reed right," Jane said. "It's

terrible that she makes such a fuss about stocking contemporary books."

"Oh, Jane," Louise said. "Something like this is only divisive."

"Well, I happen to think it's good to shake things up occasionally," Jane said. "Like this genealogy study. It's given the town something to think about and something to do."

"Nia Komonos told me that many people are going to Potterston this Friday to research genealogy at the county courthouse," Alice said.

"Why there?" Louise said.

"The courthouse has information that's difficult to get anywhere else," Alice said. "I don't suppose there's time to go, though. We have guests checking in on Friday, of course."

"I can take care of them," Jane said. "You and Louise go. I'm not that much interested in the research, anyway, other than picking up the slack when you two need some help."

Louise looked at Alice. "I have no piano lessons on Friday. I'm willing to go if you are."

Alice considered. "It might be interesting. I'd like to find more information about Father's family."

"Good. You're going," Jane said. "And you can keep an eye on Martina."

"Why do we need to do that?" Alice said.

Jane explained about Martina's desire to study her mother's genealogy and her father's desire to pursue his own.

"Maybe by Friday Martina will have told him how she feels," Louise said.

"Maybe," Jane said, but she did not sound hopeful.

"I stopped by the Humberts' on my way home from the bookstore," Alice said. "Fred's worried about Vera. He says she's exhausted. Apparently, the principal of her school wants the fifth graders to be involved in this genealogy study, and she's had to redo her lesson plans. That's difficult enough, but especially when school has only just started."

"She doesn't need that extra work on top of the wedding plans for Polly," Jane said. "She's getting crunched by everything at once."

"Exactly." Alice sighed. "Fred says that she came home from school utterly exhausted. She was resting when I stopped by."

"Perhaps we can help in some way," Louise said.

"I'm not sure how," Alice said. "Weddings involve personal choices that only the bride can make."

"Along with her mother," Jane added.

"Yes. Poor Vera," Alice said. "She's under enough stress about Polly marrying an Army man as it is."

"When I'm making dinner for us the next few nights, I'll make a little extra for Vera and Fred," Jane said. "At least they won't have to worry about cooking."

"Do you suppose that Martina would be interested in doing some cleaning for the Humberts as well as for us?" Louise asked.

"Vera does have trouble getting her housework done, with teaching school all week," Alice said. "I'm sure she could use the help, but Martina hinted that she preferred to work only one day."

"What about your ANGELs, Alice?" Jane said. "Maybe they could help with that kind of light work."

"That's a good idea. I'll mention it to them."

At their Wednesday night meeting, Alice did mention it to her girls. Almost all of them had had Vera Humbert as their fifth-grade teacher, most within the last year or two. They made a list of things they could do to help her, including cleaning. Alice was glad they would not need to ask Martina to clean for Vera. She was sure Martina had enough problems to keep her occupied. Alice also resolved to try to speak to Jeff Beckett, if possible, during the trip to Potterston.

Chapter Eight

L ouise was not surprised to see a large number of people making the trek to the Potterston courthouse on Friday. While driving there, she and Alice agreed that the town had gone genealogy happy. Several people had even closed their shops so that they could join the group at the courthouse.

The sisters had seen Ada Murdoch for just a moment that morning, when she came down from her room long enough to get a popover from the batch that she had smelled baking for breakfast. Ada seemed in such a hurry to get back to her writing that the sisters did not tell her where they were going or why, but only that Jane would be the lone sister at home for the day if Ada needed anything.

While Alice drove her car past trees dotted with brilliant autumn colors, Louise ticked off the names of Acorn Hill townspeople whom they saw on the way to Potterston. "There is Carlene Moss, covering the event for the *Nutshell*. There goes Lloyd Tynan with Aunt Ethel, of course . . . and Viola Reed . . . oh, I do hope she and Aunt Ethel don't get into a confrontation at the courthouse."

"If they do, Carlene can report on it," Alice said, only half joking.

In Potterston everyone parked and then met on the steps

of the courthouse. Louise always enjoyed going to the stately old building, but she felt a special thrill this time. She could almost understand why Alice preferred reading mysteries. She had been thinking about how little they knew about their father's family, and finding the right information seemed a bit like solving a mystery. She hoped that the courthouse would hold many clues for them.

Nia Komonos immediately took charge, marching them all inside and into the records area. She had phoned ahead to let the clerks know they were coming, so the staff was well prepared.

So were the citizens of Acorn Hill, who were clutching notebooks, pencils and sheaves of genealogy forms. All wore eager expressions, and most chatted animatedly.

Louise spotted Jeff Beckett linking up with Martina, who had ridden the bus with her classmates. Before she could say hello to them, the courthouse clerks began a brief introduction relating to the available records and how to access them. Then Nia gave the group a short pep talk.

"I know many of you will want to jump straight back to 1776 to find your ancestors, but you really have to work backward to get there. You might get lucky and find the right information, but most of the time you have no way of knowing for certain that you have traced your actual lineage if you don't follow a logical trail."

"That's not a problem with Father's family," Louise said to Alice after Nia had finished. "We don't have much to go on."

"We might be able to finish Mother's history today, though," Alice said. "We've already traced the family back to 1795, when Ethan Berry was born."

Nia overheard them talking and looked at the ancestral chart that Alice held. "See if you can find Ethan Berry listed in a vital record here at the courthouse. You might be able to find him in the 1810 census. Because he would have been only fifteen, he'd be listed under his father's name or that of another head of household. You then can use that name to trace back before 1795."

Nia walked off to help someone else, and Alice grinned. "This is rather exciting, Louise."

"I agree. Now since we only have a limited amount of time here, perhaps you should do as Nia suggested," Louise said, "while I work on Father's side of the tree."

Alice headed off toward the microfilm area, where the census records were housed. Louise looked at the ancestral chart in her hand and sighed. She had to start with her grandfather, George Howard, and work all the way back to the American Revolution. Could she do it?

"Hello there," a voice said at her elbow. Louise turned to see her aunt.

"Hello, Aunt Ethel. Are you helping Lloyd research his family?"

"I might," Ethel said, "but I'm more interested in helping you. Alice told me that she was researching your mother's family history and that you were researching your father's."

"That's right. We decided that we could cover more ground, more quickly, if we split up the research duties."

Ethel smiled. "Then I'm surprised you didn't think to ask me if I had information you might need. After all, your grandfather was my father."

Louise felt ashamed that she hadn't thought of Ethel. "Things have been moving so fast that I didn't even think to ask. Please forgive me, Auntie. Would you like to work together? We have a long way to go to get back to the American Revolution."

"Maybe we do and maybe we don't," Ethel said, smiling mysteriously. She held up several pieces of photocopied paper. "I never told you girls about this before. In fact, I'd forgotten all about it since your father died."

"What, Aunt Ethel?"

"My father and your father didn't always see eye to eye, as you know."

Louise nodded. George Howard, her grandfather, had never understood his son's desire for an education and was a very difficult, harsh man. After the death of Daniel's mother, George had married Gladys Mulligan, Ethel's mother, and thereafter had little time for the teenaged Daniel.

"When my father died, he willed the family Bible to me. By rights, it should have gone to Daniel, since he was the only son, but I think it was Father's last way of getting back at the son who pursued an education."

"He used a Bible for spite?" Louise was horrified. She was glad that she and her sisters had never shared Daniel's journal with Ethel. Though his descriptions of his father were never hurtful, they painted what seemed to be an accurate portrayal of a bitter man. Ethel did not need to hear further proof of that.

"I suppose you could call it spite," Ethel said. "Truthfully I always meant to give the Bible to Daniel. He knew about its existence, of course. Our father wasn't a churchgoing man, and he seemed to resent it when Daniel became religious."

"And so he had it specified in his will that the Bible would go to you?"

Ethel nodded. "Though your father never said anything, I think he was disappointed that Father willed it to me. I often thought about giving it to Daniel, but after I had it wrapped up and stored in the back closet, I flat forgot about it."

Anger flashed briefly through Louise. How could Aunt Ethel forget something so valuable, something that would have meant so much to Father? Ethel had left the family Bible in a *closet*?

Just as quickly, she knew that her father would not have wanted his daughters to hold a grudge over a material possession. And Aunt Ethel had been taking good care of the family heirloom. It might be in a closet, but it was still in her possession.

"Anyway," Ethel said, holding out the papers in her hands, "these are the photocopies of the family pages from the Bible. I was going to use them to do more research today."

Louise raised her eyebrows. "You have family history beyond George Howard?"

"Right here on these pages. These will give us some good information to get started." Ethel extended her right hand in a conciliatory gesture. "What do you say? Shall we work together?"

Louise looked at Ethel's outstretched hand, then took it in her own, smiling.

Louise thought about calling Alice over to look at the Howard family Bible information with them, but Alice seemed deep in thought in front of the microfilm reader. She decided she could share the Bible news with her sister later.

Ethel and Louise found an empty table where they could spread out the pages. Louise took a pencil from her purse to copy the information to her ancestral chart.

The writing photocopied from the Bible pages showed variations on a spidery cursive. "People just don't write like that anymore," Ethel said, sounding sad.

As much as she loved calligraphy and beautiful handwriting, Louise could not say that she preferred the old-time penmanship. The ink looked smeared in places, and in others, the writing was so different from current standards that Louise had difficulty distinguishing the letters.

Ethel Howard was the last entry in the Bible. Beside that was *Daniel Howard*, and above that, *George Howard* and the names of his two wives. Ethel pointed to the lines above George's. "My father's parents were William Howard, born in 1850, and Sarah Dewcroft. William's parents were Ransom Howard, born in 1818, and Julia Giles."

"Those are my great-great grandparents," Louise said, feeling as though she should whisper.

"So they are," Ethel said. "And my great-grandparents."

Louise studied the page. "It says that all these Howard men were born in Englishtown, just as Father was. It's a shame that town does not exist anymore."

"Yes," Ethel agreed. "It was primarily an agriculture town, and it grew smaller as people moved to larger towns and cities. It finally just disappeared. Fortunately, it was in this county, though, so we should be able to find some records to help us in our search."

"Do you know when the town was established?"

Ethel shook her head. "But if you look at Ransom Howard's father, James Howard, he appears to have been born in Englishtown in 1784. And that's the earliest male Howard that we have a record of," Ethel said. "James Howard is the first entry in the Bible."

Louise marveled that in a matter of minutes, she had reached back over two hundred years with her ancestors. She knew nothing about them except their names. She wondered what these men and women had been like. *What dreams did they share with their spouses and with their children? What was Englishtown, or this area of Pennsylvania, for that matter, like back then?*

"James Howard's father would have been alive during the Revolutionary War. Where do you think we should start looking?" Ethel said.

Louise thought for a moment. "Since we know that James Howard was born in Englishtown, let's start by looking for records of him any year this side of his year of birth, 1784. Maybe that will lead us to his father's name."

"How about the 1790 census?" Ethel suggested.

"Good idea," Nia Komonos said. "I couldn't help

overhearing the last part of your conversation, ladies. These are valuable Bible pages you have here, Ethel. It was wise of you to bring them."

"I didn't get to attend your genealogy talk at the library," Ethel said, "but Lloyd Tynan told me that your advice for researchers was to start at home with family records. And so I remembered the family Bible, which hasn't been opened in many, many years."

"I agree that the 1790 census is a good place to start," Nia said. "However, the census back then only showed the name of the head of the household, but there were columns where the census taker put a tick mark for different genders and age groups. We should see a tick mark for James Howard in the 'free white males under 16' column, since he was only six at the time of the census."

"And we should get his father's name, which would be listed as the head of the household," Louise said, getting caught up in the excitement.

"And we can use that to find more information," Ethel concluded. She beamed at Louise. "Let's get started."

Alice was staring into the grainy light of the microfilm reader when someone tapped her on the shoulder. "Hello, Miss Howard."

Alice turned. "Martina. How are you doing?"

"Fine, thanks. My dad's over there," she said, nodding her head in the direction of the research bookshelves.

"Are you two getting lots of information?"

Martina smiled. "We are now. We started researching his family, and he really got into it. He was asking my friend Ingrid's parents for help because they've traced their tree way back."

"Were they able to help?"

"They did," Martina said, and then paused. "But when

Mrs. Butorac gave us this assignment, I really sort of envisioned us researching my mom's family. I didn't say anything to Daddy at first because he seemed to be having so much fun. Then your sister, Ms. Howard, said I should just talk to my dad and tell him how I felt."

"Did you?" Alice said.

Martina nodded, breaking into a smile. "He was shocked. He had no idea that's how I felt. Then I cried, and he cried, and we agreed that researching Mom's tree would make us feel closer to her."

Jeff Beckett turned away from the bookshelves and smiled when he located Martina.

"I think it will make you feel closer to each other too," Alice said.

"Marti," Jeff said, calling to his daughter, "I think I found something in one of these books. You'd better have a look."

"Okay, Daddy. Be right there." She turned back to Alice. "I'd better get back to work. Are you and your sister having any luck with your research?"

"I'm not," Alice said. "I hope Louise is doing better."

Martina inclined her head toward the other side of the room. "Looks like Mrs. Smith and Mrs. Buckley are working together. Good luck, Miss Howard."

"Thank you, Martina. You too," Alice said distractedly, wondering what Louise and Ethel were doing huddled together.

She turned back to the microfilm reader, where she was looking for information on Ethan Berry. She had found information on his son, Benjamin, but nothing about Ethan, or more importantly, his parents.

Alice blinked, and then closed her eyes to get a moment's rest. *If I'm having this much trouble with the Berry side of the family, what obstacles must Louise be facing? After all, she had many more names to trace.*

"There it is," Ethel said excitedly, pointing at the microfilm screen. "There's the Howard family in the 1790 census for Englishtown."

"Yes," Louise said, marveling at the ancient record. "And just as Nia said, there is a tick mark under 'free white males under 16' column. That must be James."

"What's his father's name? Nathaniel?"

"Yes," Louise said, squinting at the florid writing of the census taker. "So now we have James's father's name."

"If he had a child in 1784, Nathaniel must have been old enough to fight in the Revolutionary War," Ethel said. "Do you suppose we could find a list of soldiers' names?"

"Let's check with Nia," Louise said.

They had to wait their turn while she helped some other town members. When she was finally free to help them, she directed them to a book, *Revolutionary War Pensions and Land Boundary Warrants*, which someone had thoughtfully brought for others to share. "The chances are," Nia said, "that if he was a veteran of the Continental Army, he would have requested a pension later. You might find information there."

Searching the book, however, revealed no Nathaniel Howards.

"That's odd," Nia said. "Like you ladies, I would have thought he'd been a soldier. Why don't you try looking for an official record like a birth, marriage or death certificate?" she suggested. "That might give you more information. That clerk over there, Mabel Walters, has been helping lots of people."

Louise and Ethel moved over to a stoop-shouldered white-haired clerk who had just finished helping Viola Reed. "This is my favorite part of the job," the clerk said, smiling broadly. "Every day when you genealogy people come in here with your little bits of information you want pieced together, it's like solving a puzzle."

"We have a bit of a puzzle all right," Louise said. "We have a name of someone who was on the 1790 census, and we need to find more information."

"We couldn't find his name listed as a soldier," Ethel added.

They showed the information they had to Mabel. "He was registered in Englishtown?"

"Yes," Louise said. "My family lived there for many generations."

"The town's no longer in existence," Mabel said.

"We know," Ethel said, bobbing her head as if to hurry the clerk. "But can you point us to earlier records of Nathaniel Howard?"

"Perhaps an earlier census?" Louise said.

Mabel shook her head. "1790 was the first year there was a federal census. What we need is a vital record. Let's look on microfilm."

Mabel pointed them toward the microfilm of 1790 and earlier: Birth, death and marriage certificates and wills were on file by years. They divided up the years from 1770 and plowed through them.

Just when Louise had begun to despair of finding any new sign of Nathaniel Howard's existence, Ethel let out a squeal. "Here! Look."

"What?" Louise said, leaning over from her chair to look into Ethel's microfilm viewer.

"It's a marriage certificate for a Nathaniel Howard and an Elizabeth Shaw in 1774."

"And the place of their marriage was"—Louise squinted to read—"Georgetown. In this county."

"I never heard of a Georgetown," Ethel said. "That's odd."

"I suppose we could keep looking for a birth certificate," Louise said, slightly disappointed. They had found the name of Nathaniel's spouse, but not his place of birth, nor if he had fought in the Revolution. The thought of looking at more microfilm was daunting.

Louise pushed back her chair. "I am going to ask the clerk if she has any other ideas. This takes too long, Ethel, and we will have to leave soon."

She found Mabel working behind a desk, and she explained the situation. "Have you ever heard of a Georgetown?" she said. "Do you have any records for it?"

"I don't have any material on Georgetown," she said, "but a dear friend of mine works at the county historical society just next door. She knows more about this county than just about anyone, including me. Her name is Grace Topham. Tell her I sent you."

"Thank you," Louise said. "You have been very helpful, Mrs. Walters."

Louise got Ethel's attention, and they headed down the steps of the courthouse and toward the historical society next door. They had not seen any sign of Alice. Louise wondered if she was having any luck tracing their mother's side of the family.

The historical society was housed in a small building that had obviously once been a residence. Grace Topham met them at the door. "You must be part of that lovely group from Acorn Hill. I've had several visitors from there today."

"We have run into a snag, and Mabel Walters at the courthouse sent us to you," Louise told her.

"What can I help you with?"

Laying out their notes on a table, Louise explained the situation, with Ethel filling in details. Grace nodded her head as they spoke.

"And so we don't know why Nathaniel Howard is not listed as a soldier or where this mysterious Georgetown was," Louise finished.

Grace smiled. "Do you know the origin of Englishtown?"

"I don't believe I've ever heard how the town came to be named, now that you mention it," Ethel said. Louise nodded in agreement.

"Englishtown was established after the Revolutionary War," Grace said. "I know because my ancestors lived there too."

"Why is its name so important?" Louise said.

"Think about the name. Englishtown. If it was established after the War, why would anyone name a town after the enemy from whom they'd just gained their independence?"

Louise and Ethel looked at each other, baffled.

"Not everybody in 1776 was in favor of a new country," Grace said. "Many still wanted to hold their allegiance with King George and England. What happened to them during and after the war?"

"If I remember my history correctly, many of them moved to Canada," Louise said.

"True, but not all of them did. Some of them stayed. You see, a sizeable portion of this county was developed on a land grant from the king. Tories, British supporters, might have owned part of that land and not wanted to give it up, even after the British lost and sailed home over the Atlantic."

"Hence the name Englishtown?"

Grace nodded. "There was a settlement called Georgetown that was home to both patriots and Tories. After the war, the patriots refused to call it Georgetown anymore. In fact, during the war they became so incensed at their Tory neighbors, that the Tories all sold out and bought land close together and started a new town. Legend has it that they picked a fancy name for it, but all the patriots derisively called it Englishtown."

"And the name stuck," Ethel said.

Grace nodded. "They didn't figure it was too much of an insult, I guess."

"What about the town of patriots?" Louise said. "Is it still in existence?"

Grace smiled. "I'm surprised you didn't know, my dear. That is your own Acorn Hill."

Louise let all the information sink in for a moment. "Nathaniel and his wife must have moved to Englishtown sometime after the Revolution, since that is where their son James was born in 1784."

"That's a possibility," Grace said.

"Thank you, Mrs. Topham," Louise said. "You have been so helpful."

"Yes, thank you," Ethel echoed.

Grace smiled. "Chances are that my family knew yours. We Tophams have been in this area for over two hundred and fifty years. If you find out we're related, give me a call. I'd like to compare ancestral charts."

Louise laughed. "This is an interesting hobby, Mrs. Topham, but I am afraid that I don't have the time to give it the full attention that it would no doubt require."

"Just the same, you can always contact me here," Grace said. "Good luck with the rest of your research."

"Thank you," Louise said. With a sigh of relief, she hoped that their research was nearly concluded. Genealogy was nerve-wracking.

Chapter Nine

O n the ride back to Acorn Hill, Alice listened to all the information that Louise had discovered. She was fascinated to learn that Ethel had been storing a Howard family Bible all these years, and even more fascinated to hear where the names in the Bible led. "So Father's ancestors . . . our ancestors . . . were Tories? British sympathizers?"

"Yes," Louise said. "How about that? I always pictured our relatives as being staunch patriots. I suppose Mother's side was, anyway."

"We don't know that," Alice said. "I couldn't find any information about Ethan Berry. It seems like a dead end."

"Grace Topham, the woman at the historical society, believes that just after the war, everyone in Acorn Hill was a patriot. So chances are Ethan's family was too."

"I don't know," Alice said. "Maybe he didn't come from Acorn Hill. I'll just have to dig a little deeper. Maybe I'll find something."

"I am sure Nia or Martina would be glad to help you do some Internet research." Louise looked over the Howard names she had managed to add to the ancestral chart. "I wonder why the family Bible began with James Howard?"

Alice shrugged. "Maybe it was a wedding gift. And speaking of weddings, I'll have to check with Vera this weekend, to see if she and Polly need any help with the wedding planning."

"That is a good idea," Louise said. "There must be something we can do to help."

"I hope we didn't leave Jane in the lurch," Alice said. "I feel guilty for making this trip to Potterston, especially when I didn't even find out any information. I might as well have stayed home and helped her register our weekend guests and look after Ada Murdoch."

"Is she still staying with us?" Louise said, smiling. "Ada is such a quiet guest and we see so little of her. If it were not for all the fuss her presence has caused with Ethel and Viola, I might not be sure she really existed."

Alice laughed and turned on the car radio to an oldies station for the rest of the drive home.

Jane registered all the guests who were visiting for the weekend. She put the Parkinses in the Sunset Room, the Leggs in the Sunrise Room, and the Springfields in the Symphony Room. The Parkinses were passing through on their way to visit a relative in Boston, the Leggs were using the inn as a base while they traveled to other places in the area, and the Springfields were celebrating their sixtieth wedding anniversary.

Jane was impressed by the Springfields. Even though her own marriage had failed, she delighted in seeing older people who had had success. As far as she could tell, it took not only a great deal of love, but a good sense of humor too.

She could see that Horace and his wife Cora had a lot of

that from the moment they had arrived at the inn, pulling up in a stretch limousine. The chauffeur had helped them out of the car and up the walkway to the inn, then gently had lifted Cora and carried her through the door, with Horace hobbling along behind.

Jane had rushed to help, certain that Cora Springfield had some infirmity, but Horace had waved her away, his eyes twinkling. "Not a thing wrong with my princess," he said, in answer to Jane's questioning look. "It's just that I'm too old to carry my bride over the threshold like I did sixty years ago. But I wanted her to know that in my heart, I still carry her every day of our marriage."

"Oh, Horace," Cora said, putting a hand over her heart as the chauffeur set her down. "That is the sweetest thing. Isn't he the sweetest thing?" she said to Jane.

Jane grinned. "He's pretty sweet."

"Nothing too good for my princess," Horace said, pinching Cora's wrinkled cheek. She blushed, and then giggled.

Jane covered a laugh of her own. Horace turned to her, his eyes still twinkling. "Our children call us incorrigible."

At last all three couples were settled in their rooms. Jane went back to the kitchen, wondering how Louise and Alice were doing with their research.

While she was preparing stuffing for the roast chicken she planned for dinner, she heard a faint rap at the back door. Vera Humbert stood outside, looking pale. "I hope I'm not bothering you," she said.

"No, Vera. Come inside." Jane opened the door and gave Vera a hug. "You look exhausted. Are you feeling all right?" she asked as she pointed Vera to a chair.

"Truth to tell, I'm not." Vera blinked, looking as if she wanted to cry.

"Oh, I'm sorry," Jane said. "Let me get you something to drink."

"I'd really like a glass of water," Vera said.

Jane put ice cubes in a glass, filled it with water and handed it to her friend. "Why don't we move into the parlor or someplace more comfortable?"

"No, I'm fine," Vera said, setting down the now half-empty glass. "I know your guests have probably arrived for the weekend, and I don't want to disturb them. I just needed to rest a spell. I came to talk to you about Polly's wedding."

"What can I do to help?" Jane drew up a chair.

Vera sighed. "She and Alex say they don't want to put a financial burden on us. They want to keep the wedding simple. But she wants me to help plan, and I'm afraid I'm so addled and scatter-brained from everything going on, that I'm not much help."

She took another sip of water, and then said, "Do you know of any good recipes for a wedding cake? Polly wants to make one herself. She wants everything to be homemade."

"I can look for some recipes, Vera, but does she really think she'll have time to make her own cake?"

Vera's eyes misted with tears. "She thinks she'll be able to make it the night before the wedding. I don't know why she's being so stubborn, Jane. I know what will happen. I'll wind up having to make it, and I'm sure I'll make a mess of things."

"You shouldn't have to make your daughter's wedding cake, Vera," Jane said, "or anything else for the wedding. Neither should Polly. You two should be able to enjoy all these moments without having to worry."

Vera nodded, wiping her eyes. "I know. And I want to. But there's so much to do. Polly came home early from college today and is over at Sylvia's Buttons right now. She's looking over dress patterns and material. I suppose she'll want me to make her dress."

Jane patted her arm. "Go join her, Vera, and let me think. For one thing, don't worry about that cake. I'll be glad to make one for you."

"I can't ask you to do that." Vera looked shocked.

"You didn't," Jane said. "I volunteered. Now go join your daughter, and let me noodle on your problem."

"Thank you, Jane," Vera said. "I can rest easier knowing that I won't have to worry about the wedding cake."

After she left, Jane went back to her stuffing, mixing sautéed onions and celery and dried cranberries with seasoned bread cubes. She heard the Springfields coming down the stairs, so she went to see if they needed help with anything.

"Oh no, dear," Cora said. "Horace and I just wanted to spend some time in your parlor, if that's all right. We love to read, and I've brought the latest Portia Keyes book for this trip." She held up a hardback novel, and Jane saw Ada's author photo on the back.

"Cora loves that woman's writing," Horace said, holding up his own hardback. "Me, I lean more toward military history, but she loves her romance novels."

"There's lots of military history in them too, Horace," Cora said, pretending to sound slighted.

"Yes, dear, I'm sure there is." He turned to Jane, smiling. "We've learned to keep the peace."

"I can see," she said, knowing that they were not in the least miffed with each other. "Feel free to use the parlor for reading, or you might want to read in the library."

"Thank you, dear," Cora said, opening her novel to read as she walked. "Oh, Horace, this is another wonderful book."

At that moment, Ada Murdoch descended the stairs. Jane glanced from her to Cora, wondering if it would be such a good idea for reader and writer to meet. Cora might turn into another Ethel and want to dog the author's every step.

Jane tried to wave Ada away, who only looked perplexed at her actions. "What's wrong, Jane?" she asked.

Standing at the parlor door, Cora glanced up from her book. "Why, hello," she said to Ada.

"Hello there," Ada said, smiling. Jane could see that her glance had fallen on the book in Cora's hands. "What are you reading?"

"It's the latest Portia Keyes novel, about the French Revolution," she said, and then sighed. "She's my favorite author." She gestured at the photo on the back cover. "She's so smart and glamorous."

"Do you think so?" Ada's smile widened.

Jane stepped forward. "Cora, this is Ada Murdoch. She's staying with us for several weeks while she"—she fumbled for the words, not wanting to give away Ada's identity—"she . . ."

"I'm working on a project," Ada said, extending her hand.

"This is Horace and Cora Springfield," Jane said to Ada. "They're celebrating their sixtieth wedding anniversary."

"Really?" Ada said, taking first Cora's hand, then Horace's. "Now *that* is a true romance story."

Cora smiled and explained, "Horace and I were just about to start our reading time. We've found that indulging our literary hobby together has helped our marriage immensely."

"Well, then, I won't keep you. It was nice to meet you," Ada said.

"Likewise," Cora said. She and Horace went into the

parlor and made themselves comfortable, leaving Jane and Ada looking at each other. They smiled, and without a word, retreated to the kitchen. Behind the closed door, they giggled.

"They're the sweetest couple I've ever met," Ada said. "They remind me of my husband and me. We were so much in love."

"I knew you wouldn't want her to know who you are," Jane said.

"It's always nice for an author to get an unsolicited opinion from her readers," Ada said, "but yes, I'm glad she didn't recognize me. That's another reason to have a glitzy author photo. No one recognizes the real you."

"Well, *I* barely recognize you now," Jane said. "We haven't seen much of you lately. I take it your writing is going well?"

Ada nodded happily. "Very well. I think I'll be able to eat dinners with you and your sisters this weekend, if that's all right."

"Of course it is," Jane said. "We'd love your company. You're welcome to eat with us in the kitchen if you'd like some privacy from our other guests."

"I'd like to do that," Ada said. "I promised your Aunt Ethel that we'd do some sightseeing and shopping around town later today, but I'd like to keep the weekend fairly quiet."

When Louise and Alice returned home, Ada had already retreated to her room. Jane filled them in on all that had happened while they were gone, and they told her what they had discovered about their family history.

"We appreciate your holding down the fort while we

went to Potterston," Alice said. "Although I must say it was a fruitless search on my part."

"You'll find out more information," Jane said. "Meanwhile, since you two are back to look after things, I'm going to head over to Sylvia's." She explained about Polly's desire to have an old-fashioned, homey wedding. "I want to see how things went at Sylvia's," she said. "I offered to make the wedding cake, and I think Vera was glad to accept. It would be a major item to cross off the wedding to-do list."

"Maybe I could volunteer to play the organ at their wedding," Louise said. "I have quite a good selection of wedding-appropriate music, and Polly could choose what she liked."

"That would be another thing to cross off the list," Jane said, clearly delighted. "Let me see what they have to say, and I'll check back with you."

On the way to Sylvia's Buttons, she saw Patsy Ley. The associate pastor's wife had a rolled-up magazine under her arm, and she was humming to herself.

"Hello there, Jane," Patsy said. "Where are you off to?"

"Sylvia's Buttons. I wanted to find out from her if Polly Humbert had found a pattern for her wedding dress."

Patsy's eyes took on a faraway look. "I think it's so romantic, don't you? I love weddings, and unfortunately, in a small town, we just don't see that many."

"Did you and Henry have a big wedding?" Jane asked.

"It wasn't particularly large, but it was beautiful." Patsy sighed. "I loved planning it, though, down to the last detail."

She looked around as though afraid of being overheard. "My secret vice is watching that reality TV show that follows couples as they plan their weddings." She held out the TV show's companion magazine. "I even buy this and read it every month. As silly as it sounds," she said, lowering her voice, "once Bible studies and mission work and such are done, I feel like I need a creative outlet."

Jane stopped. "Do you keep up on the current wedding trends?"

Patsy blushed. "Yes. Dresses, music, food, everything."

Jane took a deep breath. "Would you be willing to put your knowledge to work?"

"I don't understand," Patsy said.

"Vera wants to help Polly plan her wedding, but her teaching job keeps her very busy. And I don't think she's that interested in planning the details that make a wedding."

"I see," Patsy said.

"If Polly agrees, would you be interested in helping her plan her wedding? She needs someone to go over ideas with her and someone to take care of the little details while she's back at college during the week. And Vera needs the rest."

"I'd be delighted. Even with my church work, I still have time on my hands occasionally. This would be doing something I love, and it might truly help the Humberts."

"Isn't it great how God hooks up a needy person with a gifted person so that they both benefit?" Jane said. "Let's head for Vera's."

Jane expected to see the Humberts' house in its usual disarray, since this was a Friday and Saturday was Vera's regular cleaning day. But she stifled a gasp when Polly opened the door. Besides the usual weekly clutter, the Humberts' living room was littered with pages ripped from bridal magazines, swatches of satin, taffeta and chiffon, and several separate yard-lengths of various colored ribbons. The ANGELs may have helped clean during an earlier week, but obviously not this one.

"Oh dear," Patsy whispered to Jane.

"What brings you here, Mrs. Ley, Ms. Howard?" Polly asked. Her eyes were shining and her face glowing. She did not acknowledge or even appear to notice that anything was amiss in the house.

"We'd like to talk to your mother and you," Jane said.

"She's in the kitchen. I'll go get her." Polly left the room, and in a moment returned with Vera.

"Hi, Jane, Patsy. What's up?" Vera asked.

Jane cleared off spaces on the couch for them to sit. "I hope you don't think I'm interfering, but I know you are pressed for time and I've had an idea. Weddings are Patsy's special hobby, and she's very knowledgeable about everything that goes into organizing one. She is willing to serve as your wedding planner, Polly. Vera, that would free you up to get your lesson plans and other schoolwork done. You wouldn't have to be responsible for planning the wedding, and you and Polly would have more time to do mother-daughter things. Patsy's up on all the latest wedding trends and can give you lots of good ideas. When you're back at school during the week, she can be organizing things."

Polly looked skeptical. "I really wanted Mom to help me."

Vera looked guilty and opened her mouth, but Jane quickly cut in. "She *can* still help, Polly. She can still be your consultant. I know you've been busy with school and the wedding, but I'm not sure that you've noticed that your mother is exhausted."

Polly turned to Vera. "Is that true, Mom?"

Vera looked down, as though ashamed. Then she raised

her head and looked Polly straight in the eye. "Yes, it is. I want you to have the wedding of your dreams, but there are so many details, and having everything be homemade is unrealistic."

"Forgive me for interrupting," Patsy said, "but some things could be homemade. It seems to me that everything you need for a wedding can be found right here in Acorn Hill. Each item would be made by someone who knows you, Polly. The whole town loves you, and that love would go into each stitch on your dress, each note of music—"

"—and each morsel of food," Jane said. "And Patsy would work with you to make sure you have exactly what you want."

Polly looked at her mother. "Would you still help me decide, if I can't make up my mind?"

Smiling, Vera patted Polly's hand. "Of course I will. You're my daughter." Her eyes misted with tears.

"Oh, Mom." Polly threw her arms around her mother, and they both broke into sobs, interspersed with laughter. "I can't believe I'm getting married."

"I can't either," Vera said, holding Polly close while she stroked her long, blond hair. "My baby."

Jane wiped her eyes. Patsy did too. Though nothing had been said regarding a decision, she knew it was settled. Vera would get her much-needed rest, and Patsy would become Polly's wedding planner.

While Jane was at the Humberts', Louise took her genealogy notes to Daniel's library. She had just spread them out on the desk when Ethel stuck her head in the doorway. "Oh, there you are. I've been looking for you."

Louise set down her pencil. "How was your trip back from Potterston with Lloyd, Aunt Ethel?"

"That man," she said, flopping down into a chair. "He either drives too fast or too slow. He's like a teenager taking driver's training."

"But you made it back safely," Louise pointed out.

"Yes, well, Lloyd did buy me an ice cream cone at one of those roadside malt shops," Ethel said. "I know it was just to mollify me, but it made me feel better about his driving." She studied the pages Louise had spread in front of her on Daniel Howard's desk. "Did you tell your sisters about our discovery?"

Louise nodded. "They were very interested."

"That's good." She rose as if to leave, then turned back. "Do you and your sisters have any plans for this evening after dinner?"

"I don't believe so. Unless one of our guests needs something. Why?"

"I'd like to see you about something, if I may."

Louise thought her request peculiar. Unless she was invited for dinner, Ethel did not usually come to the house in the evening. "Certainly, Aunt Ethel. You know that you're welcome anytime."

"Ethel?" Ada Murdoch stepped into the library. "Oh, I didn't mean to disturb you ladies."

"Not at all," Ethel said. "I just needed a word with Louise, but now I'm ready to head out on our excursion, Ada."

"Where are you two going?" Louise asked.

"Ethel has graciously agreed to show me Acorn Hill's Town Hall," Ada said. "I'm looking forward to seeing the town display."

"Lloyd's agreed to share a bit of history about the town too. At Ada's request," Ethel added, as if Louise might think Ethel had pushed the idea herself.

"You ladies have fun," Louise said. "Ada, will we see you for dinner?"

"Yes, indeed," she said. "I already spoke to Jane about it."

"Ethel, would you like to join us tonight?" Louise asked.

"No thank you," Ethel said. "I'm cooking for Lloyd tonight. He has a meeting right after, so I'll stop by after dinner. Ada, are you ready?"

"I am," the author said. "I've been looking for an afternoon off. Acorn Hill, here we come."

Friday evening, after they had returned from their various dining places, all the guests migrated to the parlor. At Horace and Cora Springfield's request, Jane brewed strong coffee.

"I don't know how they drink that stuff this late in the day," she confided, back in the kitchen with Louise, Alice and Ada.

"Maybe that's the secret to their long lives and happy marriage," Ada said, sipping her herbal tea thoughtfully.

"I don't know, but they seem to be enjoying themselves with the Leggs and the Parkinses. They were talking about playing a card game."

"What game?" Ada asked, with an excited look in her eyes. "I love cards." She slumped in her chair. "But I suppose I should get back to work. I had far too much fun this afternoon with your aunt. I'll get lazy."

"If you do not mind my saying so," Louise said, "you have an admirably strong work ethic."

"But perhaps too strong," Jane offered. "Would it hurt to indulge yourself in a little fun?"

"All work and no play make Ada a more disciplined writer," she said. "And a happier grandmother when she's relaxing in Florida for the winter. Jane, that was the best crème brûlée I ever had. If I keep eating like this, I won't be able to fit into my swimsuit next month."

"I'll leave the rest in the refrigerator. You're welcome to have a midnight snack," Jane said.

"Heavens no, I wouldn't dream of it," Ada said, rising.

"More discipline?" Alice asked.

Ada winked at her. "You'd better believe it, kiddo. That's the only thing keeping me from diving into more of that heavenly dessert. Good night, ladies."

"Good night, Ada," they chorused.

After Jane had delivered the coffee to the parlor, where the three couples were involved in a spirited game of charades, which they decided upon instead of cards, Alice and Louise made Jane sit at the kitchen table with her own pot of Wilhelm Wood's special after-dinner tea blend called Winding Down.

Jane sipped the brew, and then stretched her feet out under the table while her sisters tidied up the kitchen. "You know, a girl could get accustomed to this good life. Good meal, good tea, good sisters to clean up—"

"Yoo hoo!"

Jane sat up straight, drained her teacup, and then sighed. "I knew it was too good to last."

"Hello, girls," Ethel said, entering the kitchen. She set a large white box, wrapped in a big red bow, on the table and then stood back and smiled.

Alice and Louise dried their hands on dishtowels and

came over to investigate. Jane fingered the ribbon, her eyes gleaming. "And I thought you'd forgotten Alice's birthday."

Ethel's face fell. "It isn't today, is it, Alice?"

Alice smiled. "No, Aunt Ethel. Jane is just kidding you."

Ethel looked relieved. "I brought this for all three of you."

"What is it?" Alice asked.

"Open it and see," Ethel said, smiling.

Jane carefully unworked the bow so that she could save the ribbon. Louise lifted the lid and pushed away scads of tissue paper. Her eyes grew wide as she lifted out a large, aged, brown leather book. "Oh, Aunt Ethel . . ."

"What is it?" Alice asked again, craning her neck to see.

Louise set the book on the table, her eyes misting with tears. She reverently brushed her hand across the cover, over what were surely once brightly gilded letters reading "Holy Bible."

"The Howard family Bible," Jane said, standing to get a better look. She and Alice crowded around Louise, who opened the book as carefully as though it were a Gutenberg.

"Louise told you the story about my father willing it to me?" Ethel asked.

They nodded, unable to take their eyes off the family heirloom.

"It should have gone to my brother Daniel a long time ago," Ethel said. "But better late than never, I say. I want you girls to have it."

Louise looked up. "Are you sure, Aunt Ethel? Your children might want this to pass along to their children one day."

Ethel shook her head. "The Bible should stay in this area, and my children don't live in Acorn Hill and probably never will."

"Look at this," Alice said in an awestruck tone. "Here are all the pages you photocopied from the front of the Bible, Ethel. And, oh, look! If you flip through the pages, you can see names and birth dates written beside certain verses in the Bible."

"Perhaps these were verses that someone prayed over the newborns," Louise said.

"I had forgotten all about those," Ethel said, crowding closer. "I can't say that I've looked inside this old Bible since my father showed it to me when I was just a girl. I wasn't allowed to look at it without him or Mother present."

"Here's an entry for Ransom Howard. His birth date is noted as July 12, 1818, right beside Proverbs 16:3," Alice said, "'Commit thy works unto the Lord, and thy thoughts shall be established.'"

Louise carefully turned some of the pages. "Here is an entry for his father, James Howard, but there's no birth date. It is beside Isaiah 43:19. 'Behold, I will do a new thing; now it shall spring forth; shall ye not know it? I will even make a way in the wilderness, and rivers in the desert.' Do you suppose he selected that verse for himself?"

"Maybe his parents selected it for him when he was born and he wanted to record it," Jane said.

Louise shrugged. "We may never know. At any rate, Aunt Ethel, you have given us a priceless gift."

"Yes, thank you, Auntie," Jane said. She kissed Ethel on the cheek.

Ethel smiled, and then pulled all three women into her embrace. "Thank you, girls. Your presence in Acorn Hill has been a precious gift to me as well."

Chapter Ten

The next day, Saturday, Alice worked on tracing Madeleine Howard's side of the family. She went to the library, where Nia Komonos had obtained free access to online genealogical Web sites.

"But I looked at so many censuses at the courthouse, Nia. I found the people we already know about, but not anyone earlier than Ethan Berry, who was born in 1795."

"You'll have to check places other than censuses," Nia said, "since the first one was taken in 1790. You might also try e-mailing that nice woman Louise talked to at the county historical society. She might know something. Or the Daughters of the American Revolution."

"The DAR?"

Nia nodded. "I wish I'd thought to have them talk to us while we were in Potterston. That's the closest local chapter. I have their Web site and e-mail address, though."

"I don't even have an e-mail address," Alice confessed. "I'm one of those old dogs that can't learn new tricks."

"Nonsense," Nia said, smiling. "You know that you're only as old as you feel. I can set you up with a free e-mail account in no time."

Alice soon found herself with a cyber address, a place where she could receive e-mail. Her ANGELs had suggested a long time ago that she get such an account so that she could e-mail them information. Now she could be the hub to pass along emergency prayer requests or last-minute schedule changes.

"I'm not sure about all these new forms of communication," Alice said. "The next thing you know, I'll be pressured into getting a cell phone."

"It's not a bad thing to have," Nia said, "especially since you travel alone from Potterston to Acorn Hill so many times a week for work."

Alice smiled. "If I had any car trouble, I'm sure that someone I know would come along to help me out. Just like you're helping me now."

"I do what I can," Nia said. "I'm so glad to see Acorn Hill take an interest in its past. Now let's see what more we can find out about yours."

She showed Alice how to access the national DAR Web site so that she could check their library. "You can search by family name here," Nia said, pointing to a list on the library's page. "Or by subject. Something like Pennsylvania—Revolution would give you a broad list of resources, I imagine."

"I'll try the Berry family name first, then," Alice said.

"Call me if you need any help," Nia said, moving away to assist other patrons.

Alice felt a little nervous at the computer keyboard. Her Internet surfing experience had been severely limited, mostly just observation as Jane established Grace Chapel Inn's Web site. But the Web page seemed friendly enough, and she soon found the place to type in "Berry Family." Unfortunately, the information that the computer returned was scant, and it only listed Berry families in other states. Nothing for Pennsylvania.

Alice realized she was going to have to cast a wider net and typed "Pennsylvania—Revolution." This time, she got more than thirty hits, as Nia called them, and she scrolled through the information, her heart sinking. *Pennsylvania—Revolution—Campaigns, Pennsylvania—Revolution—Capitalists and Financiers . . . How will I know what to select?"*

Then she saw Pennsylvania—Revolution—Military Records. "I might as well start somewhere," she murmured to herself and clicked on the subject title. She received several results that included book titles, which she wrote down on a piece of paper.

Patiently, she went through a number of other subject headings under Pennsylvania—Revolution and got other titles of books and periodicals to check. When she showed her information to Nia, the librarian smiled. "Now that you have that, let's go to the Pennsylvania State Archives home page and see if you can find those books and periodicals online."

Alice's heart beat a little faster as she searched the information at the archives Web site. She hoped that she was not wasting her time.

She scoured the information about military records and was about to give up, when she found a request for a pension by a Jeremiah Berry in Acorn Hill's county. *Could this be Ethan Berry's father?*

Armed with a name now, she dug deeper into the records.

Jane decided to stop by the Good Apple Bakery. She did not feel the need to do *all* the cooking at Grace Chapel Inn, especially where pastries were concerned. Today, she had a craving for éclairs, and she knew she could count on Clarissa Cottrell at the Good Apple Bakery. Sure enough, there in the glass case were many éclairs, plump with *crème pâtissière* filling and frosted with chocolate.

"I'll take one dozen," she said to Clarissa.

"How's the inn doing?" Clarissa asked.

"We're busy again this weekend. It'll probably stay like this until after New Year's. How about you?"

"The bakery keeps me busy."

She carefully boxed the éclairs and handed them across the counter to Jane. "Here you go. I hope you enjoy them."

"I'm sure we will," Jane said. "I've never heard any complaints about the Good Apple Bakery."

She left the Good Apple and headed toward Sylvia's Buttons. Jane sold some handmade jewelry there, and she wanted to check on the stock. During the winter months, when there was less to do outdoors, she usually found more time to create her jewelry.

Inside Sylvia's, she was pleasantly surprised to find Patsy Ley and Polly Humbert poring over wedding dress patterns. At some times Sylvia hovered over them like a mother bird, at others she flitted around her shop to bring swatches of fabrics and ribbons for their perusal.

After they greeted Jane, they quickly returned to their planning. "I like this style," Polly said, pointing to a picture in the pattern book.

"I think that basque waistline would look good on your slim figure," Patsy said. "And I like the simplicity of the straight long sleeves."

"That would be nice in satin," Sylvia said, laying a white swatch beside the pattern.

Polly studied it critically. "I don't like the neckline off the shoulder, though."

"I can remedy that," Sylvia said. "What kind of neckline do you like?"

Polly studied several other patterns in the book until she found one she liked. "This one with the slight curve. What's that?"

"That's called a boat, or *bateau*, neckline," Sylvia said.

"Oh, I like your choice. It's demure and attractive," Patsy said. "I don't like wedding dresses that make the bride look like a Hollywood starlet. A bride should be soft and feminine, not daring."

Polly studied the picture again. "I don't like the train, either. In fact, I don't want a train at all."

"You just want the hemline touching the floor, with a touch of fullness in the skirt, right?" Sylvia asked.

Polly nodded.

"*Hmm*." Sylvia tapped a finger against her chin. "I could make an underskirt with a little netting. That would make the dress stand out a bit, but not make you look like a ballerina."

Patsy sighed. "It sounds heavenly, Sylvia. I know you'll do a great job. Polly, I know you'll look beautiful."

"What about a veil?" Jane asked, finding herself drawn into the plans.

"Well," Polly said slowly. "You know that veil that brides wear over their faces and when it comes time for the groom to kiss her, he lifts it over her head?"

"A blusher," Sylvia said.

"I want one of those," Polly said.

"I can create a fingertip-length veil and attach a blusher veil to it with a half-wreath headpiece." Sylvia said.

"Look at that veil edged in ribbon. Do you want that or something with a lace design?" Patsy asked.

"I like the ribbon," she said, her eyes shining. "I think it all looks pretty. I can't believe it's going to be for me. For my wedding."

"You're going to be a beautiful bride," Jane said.

Polly smiled at Patsy. "Mrs. Ley is really helping me. We're getting lots of items crossed off our list." She counted on her fingers. "We have the dress pattern picked out. You had told Mom that you'd make my wedding cake."

"And that offer still stands," Jane said.

Polly nodded, still counting off fingers. "I need to talk to Mrs. Smith about playing the organ for the wedding. But our next biggest need is finding someone to sing."

"Do you have anyone in mind?"

Polly shook her head, looking worried. "Not really."

"I'm sure you'll find someone," Jane said, glancing at her watch. "Oh dear. I'd better get back to the inn. I'm glad I was here to see you design the wedding dress, but I really just popped in to check on my jewelry. Do you need any more, Sylvia?"

She shook her head. "Check back in a month, though. With all the extra tourists in the fall, it may start selling fast."

Jane promised that she would, then headed for home with the éclairs.

The inn's guests were gone during the day, off on adventures in Acorn Hill and surrounding towns. That night they all reported back, tired from their shopping and sightseeing.

Louise met the Springfields at the front door when they returned. Some friends had driven to Acorn Hill to pick them up for a round of golf at a country club outside of Potterston. "It may be the last time we play before the cold weather sets in," Horace said.

"We do love our golf," Cora added, smiling up at her husband.

"But we're not such old fogies that we're too tired to go out to dinner with the Parkinses and the Leggs tonight," Horace said. "We had such fun together last night playing charades that we decided to have dinner together and then come back here and play more games."

"That sounds like fun," Louise said, bemused. It was delightful to see their guests become friends, but she was beginning to wonder if the Howard sisters were running a resort rather than a bed and breakfast.

"They'll never have room for these éclairs after eating at Zachary's," Jane said when Louise told her about their guests' plans. "I guess we'll just have to eat them ourselves."

"An entire dozen? Perhaps we should invite someone over for dessert and coffee," Louise said.

"That's a great idea. Let's invite Lloyd and Aunt Ethel," Jane suggested.

"How about Viola?" Louise asked.

"Do you think she and Ethel will be on speaking terms, after the Portia Keyes book-signing disagreement?"

"Perhaps this will be a good way for them to settle their differences," Louise said.

"All right, then. We have Lloyd, Ethel and Viola. How about Dr. Bentley and his wife, Kathy?" Jane asked. "I hate to think that the only time I see him is when I have medical trouble, and I don't know her as well as I'd like. And do you think Pastor Ken would like to join us? That would make six guests."

"It sounds lovely, Jane. Shall we start calling?"

Everyone had been delighted to accept the invitation for dessert, and Jane and Louise talked about it as they set the kitchen table for dinner.

They heard the front door open and then Alice say, "Jane? Louise?"

"In the kitchen," Jane called.

Alice bustled in, her face glowing. "I found Ethan Berry's father."

Louise looked at her in surprise. "But you couldn't find anything at the courthouse."

"Nia showed me several Web sites to check, and . . . " She

looked around the kitchen, noticing their dinner preparations. "Is it time to eat already?"

Louise laughed. "Alice has turned into a die-hard genealogy buff. She is starting to lose track of time."

"I didn't realize it was so late," Alice said. "My news will
have to wait."

"I bought a dozen éclairs at the Good Apple Bakery, but
then discovered that our guests are all eating at Zachary's
and probably won't have room for an evening snack," Jane
said. "So Louise and I have invited some guests for dessert
tonight."

"That sounds like fun," Alice said. "Who are we
entertaining?"

"Lloyd, Aunt Ethel, Pastor Ken, Viola, and Dr. and
Kathy Bentley."

"Am I invited?"

They turned to find Ada Murdoch standing in the
doorway. "Or have you forgotten that I told you yesterday I
could eat dinner with you ladies every night this weekend?"
she asked.

Louise and Jane looked nervously at each other. They
had completely forgotten. And now they would have Aunt
Ethel, Viola *and* Ada in the same room. Ada Murdoch would
comport herself beautifully, but the casual get-together could
turn uncomfortable if Ethel decided to pursue the Portia
Keyes book-signing issue.

"Of course you're invited," Alice said. "As you can see,
we're just about to sit down to dinner."

"Then chocolate éclairs and company for dessert," Jane
said, in what she hoped was a breezy manner.

"Sounds wonderful." Ada seated herself at the table.
"Chocolate is my particular indulgence, especially when I'm
under a deadline."

"You'll have to try some of Jane's truffles," Louise said. "She makes them for us, of course, but she also sells them at Wilhelm Wood's."

"The gentleman that owns Time for Tea?" Ada said. "He's a nice man. His mother is sweet too. Your Aunt Ethel and I visited there yesterday. He showed me some lovely tea services. Then we went to that antique store in town and met the owners, the Holzmanns. Rachel told me that her father was a glassblower."

Jane set dinner on the table, and all the sisters sat. "Are you interested in glassblowing, Ada?"

"Could be," she said, staring into space as if thinking about something. "You never know when that occupation might work itself into one of my books."

When the sisters cleared the table after dinner, Ada insisted on helping. She brushed off their entreaties to rest with an emphatic refusal. "I should be getting more exercise, anyway. Besides, you gals make me feel like I'm part of your family."

"That's how we want all our guests to feel," Alice said.

After the kitchen was cleared, Jane set the coffee pot to brew a French vanilla decaf, and Alice put water in the kettle for herbal tea. Louise arranged the best china service, their mother's white on blue Wedgwood, in the parlor. Ada scooted upstairs "to change into something a little more presentable."

The guests arrived, first Lloyd and Ethel, then Dr. Hart and Kathy Bentley. Before Alice could hang up Kathy's sweater, Rev. Thompson was at the door, followed by Viola Reed.

Louise shot Jane a look as Viola and Ethel warily greeted each other. She knew then that they had not patched up their differences. She was beginning to think that Ada had gone back to writing or at least forgotten about the coffee, when the author walked into the parlor.

"Ada," Pastor Ken said, rising from his seat. "I didn't know you would be joining us. What a treat to have a published writer among us."

Viola's head snapped around. "Is *this* the famous author I've heard so much about?"

Louise glanced at Ethel, who seemed to be pressing her lips together.

"You must be the bookseller," Ada said, cordially holding out her hand. "I've met everyone else here in town, but not you. It's a pleasure."

Viola shook her hand, but did not look too pleased. "My name is Viola Reed."

"Ada Murdoch," she replied, and then winked. "Though some folks call me by my pen name, Portia Keyes. It doesn't matter which. I answer to both."

Everyone laughed lightly, and Ethel moved to her side. "I'm so glad you could join us tonight. Lloyd and I have been talking about you so much. He's started reading one of your books. From the *library*," she said, casting a glance in Viola's direction.

Viola's face flushed, and she opened her mouth to speak, but Jane cut in. "Have a seat everyone. I have the éclairs all ready. Louise, would you mind helping me in the kitchen?"

"Not at all," she said, delighted to follow her sister.

"What are we going to do?" Jane hissed, once they were in the safety of the kitchen. "Aunt Ethel and Viola are ready to go at it. I don't want Ada to get caught in the crossfire."

"How about if I play the piano? It will be more difficult for everyone to talk that way," Louise said.

"Good idea." Jane arranged the éclairs on a Wedgwood serving platter and handed it to Louise. "Take these in there so they'll have something to occupy their mouths for the time being, at least. I'll bring the coffee and tea. After that, I'll ask you to play. Agreed?"

Louise nodded, heading back into what she felt certain was a looming fray. Fortunately, the discussion had turned to the town's genealogy research.

"I haven't accomplished much on the British side of my family," Rev. Thompson was saying. "But the other side of my family was in Boston during the American Revolution. One of my relatives even worked for a time in Paul Revere's silversmith shop."

"How fascinating," Alice said. "So I suppose he was a patriot?"

Rev. Thompson nodded. "It would be interesting to find out how my relatives in Great Britain viewed the colonial rebellion."

"I know how mine felt," Dr. Bentley said. "I have a letter from a British relative who was in America to quash the rebellion. He died at Bunker Hill."

"I also have a relative who died at Bunker Hill," Lloyd Tynan said, frowning, "but he was a patriot who died fighting the lobsterbacks."

Hart Bentley's expression darkened at Lloyd's use of the derisive term for the British soldiers.

Oh dear, thought Louise, *this evening has the potential for several skirmishes among our guests.*

"We found out that our family tree had British sympathizers," Alice said hastily. "Today I found out that, at the same time, we had a patriot ancestor. Practically in the same area, this part of Pennsylvania."

Rev. Thompson leaned forward. "Tell us what you discovered," he said, as though trying to smooth out the rough words between Dr. Bentley and Lloyd.

"Yes, Alice," Jane entered the room with coffee and tea. "I'll pour and Louise will pass around the éclairs while you tell."

Alice glanced around the room, looking intimidated by her captive audience. "Our great-grandmother was Emily Charters Berry and her father-in-law was Ethan Berry. That was as far back as we knew about Mother's side of the family. Nia helped me find information today that indicated Ethan's father was Jeremiah Berry. He was a member of the Continental Army. He didn't get married until after the Revolution was over and he was settled in this area."

"At the same time," Louise said, "we had a relative who was one of the founding members of Englishtown. Did you know that that town was organized by Tories who decided to stay in America after the war?"

"Interesting," Rev. Thompson said, stroking his chin. "There they were living in separate but close towns. They never would have imagined that their descendants, your mother and father, would eventually marry."

"Isn't that romantic?" Ada said softly.

Viola smirked. "It's just life, is what it is."

"That's what I like best to write about," Ada said cheerfully. "But tell me, what's with all the genealogy talk?"

Rev. Thompson explained about the town's interest in researching its roots because of the high school history teacher's assignment. "I'm afraid we've all become a bit too caught up in it," he said, glancing at Lloyd and Dr. Bentley, who refused to look at each other.

"I would like to hear from other people whose families weren't in this area during the Revolution," Alice said. "The Holzmanns, for example, have German roots. Nia's family was in Greece. I believe Dee Butorac's family came from what was once Yugoslavia."

No one responded, though Lloyd looked thoughtful. Louise and Alice exchanged a worried glance. Besides Lloyd and Hart Bentley not speaking, Viola Reed ate her éclair with gusto, glancing at Ethel and Ada over each bite.

Jane, noticing the tension, said in what Louise recognized as her most polite hostess voice, "Louise, would you consider playing something for us on the piano?"

Chapter Eleven

On Sunday afternoon, her sisters busy with other things, Jane bid farewell to their weekend guests. The Leggs and the Parkinses said that they had had a wonderful time and would tell all their friends about Grace Chapel Inn. The Springfields were equally complimentary. After hugging Jane, Cora Springfield said, "Thank you for allowing your inn to bring a little romance into our lives."

Jane arched a brow. "I don't think you needed any help there. I've never seen two people so much in love."

"You mean two people of our antiquity, huh?" Horace said, winking. He put his arm around Cora's shoulder and pulled her close for a little squeeze.

She giggled. "Oh, Horace. Stop that. Act your age."

He pretended to look shocked. "I am, Cora. I am. With you by my side, I'm always young at heart." He guided her toward the front door, winking. "Thank you, and please give our thanks to your sisters."

Jane watched Horace chivalrously open the car door for Cora and settle her into the back seat of the chauffeured limousine. The driver honked the horn as they drove away from the curb, and Jane waved after them. Too bad Ada Murdoch had not been downstairs to bid them farewell.

She probably could have taken notes for one of her romance novels.

Jane started to shut the door when she saw Patsy Ley's white Ford Taurus pull up at the curb. Patsy and Polly Humbert hustled up the walk, their arms filled with notebooks, bridal magazines and brochures.

"Jane!" Patsy said. "Thank goodness you're here. Polly has to drive back to school within the hour, and we were hoping to catch you."

"Come inside," she said. "Hi, Polly."

"Hi, Ms. Howard." Polly's long blond hair bounced as she breezed through the door with Patsy in her wake.

"Have a seat in the parlor," Jane said. "Would you like something to drink?"

Patsy shook her head, laying a hand over her heart as though to catch her breath. "No time. We drove to Philadelphia for a bridal show yesterday, and we've spent all day discussing what we saw. We have some wonderful ideas, but I'm afraid we've gotten carried away with the time."

"Alex will be in Acorn Hill within the hour to take me back to State College," Polly said. "I still have a few things to throw in my suitcase."

"Let's get right down to business then," Jane said, perching on the edge of Louise's baby grand piano bench so that she could be close to the women sitting in the Eastlake chairs. "How can I help?"

Polly looked at Patsy as though she was the leader. "We wanted to know, first of all, if you were serious when you told Vera that you'd make Polly and Alex's wedding cake."

"Quite serious," Jane said. "It would be my honor."

Polly bit her lip, and then looked down. Wendell leaped into her lap, and she absently stroked the tabby's head in a rhythmic pattern.

"What's wrong?" Jane asked.

Patsy uncrossed her legs, balanced the notebooks and magazines on her knees, and then looked Jane straight in the eye. "We hope you won't be offended if we decline your offer."

Polly glanced up, her blue eyes pleading. "Please don't be upset, Ms. Howard. I love your cooking. It's the best in town. But I know first of all that you made that offer to Mom so that she wouldn't have to make my cake. I thought I wanted my wedding to be homemade, but I realize now that I don't."

Jane was taken aback. She had never thought of *home-made* as a bad thing. Did Polly want to go to an impersonal bakery chain?

"It's just that . . . that . . ." Polly wrung her hands in her lap.

Patsy finished the explanation. "When Polly was a girl, she dreamed of having her wedding cake come from the Good Apple."

"I know you could make one just as beautiful," Polly said to Jane, "but I had always pictured Clarissa making my wedding cake, like she made all of my birthday cakes when I was a kid. I showed this picture of a three-layer Italian cream cake to Clarissa, and she agreed that she could make it for me in a snap. Take a look at this picture Patsy found."

"It came from the *Making Vows* Web site," Patsy said, referencing the reality wedding show she loved to watch.

Jane glanced at the photo. The layers, covered with luscious-looking, white, butter cream frosting, were separated with a gold wire ring of connecting hearts. The sides of the cake layers were piped with pale pink hearts and fancy scrollwork. "That's a beautiful cake, and the Good Apple will make it just right. I'm not offended, just relieved. For a minute there, I thought you wanted to get your cake from a grocery store."

Polly put her hand over her mouth and gasped. Patsy

grinned. "I'm glad you understand, Jane. That's a load off my mind."

"We do have one other question, though," Polly said. "Would you consider catering our reception? Not including the cake, that is."

"I wouldn't consider it at all. I accept the assignment without question," Jane said.

Polly and Patsy beamed at each other, and then Patsy opened a notebook. "Here's a list of the food we're considering. We value your input, of course. You don't have to tell us now. We can talk about it when Polly's in town next weekend."

Jane took the paper, studying the list. "Where will the wedding be?"

"Grace Chapel, of course."

"And the reception?"

"In the chapel's Assembly Room," Polly said. "We've already spoken to Rev. Thompson and he said that was okay."

"I'm in charge of decorations," Patsy said, "with Polly's approval of course. We're still working on that."

"What about the ceremony?" Jane asked. "Have you decided on decorations for the chapel and music and vows?"

Polly looked worried. "We only have a few weeks left, but we're still working on that, too. I want to carry the same decoration theme in the chapel as in the reception area."

"Craig Tracy told me that he can get whatever we want in the way of decorations—not only flowers but candles or a gazebo or whatever. He has a special arrangement with his florist association, which includes a rental shop in Potterston," Patsy said.

"I haven't figured out what music I want. I can't decide between prerecorded music, a string quartet, the piano or the organ." Polly's face crumpled. "Oh dear. There's still so much to do, and I want everything to be just perfect."

"If it helps," Jane said. "Louise would probably be delighted to play the piano or the organ, if that's your choice."

"Do you really think she would?" Polly asked.

Jane nodded.

"Great!" Polly clapped her hands together, startling Wendell. He jumped down from her lap and raced out of the parlor. Polly lowered her voice as if to compensate. "I have a friend with a beautiful voice who's a music major, but she starts a new job that weekend and can't get the time off. I really want someone to sing at my wedding. I definitely want someone to sing 'The Lord's Prayer' and a couple of my favorite songs."

Jane looked at Patsy. "What about you? You enjoyed playing the show tunes at our winter costume party, and I heard you sing. You have a lovely voice."

Patsy shook her head. "I'm not a soloist. And I certainly don't have the volume for the chapel. We need to find someone who can really fill that space."

Jane sighed. "That's a big order. Do you know any opera singers?"

Polly giggled, gathering up her belongings. "No, but I'll keep looking for someone. Patsy said she would too."

"Maybe you could post a notice at the music department at Penn State," Jane suggested.

"That's an idea," Polly said, "but I really don't have time to audition people even if I find someone at college. Patsy's hoping to find somebody this week so that I can listen to them next weekend."

"By the way, Jane," Patsy said. "Here's an estimate of what we are able to pay for your catering services. It's as high as we could go, since Polly wants to stay on budget. I hope it's acceptable to you."

Across the large notebook on her lap, she pushed a piece of paper closer to Jane. Without looking at it, Jane pushed it back. "This is my gift to Polly and Alex. They can pay for the food itself, but the labor is on me."

Polly's eyes widened. "Do you mean that? I don't want to take advantage of your professional training, Ms. Howard."

"You're not," Jane said, grinning. "And now if you don't mind my saying so, if you hurry, you might be able to catch Clarissa over at the Good Apple and order that cake."

Polly swallowed several times in rapid succession, apparently overcome. "Thank you for your gift," she managed to say. She jumped up and hugged a surprised Jane, then bounded toward the door.

Jane walked Patsy to the door. "Good luck with the rest of your plans. Let me know if I can help."

Like Polly, Patsy gave Jane a brief hug. "You already have."

After they left, Jane studied the sky. The days were growing shorter, and she wanted to get in a jog. If she went right now, she would have time. She had been neglecting her exercise in recent weeks, and her body and mind needed refreshing. It would be so easy to settle in for a lazy Sunday afternoon with the Philadelphia newspaper or a good book, but autumn was not the time to get lazy. There would be enough days of bad winter weather when she would be forced to stay indoors.

Perhaps I should consider getting a treadmill. How Louise would love it if I suggested setting it up in the parlor alongside the baby grand. Jane smiled as she put on her running clothes and laced up her running shoes.

She headed out for her jog and passed the carriage house where Ethel Buckley lived, behind Grace Chapel Inn. Jane could see that Ethel's small porch and rocking chairs were empty, but as she passed by, the front door opened.

"*Yoo hoo!* " Ethel called. "Jane!"

Jane groaned inwardly. She really needed this run. But

Ethel was her aunt, and she especially felt sorry for the way Viola had snubbed the old dear the night before. She slowed until she was jogging in place in front of Ethel's house. "Hello, Aunt Ethel," she called.

Ethel cupped her hands around her mouth. "Come inside, Jane. I have something to tell you."

"Can it wait?" she asked hopefully.

She could tell even from the distance that Ethel's face fell. "I suppose so, but Lloyd's here, and he has some wonderful news. Dee Butorac is here too."

Jane sighed. If she did not go in, she would disappoint Ethel and probably Lloyd Tynan and the history teacher, too. She might as well get it over with. Maybe there would still be time to get in her run.

She had not even begun to breathe hard or perspire, yet Ethel wrinkled her nose as Jane stepped into the house. "*Tsk, tsk*. I don't know why you want to do that, dear," Ethel said quietly. "Heavy exercise is not ladylike."

"Better a healthy woman than a dead lady," Jane said cheerfully. "Running is good for the body and soul, Aunt Ethel."

"I suppose," she said skeptically. "Especially if you don't mind *muscles*."

She said it as if it was a foul word, but Jane let the comment pass. Lloyd greeted her as he rose from the rocker. "Hello, Jane. I had a great time at your éclair fest last night. Thank you for inviting me."

"We're always delighted to see you, Lloyd," Jane said. *Well, maybe not just now, particularly. I need my run.*

"Hi, Jane." Dee Butorac rose from the sofa. "I haven't seen you in a long time. I saw your sisters at my genealogy instruction class and then again on our courthouse trip, but not you."

"Louise and Alice decided to do the family research for all of us," Jane said. "They're keeping me informed."

"That's good." Dee rubbed her hands together. "I'm hoping many people will inform us."

Jane looked puzzled.

"Lloyd has a marvelous idea," Ethel said. "Tell her, Lloyd."

"Oh, Ethel," Lloyd said. "It's not that much. I think Dee should be the one to tell."

"It was your suggestion, Lloyd," Dee said, demurring.

Jane tapped her foot. "Somebody please tell me."

Lloyd handed her a bright blue flyer from a multicolored stack on the end table. "I just had these printed up this afternoon in Potterston. The *Nutshell* won't come out until Wednesday, and I wanted to give people notice as soon as possible."

"'Come one, come all to an Acorn Hill genealogical assembly this Friday at seven PM at Town Hall,'" Jane read aloud. "'We hope to hear from everyone whose family was in the Acorn Hill area at the time of the American Revolution, but we want to hear from anybody who has traced back his family tree over two hundred years. We are a town with deep roots.'"

"Lloyd suggested we make a town assembly out of my class's genealogy presentation," Dee said. "He thought it would be fun to hear from the students and then from other town members. Anyone who wants to speak about his or her Revolutionary-era ancestors will be allowed to participate."

Jane faked a smile. "It sounds like fun."

Dee's short hair bobbed as she nodded. "At first my students grumbled about this assignment, but they've really gotten into it. It's even brought several families closer together."

"I'm sure that's true," Jane said politely. She held up the flyer. "May I keep this to show Alice and Louise or do you need it back?"

"Oh no, you keep that," Lloyd said. "It was Alice who gave me the idea last night when she said she'd like to hear from people whose families weren't in this area during the

Revolution. Start spreading the word. It's short notice, and we want a lot of people to be there. We'd hold it later, but the students will be wrapping up their assignment this week. It's best to have them make their presentation while it's still fresh."

"We're going to distribute these flyers today and tomorrow," Dee said. "Take that one to your sisters."

"Thanks," Jane said, folding it into tiny squares. "To tuck in my pocket," she said by way of explanation, when the others looked at her strangely. "I'm sure you have many plans, and I need to get back to my run."

"Thanks for stopping in," Ethel said, showing Jane to the door. She leaned closer and whispered, "Don't run too far. You might hurt yourself."

"Yes, Aunt Ethel," Jane said, squashing the impulse to reply sarcastically. "Bye Lloyd, Dee."

Back on the road, she eased into a run, thinking about the upcoming assembly. *Oh dear. Hours and hours of other families' genealogy information. What a snoozer!*

She knew Dee was right that several families had grown closer because of their genealogy research. Martina Beckett and her father had used it to help work themselves through their mutual grief, so that was a good thing. But Jane still was not sure why she had to endure hours of "my great-great-great-great-grandfather" because of a high-school assignment. What interest could she, or anyone else have, in someone else's family tree?

After she had returned home, taken a shower and dressed, Jane read the flyer aloud to Alice and Louise, who listened attentively.

"I like the part about our being a town of many roots," Alice said.

"When we were growing up, it seemed as though everyone

in Acorn Hill had lived here longer than anyone else could remember. It will be nice to know about those original relatives," Louise said.

"As well as where current town residents' ancestors are from," Alice said. "We've had a lot of outsiders, as Lloyd used to call them, move in. I'm looking forward to learning about their roots."

Louise nodded in agreement.

Jane pressed her lips together so that she would not say anything that offended Louise or Alice. She could not think of anything more boring than hearing about the research for ancestors. Where they came from did not hold any fascination for her. Maybe she could pretend to be ill the night of the assembly.

On Sunday nights, Jane usually fixed a light meal, sometimes pancakes or waffles, other times soup and salad. Tonight she felt particularly uninspired, so she gathered the ingredients for French toast and bacon. She put the bacon in the microwave, and then halfheartedly dipped slices of bread into an egg yolk and milk mixture to fry for the French toast.

While she was slicing up strawberries to serve on top with powdered sugar, Ada Murdoch entered the kitchen. She sniffed the air appreciatively. "I knew something smelled wonderful."

"It's just something I'm throwing together," Jane said.

"It sure smells good," Ada said. "Mind if I fix myself a pot of good strong coffee? I've got a long night ahead of me."

"Help yourself," Jane said. "You can find coffee beans in the pantry. They're separated by blends."

Ada disappeared into the pantry then returned with a canister in hand. "You weren't kidding," she said. "You must have eight kinds of coffee in there."

"I never know what our guests will want," Jane said. "What did you pick?"

"I decided not to go for too strong a blend after all," Ada said. "I chose Southern pecan."

"Ah, are you dreaming about Florida?"

Ada measured and poured the beans into the grinder. When they were done, she poured the ground beans into a filter in the coffeemaker's basket. "Now that you mention it, I am looking forward to visiting my daughter and her family. And the air had a bit of a nip in it today, did you notice?"

Jane paused to consider. "I don't think so."

"When you get as old as I, your bones get more sensitive. And mine are telling me that the weather is changing and there's a shift in the wind."

Jane laughed. "It sounds like Mary Poppins is about to descend."

Ada laughed along with her. "Just the opposite. It's almost time for me to go. I've loved my time here, but I'll soon be finished with my book." She poured water into the coffeemaker and then hit the "On" switch. "I'll miss you and your sisters."

"We'll miss you too, Ada. We've tried to stay out of your way so that you could work, but we've enjoyed the time you've been able to share with us."

"I wish it could have been more. It's hard to be disciplined."

"You certainly made Aunt Ethel happy," Jane said. "I'm glad you were able to spend some time with her."

"Ah, Ethel." Ada leaned against the counter and crossed her arms. "She's easy to like. I would really like to do something special for her before I leave."

Jane heated the griddle for the French toast. "What she'd like more than anything is to get Viola Reed to agree to a book signing for you."

"She does see that as a personal cause," Ada said. "I

don't care about the dog and pony show of a book signing. One of the reasons I came to Acorn Hill was precisely because Viola didn't stock my books."

"Are they usually mobbed?" Jane asked.

"Sometimes," Ada said. "Other times, the literary world is like your friend Viola, looking down its collective nose at what it feels are trashy little books. It has no idea of the amount of historical research I use."

"Well, I know about it," Jane said. "I know how much time you've spent up in that room. You can't be writing the entire time."

"Heavens, no," Ada said, chuckling. "For me, writing is only about forty percent of the work. The other sixty percent is reading tedious, boring books about whatever period or location my current work in progress is set in. I read everything from political histories to personal letters so that I can truly immerse myself in the subject. By the time I'm finished with a novel, I'm close to being an expert."

"That sounds like it'd be right up Viola Reed's literary alley," Jane said.

"That woman may be prejudiced against popular fiction," Ada said, "but I hear she at least keeps after everyone to read. That librarian too. She and I had a great conversation the other day, and she knows her books."

Ada took a seat at the table. The flyer announcing Acorn Hill's genealogical assembly lay on top. She picked it up and scanned it. "This assembly sounds interesting."

"What?" Jane turned away to drain the bacon. "Oh, that. Yes, I suppose. If you like family history."

"Don't you?"

"Sure," Jane said, shrugging. "I just don't like to hear about all the research for hours on end. I'm afraid that's what the assembly will turn into. You should have heard Louise, Alice and Ethel when they got back from their courthouse research trip. They went on and on about every little research detail. Where they looked, what was a dead end and so on. I just like to hear about the people, but I can't believe that there will be that many interesting stories at the assembly."

"That's what I try to accomplish in my writing," Ada said. "I weave in the history so that people don't realize they're getting a good history lesson. The past is always more exciting when we can put faces to it. Real people with real lives."

"But your characters are fictional."

"Yes, but they're based on facts. Let me ask you a question: how much would you think your Aunt Ethel knows about the French Revolution?"

Jane shrugged, lifting several pieces of French toast onto a plate. "Probably not much," she admitted.

"We had a conversation about it the other day. If I can say so, without sounding immodest, she knows quite a bit about it because of my novel. She has a grasp of the prevailing political, cultural and economic climate in France that led to the Revolution. She talked about it from my characters' perspective, of course, but she understands."

"Someone should tell Viola that."

Ada laughed. "Would she respect me as a writer more? I doubt it, sweetie. Trust me. I don't take it personally. I've heard it all."

Jane blushed, remembering how she and her sisters had joked about Aunt Ethel's fondness for romance novels. Then Ada Murdoch had changed their attitudes by not being who they had imagined she would be.

Jane set a small pitcher of warmed syrup along with powdered sugar and sliced strawberries on the table. She grinned at Ada, and then gestured with the platter of French toast and bacon before setting it down. "*Bon appétit*," she said. "I'd better call my sisters to supper."

Chapter Twelve

The rest of the town was as excited about Lloyd's idea as he was. The assembly was scheduled the weekend before Polly Humbert's wedding, so Acorn Hill had much to anticipate.

While Alice was at work on Monday, Louise took her turn at the library for more genealogy research. She was curious to see if she could find more information about Jeremiah Berry, their mother's ancestor, or Nathaniel Howard, their father's.

Since they were so close to the date of the town assembly, she and Alice had agreed that now was the time for either sister to work on either side of the family. Louise opted to pick up the trail to Jeremiah Berry.

She decided to try the library's connection to a genealogy search engine and typed in the name Jeremiah Berry. It brought up many suggestions for her to explore, including military history, a long list of others with the last name of Berry, and too many dates to check out at one sitting.

Sighing, she cleared the search results. She could always go back there later if she was unable to find anything else.

On a whim, she decided to try a cross reference of the two men, and she typed in both Jeremiah's and Nathaniel's names to see if they were possibly listed in the same source.

Though she did not have their exact birth dates, the two men had probably been contemporaries. It intrigued her to think that they had lived in neighboring towns, yet perhaps had never met. Today she and her sisters could cover the distance between Acorn Hill and what was once Englishtown in a few minutes by car.

The computer screen showed three suggestions. Louise sat straight up, picked up a pencil and started clicking the computer mouse to check the results.

Jane met Martina at the door when she came for her weekly cleaning. "You don't mind staying here by yourself while I go to the General Store, do you?" she asked the girl. "Alice is still at work, Louise is at the library, and Ada Murdoch has gone to Philadelphia for what she called emergency research."

"I don't mind." Martina shrugged, blowing a bubble with her gum, and then smiling. "If Mrs. Murdoch is gone, it'll give me a chance to clean her room thoroughly. I hate bothering her when she's writing up there."

"Well, she said that she wouldn't be back until evening, so you don't have to rush. I'll turn on the answering machine, in case anyone calls," Jane said. "I wouldn't even need to go except that I'm just about out of sugar and some other essentials."

"Take your time," Martina said, twirling her cleaning pail. "I've got plenty of work to keep me busy."

Jane's trip took longer than she had expected. Shadows were falling when she struggled through the back door with three large bags of groceries. She hefted them onto the kitchen table, and then proceeded to put away the items. As she did, she glanced at the clock and realized that it was past time for Martina to have gone home, yet still too early for Alice to be home since she was running some errands after work.

Stretching on tiptoe to put away a bag of cornmeal, she paused, turned toward the stairs, and cocked an ear. That was odd. She had not noticed that music before she left. Maybe Martina turned on Ada's clock radio while she was cleaning and forgot to shut it off. She would have to speak to her about that.

Jane put away the rest of the groceries, finding herself humming to the tune she heard, "All I Ask of You," from *Phantom of the Opera.* The music seemed to grow louder, and when she finished her chore, she headed up the stairs to shut off the radio.

Before she reached the second landing, however, she realized it was no radio. It was live singing. Ada must have come home early.

"Wow. The old gal can really belt out a tune," Jane said to herself, impressed. Ada Murdoch was apparently talented in more than one art.

The song ended as Jane reached the top of the stairs. She applauded wildly and said aloud, "That was wonderful!"

Ever so slowly, Martina emerged from a guest room, dust cloth in hand. "You heard me?"

"That was *you?*" Jane rushed forward, delighted. "I thought it was Ada. That was beautiful."

"Thank you," she said. "I didn't know anyone was home, or I wouldn't have sung so loudly. I never wanted to bother anyone, but this big old house has great acoustics."

Jane laughed. "You've blessed the inn with your voice, that's for certain. Where did you learn to sing like that?"

"I've been taking voice lessons for four years."

All this time, this talented girl had been, what, scrubbing bathrooms? Jane thought. *She needs to be on the stage. She needs an agent.* "Why didn't you tell us?" she said aloud.

Martina grinned. "You never asked, Ms. Howard. Actually, I'm about to join a professional Christian singing group. I took this cleaning job so that I could go with them to Europe next summer after graduation."

Jane shook her head, amazed. "And we thought you only wanted the job for spending money."

"I do." Martina stripped off her rubber work gloves and popped them into the cleaning bucket. "I want to spend it on a trip to Europe."

Jane grinned. "I know another way you might be able to earn money. Something more suited to your talents than cleaning. Have you sung at any weddings?"

"No, but I'm sure I could. Why?"

"Do you know Polly, Vera Humbert's daughter?

Martina nodded. "I know of her. Everybody in town is excited about her wedding."

"She's looking for a soloist, and her wedding is in less than two weeks. Can you make it?"

Martina nodded. "If she's interested, of course."

"When she hears your voice she will be interested. She and Patsy Ley, who's helping to plan her wedding, were just here yesterday telling me they needed to find someone and soon. I never dreamed it would be the next day."

Martina removed her bandana and shook it out. "Sometimes God's answers are pretty quick, and sometimes they're slow. But He always has a way of letting you know He's still around."

Jane thought that Martina's comment was uncommonly wise, especially for an eighteen-year-old. How much of the girl's wisdom had been the silver lining from the dark cloud of her mother's death? She hugged the teenager and smiled. "He does have a way of letting us know He's still around, Martina."

Martina left soon afterward, and Jane raced to phone Patsy Ley. Patsy was so excited that she said she would call Polly Humbert long distance immediately to give her the good news. Jane knew that Polly would be glad to have one more thing to cross off her list, and she knew the bride-to-be would be even more delighted when she actually heard Martina Beckett sing.

Alice and Louise arrived home at nearly the same time. Jane was in the garden, dressed in her overalls and straw hat as she worked the soil. Fred Humbert had loaned her a rototiller from his hardware store, and she plowed under the summer garden. When she saw Alice and Louise, she shut off the tiller and waved.

Alice looked tired. Louise, on the other hand, was practically bubbling with excitement. "I'm glad I've got you both here together," she said.

"Me too," Jane said. "You won't believe what I found out."

"You will not believe what *I* found out," Louise responded.

"Can you both tell me what you found out after I've had a quick shower?" Alice asked. "It was an especially busy day, and I'd like to freshen up."

Jane glanced down at her dirty overalls. "I guess I'd better clean up too."

Louise glanced at her wristwatch. "Let's meet in thirty minutes in the library."

"Can we make it an hour? I'd like to finish my tilling here," Jane said.

"Fine." Louise and Alice headed inside, and Jane went back to the tiller. She tried to work faster, knowing that there was lots of news to share.

When she was finished, she stored the equipment in the garden shed, and then took one more look at the newly plowed garden. It gave her a feeling of satisfaction to know that new plants would bloom there again in spring, in a new growing season. As she was about to go inside, she realized that she had not collected the day's mail from the box at the end of the inn's driveway. Walking to the curb, she reached in and pulled out several items: Louise's Philadelphia fine arts magazine, a postcard from a San Francisco friend, a flyer from a bed-and-breakfast supplier, and a letter to Alice.

As she walked back to the house, Jane smiled, tapping the envelope thoughtfully. Maybe this letter would lift Alice's weary spirits after a hard day at work. She placed the letter, along with the rest of the mail, on the kitchen table and headed for a quick shower.

"Jane?" Alice entered the kitchen, looking for her younger sister. Jane had not been in the library with Louise and did not seem to be anywhere else, so Alice assumed she was still upstairs getting ready.

As she turned to leave the room, her gaze fell on the table. On top of the stack was a letter addressed to her from Mark Graves. It had been a while since Alice had heard from her old beau. He had popped back unexpectedly into her life not long ago. He lived in Philadelphia, but they had enjoyed reconnecting.

Alice's fingers trembled as she worked at the envelope flap, and she finally put down the letter. This was ridiculous. She was acting like a schoolgirl.

"Alice?" Louise poked her head into the kitchen doorway. "Jane's in the library. Are you ready?"

"Sure," Alice said. "I'm coming."

When Louise had turned away, Alice scooped the letter into her pocket. It was probably better that she read this by herself later anyway. She could not always trust her emotions where Mark Graves was concerned.

"There she is," Jane said when Alice entered the library. "Louise and I drew straws to see who should share her news first. I won."

"Great," Alice said, feeling more lighthearted now that she knew she had a letter from Mark Graves waiting to be read. The cares of the day seemed to slide from her shoulders, and she focused her attention on her younger sister.

"I found a soloist for Polly Humbert's wedding. You won't believe who it is," Jane said, her eyes shining.

"Don't keep us in suspense, Jane. Is it someone we know?" Louise asked.

"Is it ever. It's Martina Beckett."

A stunned silence followed. Alice considered the information, trying to picture Martina singing at a church wedding.

"Are you certain?" Louise asked. "Did she just tell you that she likes to sing?"

"She *does* like to sing," Jane said, "but I heard her myself. When I came home from the store, she was upstairs cleaning. I could hear her all the way down here." Jane rose up from the edge of Daniel Howard's desk, where she had been perching. "That girl has a powerful voice. It was beautiful. She was singing a number from *Phantom of the Opera.*"

"I do remember her saying that she liked that musical," Louise said. "I never dreamed she was a singer herself. Are you *certain,* Jane?"

"Yes. She's joining a professional Christian group's tour next summer, and that's why she wanted to work here. She needs the money to go to Europe."

"Oh my," Alice said softly. "I had no idea."

"Nor had I," Louise said. She and Alice looked at each other with some embarrassment.

Jane crossed her arms. "I think you're coming to the same conclusion that I did. We've been more than a bit prejudiced if we find it so hard to believe that Martina is a classical singer."

"Just as we were prejudiced about Ada Murdoch as being a romance writer," Louise said softly. "I feel ashamed."

"Me too," Alice said. "Father would admonish us for prejudging people."

"And judging them by their appearances," Jane said. "I thought the same thing."

"Did you tell Patsy Ley?" Alice asked.

Jane nodded. "She was going to call Polly Humbert immediately. I'm sure she'll want to hear Martina sing this weekend when she's in town."

"Perhaps we could have the Humberts and the Becketts over for coffee after the assembly," Louise said. "I could play for Martina while she sings."

"That's a great idea. I'll invite them and the Leys, as well," Jane said. "And now, Louise, what's your big news?"

Louise straightened. "I found out information not only about Nathaniel Howard but Jeremiah Berry."

"Really?" Alice said. "Where? What?"

"I used the library's genealogy search engine. There was too much information on—"

"What did you find out?" Jane interrupted, clearly impatient.

"We'd like to hear about your research efforts later, Louise. Perhaps you should just tell us what you discovered," added Alice.

Louise came to the point. "Nathaniel and Jeremiah were not only contemporaries, they came from the same town, Georgetown."

"Then they must have known each other," Alice said.

Louise nodded. "They did know each other. Remember when I told you that the woman at the historical society talked about Georgetown? Well, that town was divided. Most of the inhabitants were patriots, but some were Tory sympathizers. We knew from Alice's research that Jeremiah was a patriot soldier, but what we did not know was that either he was injured or became ill and could no longer fight. He started helping other town members—men, women and children—who secretly collected metals to create musket balls for the patriot army."

"Right under the noses of the British," Jane said, fascinated.

"Exactly," Louise said. "Jeremiah was caught and sentenced to hang, but the war ended before the sentence could be carried out."

"What about Nathaniel Howard?" Alice asked. "Did he know Jeremiah?"

"This is where it gets really interesting," Louise said. "Because the British army had no place to keep Jeremiah as a prisoner, they housed him with Nathaniel and his family, who were Tories. Apparently, Nathaniel treated Jeremiah kindly while he was a prisoner. I like to think that Jeremiah encouraged Nathaniel to stay in the area after the war, but that is just speculation on my part."

"At any rate, that is when the British sympathizers started their own Englishtown, and the patriots founded Acorn Hill," Alice said.

Louise nodded. "Just as Grace Topham from the county historical society told us when we took that trip to Potterston. The Tories actually called it by another name, but it was the derisive nickname given by the patriots that eventually stuck."

"And long, long after, Father traveled through Acorn Hill, where his car plowed into a snowbank outside Mother's home," Alice said.

"And Nathaniel and Jeremiah's descendants met, fell in love, and eventually married," Jane finished. "Oh, isn't that romantic? How wonderful that their kindness to each other came full circle."

Alice smiled. "Father and Mother would have loved to know their family histories," she said. "I'm so proud of you, Louise, for finding all this out."

"Where did you get all the information?" Jane asked.

Louise cast her an appraising glance. "I thought you wouldn't be interested."

"Maybe you could spare me the most boring details," Jane said.

Louise smiled. "I used the library's genealogy search engine. When I typed in the men's names together, I was directed to a Web site at an obscure state college. Apparently, someone on the faculty there in the early twentieth century had written a book about the American Revolution in this part of Pennsylvania. Fortunately, the book was heavily indexed, with references to Nathaniel and Jeremiah."

"It might be interesting to learn more about their families," Alice said. "Their wives and their children."

"That will have to wait for another day," Louise said. "I am stopping with this information. It will make a nice story to tell at the assembly this weekend."

"Maybe someone else will have some more information about Englishtown and the early Acorn Hill," Alice suggested.

Jane sighed. "You two are welcome to do the research. It's too detail-oriented for me."

Alice patted her hand. "You do what you do best, Jane, which involves much more creativity than I'm capable of. How did your garden work go?"

"Good. I'm done with the tilling. I wanted to do it now, before getting involved in all the activities we have coming up."

"Yes," Louise said. "We have the assembly this Friday, and then the gathering with the Humberts, the Becketts and the Leys afterward."

"And next week we have Polly's shower and her wedding," Jane said. "She gave me her suggested menu list for the reception. It's mostly hors d'oeuvres, but that will still take time."

"I think it is wonderful that you are giving your time as a wedding gift," Louise said. "If Polly would like me to play at their wedding, I would give my services as a gift too."

"Polly and Alex *are* on a budget," Jane said, "and I'm sure they'll be that way for a long while. Particularly if he is sent overseas."

The sisters were quiet for a moment. "I keep thinking that Polly is not only the daughter of a good friend, but she is also marrying a man who potentially could be putting his life on the line for our country," Alice said.

"That is true," Louise said. "He is volunteering to protect us and our freedom just as our ancestors did. It is a sobering thought that Polly and Alex are starting out their marriage with that knowledge," Louise said softly.

"Yes, it is, but let's face facts, ladies," Jane said, smiling. "They're in love. They're probably not thinking about much else at the moment. And speaking of love." She turned to Alice. "Did you see the letter for you on the kitchen table?"

Alice blushed. "I saw it."

"And?" Jane said, obviously pressing for details. "How is Mr. Graves?"

"I don't know," Alice admitted. "I haven't read the letter yet."

Louise raised an eyebrow.

Jane giggled. "I think you'd better take yourself right up to the quiet of your room and see what the gentleman has to say."

"That was my plan," Alice said, "after you two shared your big news."

"Consider it shared," Jane said. "Now go read that letter. We'll expect a full report at dinner."

Louise shot her a glance. Jane smiled. "Well, maybe not a *full* report. I mean, we want to know how Mark is doing. We haven't heard much about him lately, you know. I'd love to hear how his work is going."

"Jane," Louise said sternly. "Let Alice read her letter in peace."

Grateful for the chance to slip away, Alice headed upstairs. As interesting as Louise's and Jane's news had been, the letter had been a weight in her pocket. When she was alone behind her bedroom door, she sat on the edge of her bed and carefully slit the envelope with an opener and unfolded the letter. It began:

Dear Alice,

It seems like such a long time since we've talked. There's so much to tell that I'm afraid I don't have enough paper or time to fill you in on all that's been happening. The work here has been very exciting, but I must admit that I'm looking forward to getting back to the zoo in Philadelphia . . . .

Alice finished the letter, and then read it again. She realized her heart was beating a little faster at the thought of Mark Graves.

Alice set the letter on her antique patchwork quilt, propped her feet on the bed frame, and wrapped her arms around her knees, thinking about Mark, which led to thoughts of romance. It had been such a long time since she had attended a wedding. Acorn Hill was not a large town, and it was rare for a wedding to be held in Grace Chapel.

Over the years, though, she had loved watching Daniel Howard perform marriage ceremonies. When she was much younger, she had dreamed of her father pronouncing the sacred words over herself and her groom. But the dream had faded.

Will I ever have a chance to get married? What would it be like to plan my own wedding, as Polly is now?

The instant the thought ran through her mind, she felt herself blush. Thinking about marriage, especially with

Mark, was more than wishful thinking, it was prideful. Why would either of them be interested in marrying at this late date in their lives? And how could she consider giving up the single life she had always known? Not to mention now that she was reunited with her sisters. Could she give up her family so easily?

Alice tucked the letter back into the envelope and placed it carefully into her top drawer.

Chapter Thirteen

Of course Jane pressed Alice for details about Mark's letter, but Louise had spoken to her about teasing Alice. After Alice related the letter's practical details, the subject was dropped.

Alice's week at the hospital continued to be busy; however, when her shift was over on Thursday, the last day of her workweek, she decided to stop by Vera's. She had not seen her friend for a while, and she wanted to see if she was feeling more relaxed.

She went home, changed clothes and consulted with Louise and Jane about the guests for the coming weekend. Grace Chapel Inn was booked solid again, but thanks to Martina's cleaning job, the rooms were sparkling clean and ready. When she knew Vera would be home from the elementary school, Alice headed for the Humberts' house.

"Alice!" Vera said, her face lighting into a smile when she opened the front door. "Come in and sit awhile. It's so good to see you. I've been so busy lately, I haven't had a chance to hook up with you for our walks. If I'd known you were coming, I would have 'red up' the house."

"I'm a friend, Vera," Alice said. "You know you never

have to tidy up on my account. As a matter of fact, your house looks just fine."

She never had seen it looking so orderly, particularly on a weekday. Everything was in place and tidy.

"Fred has agreed to share household duties with me during the week," she said. "Once the stress of planning Polly's wedding was off, we were able to concentrate on our home. We realized that he's a straightener and I'm a cleaner."

"I beg your pardon?" Alice said, wondering if Vera had just referred to some new personality type.

"My mother used to say that everybody had a pet cleaning peeve. People were either cleaners who didn't like dirt, or they were straighteners who didn't like clutter. Since Fred doesn't like clutter, he's in charge of keeping things sorted, picked up and put away. I don't like dirt, so I clean the bathrooms, run the sweeper and dust."

Alice smiled. "Who does the windows?"

"We've agreed to do them twice a year." Vera winked. "His turn is coming up first."

Alice laughed along with her friend. "I've missed our walks, Vera. Do you think we could get started again soon?"

"I've missed them too. I think that's part of the reason I was so tense."

"It's important not to neglect exercise, even when you're going through a stressful time," Alice said gently. "But you had much more going on in your life than just routine stress. Planning a wedding is serious business, not to mention your daily schoolwork. How is your class's genealogy project coming?"

"It turned out to be fun for everybody. My students have worked very hard. Of course, the ones who had it the easiest were those who had older brothers or sisters in Dee Butorac's high-school class."

"And those who didn't?"

"Bless their hearts, all my students were at least able to find something about their family," Vera said. "Some of them will be participating in the assembly this Friday. I offered extra credit to those who do."

Alice fingered a red, white and blue cross-stitched pillow. "How are Polly's wedding plans?"

Vera smiled. "Patsy Ley has been a godsend. I am so thankful that Jane recommended her to us. Patsy is just as excited about this wedding as Polly. She's over here every day with a new swatch of fabric or a floral arrangement photo. We've faxed a few things to Polly, and she's been able to make certain decisions right away."

Vera plucked a folder from a desk drawer and handed it to Alice. Inside were photos printed from Internet Web pages or cut out of magazines of flowers, wedding cakes and dresses.

"What a modern world we live in," Alice murmured. "Are these the bridesmaid dresses?" she asked, pointing to a page taken from a bridal magazine.

Vera scooted closer on the sofa so that she could see. "Yes. Isn't that a lovely pattern? The bridesmaids are all getting the same dress, but in different colors."

The dresses were simple but elegant. Each had an A-line velvet skirt with a pastel satin top with a square neck and cap sleeves.

Alice studied several wedding dress photos taken from a Web site. "How is Sylvia coming along with Polly's dress?"

"She says it will be ready this weekend for a final fitting." Vera said. "I went by her shop after school today, just for a peek, mind you, and Sylvia was working on it. It is the most beautiful . . . the most beautiful . . . " Her voice faltered, and she dabbed a handkerchief against the corner of one eye. She tried to speak again and could not. "She said . . . she said . . ." Her eyes filled with tears.

"Take your time, Vera," Alice said, putting a hand over Vera's.

Vera drew a deep breath, laying a hand over her heart. "I'm sorry. I get so choked up. It's my baby getting married, of course, but more than that . . ." She drew another deep breath. "Sylvia is making Polly the wedding dress as a gift. Imagine all the time and love. It's like Jane's giving Polly and Alex her catering services as a gift. Fred and I are overwhelmed."

"Everyone loves Polly," Alice said. "They are glad to contribute their talents and gifts in her behalf."

Vera sniffled, dabbing at an eye. "Alex said he feels like he's not only marrying into the Humbert family but that he's marrying into Acorn Hill too."

"I'm glad he feels that way," Alice said. "I hope we see a lot of him and Polly."

"I hope so too . . . once he gets out of the Army." Vera teared up and blew her nose into her handkerchief. Her shoulders shook slightly.

"Polly is marrying a good man," Alice said. "Louise and I were talking about what great sacrifices brave men and women have made down through the years for our country. I know you and Fred are proud to welcome Alex into your family."

"We are," Vera said, smiling through the last of her sniffles. "Oh, we are."

"Have you met his parents?" Alice asked.

Vera nodded. "Just once, at a Penn State event. Of course, he and Polly weren't serious about each other then."

"Where are his parents from?"

"Just outside Philadelphia. His father is a television director for a news station, and his mother is a school librarian."

"How wonderful," Alice said. "You two must have a lot to talk about."

"Yes," Vera said, swiping at her eyes one last time, "and now we'll have our children to discuss too."

Louise finished her last piano lesson for Thursday afternoon, a difficult session with Amy Tutwiler. Amy was a junior high girl who had shown a certain talent for playing, but also a distinct lack of discipline. Consequently, she frequently showed up ill-prepared for her lessons.

It seemed to Louise that every other week she was having to reprimand the girl for lack of attention to her musical gifts. If there was one bit of wisdom that Louise tried to pass along to all her students, it was that God did not create musicians overnight. Musical ability was a partnership between the Creator and the artist that included a decided amount of discipline on the latter's part.

Amy's playing had been particularly discordant this week, and Louise could feel a tension headache brewing. She took two aspirin and wandered downstairs to the kitchen to find something cold to drink, when she heard the back door open.

"*Yoo hoo!*"

"Hello, Aunt Ethel," she said, putting a palm against her forehead.

"Hello, dear. What's the matter?"

"I am afraid I am getting a headache," Louise said.

"Hello, ladies." Ada Murdoch entered the room, her smile fading when she saw Louise slumped at the table. "What's wrong?"

"Headache," Louise mumbled. She hated to be rude, but she did not feel up to chatting.

"I've got just the thing," Ada said.

"Did you take some aspirin?" Ethel asked.

Louise nodded.

"Try this," Ada said. "Take the thumb and index finger of your right hand and massage that web of skin between the thumb and index finger of your left hand."

Louise did as Ada suggested. "It doesn't seem to be working."

"Keep it up for a while," Ada said, turning to Ethel. "How are you?"

"*Hmmph*," Ethel responded. "If you want to know the truth, I'm miffed."

"About what?"

"Oh, that Viola Reed," Ethel said. "I passed her on the street today, and I asked her if she would order some of your books and if she would *please* have a book signing in your honor."

"What did she say?" Louise asked, still rubbing her left hand.

Ethel glanced at Ada. "She said that she couldn't possibly sell enough of Portia Keyes's books to make their purchase *or* a book signing worth her while."

"Does that surprise you?" Ada asked.

"Frankly, it does," Ethel said. "Vera is always touting the benefits of reading, but apparently it's only *her* kind of books that a person is allowed to enjoy. No wonder some people don't like to read. Not everybody likes those classics and biographies and histories that she's always trying to push on this town."

"You shouldn't take it personally, Aunt Ethel," Louise said.

Ethel sniffed. "Well, I do. She's barely spoken to me since she found out I liked Portia Keyes's books."

Louise wondered if Ethel realized that she was indirectly insulting Ada, but knew that her aunt was often given to speaking without thinking. Ada did not seem hurt, Louise noticed, but her face did look a bit clouded.

"You know what I would do, Ethel?" Ada said.

"No, what?" Ethel looked at Ada, her expression indicating that she was hanging on the author's advice.

Ada took her arm and propelled her toward the back door. "I'd go home, drink a cold cola, and then lie down for at least thirty minutes."

"Why, whatever good would that do?" Ethel asked, clearly puzzled.

Ada smiled. "My mama was from the South, and whenever I was upset about something, that's what she would recommend. It sounds crazy, but it works wonders. Try it and see."

Ethel nodded. "Thank you, Ada. I believe I will. It sounds like good advice to me. Earlier this week, I put a six-pack of soda in my refrigerator."

"Then it's good and cold. Go get yourself one and drink it nice and slow. Then remember: thirty minutes lying down. That should do the trick."

Ethel looked at Ada with a worshipful expression, and then headed out the back door. When she was gone, Louise stopped rubbing the skin between her thumb and index finger. Her headache had vanished.

"You feel better too, don't you?" Ada asked.

"As a matter of fact, I do. Should I drink a cola and lie down?" Louise said, smiling.

"I was counting on your paying a visit with me to Viola Reed at Nine Lives Bookstore."

Louise looked surprised. "What do you plan to do?"

"Make Viola an offer she can't refuse," Ada said sweetly. "I'd like you to go with me, if you can. The Bible says that if you can't reason with your brother, you should take someone else with you. It seems like that time has come. I know that you and Viola are friends. Will you come with me?"

Not certain what to expect, Louise nonetheless found herself nodding. She thought that Ada would walk to Nine Lives since the distance was not great, but to her surprise, Ada headed for the parking lot.

"Would you like me to drive?" Louise asked politely.

"No, thanks," Ada said. "Although I wouldn't mind a ride sometime in that Caddy of yours. It's a beaut. How old is it?"

"Twenty years."

Ada whistled. "You've taken good care of it." She used a remote control to unlock the door of her own car. "I like a lot of metal around me when I drive," she said, "just like your Cadillac."

A short while later, Ada Murdoch parked the SUV outside the Nine Lives Bookstore. Louise headed straight for the door, and then realized that Ada was opening her trunk. "I've brought a little gift for Viola Reed," she said, winking.

"Little?" Louise said skeptically. Ada hefted out a very large, obviously very heavy cardboard box.

"Yes. *Oof,*" Ada said, adjusting the box in her arms. "Would you mind shutting the trunk for me? Thank you."

Louise did as she was asked, bewildered, and hurried to open the door to Nine Lives for Ada. Viola came to the front of the store when she heard the bell ring. "Hello, Louise. Hello, Mrs. Murdoch," she said frostily. Her gaze went to the large box in Ada's arms, but she did not say anything.

Ada set the box on the floor, and then dusted her hands. "*Whew.* There you go."

Viola frowned. "What's all this?"

"Hello, Viola," Louise said, unsure about what to say. "Ada and I . . . "

"That's all right, Louise," Ada said quietly, then turned to Viola. "Ms. Reed, it doesn't take any intuition to know that you don't like my writing."

Viola stiffened. "It has its place with certain readers, I suppose."

"Yes, it does, and one of those readers is Ethel Buckley." Ada crossed her arms. "Ethel is a fan of my writing, but more than that, she's become my friend. For some reason, she's dead set on seeing me at a book signing here in Acorn Hill.

I don't give a hoot and a half about such an event, myself. They're a waste of my time, and my hand usually winds up hurting for days after signing so many books."

"I don't think that would be a problem here in Acorn Hill. Not that many people read your books," Viola said.

Ada laughed. "If they don't read them, it's because you won't stock them. From what I hear, you spend so much time telling people what they should and shouldn't read, you're like the book police."

"*Book police!*" Viola puffed up, and her mouth worked itself open and closed several times.

"Now, now, don't get your dander up," Ada said. "I know you've got your likes and dislikes same as any other bookseller or reader. Look, I've brought this box full of my books. If you'll allow me to sit at a table in your store here for a little while on Saturday, I'll sell and sign those books for whoever wants one. You can charge the cover price and keep all the money yourself, or better yet, donate all the proceeds to the charity of your choice."

Viola seemed to deflate a bit. "Why would you do that?"

"To make Ethel Buckley happy. What do you say, Ms. Reed? Do you want to make some extra money?"

Viola paused to consider. "The local literacy program could use funds," she said grudgingly.

"There you go," Ada said, pleased, but not gloating. "How about ten on Saturday morning? Set me up a table here by the front door and set up a few books for display. I'll be out of your hair by noon, all right?"

Viola looked at Louise as though for support. Louise shrugged, smiling back at her friend. Viola could not say no to a charity event. "All right," Viola said. "But only until noon."

"Thanks," Ada said, beaming. "I appreciate it. If you'll put a flyer in the front window, I'll let word of mouth take care of the rest."

Once outside Nine Lives, Louise had to ask, "What word of mouth are you counting on, Ada?"

The author unlocked the car door with a flick of her keyless entry button. "Why, your Aunt Ethel, of course."

Louise smiled as she got into the passenger seat. "She'll have ample opportunity to tell everyone tomorrow night at the assembly."

"I think the meeting sounds interesting," Ada said thoughtfully. "There are probably lots of good stories about people from this area."

"And people from elsewhere," Louise said. "Not everyone is originally from Acorn Hill, of course."

"Of course," Ada said. "People have become so transient in the last hundred years or so. It's rare to find a family that's stayed in one place."

"It didn't even happen in our family," Louise said. "Jane and I moved away years ago and came back after Father died."

She swiftly recounted the story of their return to Acorn Hill and how Grace Chapel Inn became a bed and breakfast. Ada steered the car into the parking lot and shut off the engine.

She turned in her seat and looked at Louise. "You and your sisters have a wonderful place. It's easy to see that your concern for each other and for this town seeps into how you manage Grace Chapel Inn."

"Thank you," Louise said, taken slightly aback. "You make it sound quite noble."

"It is," Ada said. "Most places you go, service is impersonal and cold, if you get it at all. I almost wish everywhere could be like Acorn Hill."

Louise smiled. "We love it, but I wonder if you wouldn't miss the big cities and entertainment after a while."

Ada just smiled in return.

Chapter Fourteen

$\mathbf{A}$ corn Hill was buzzing all day Friday. Everyone enjoyed a town event, and people had been talking about information that might be presented at the genealogy assembly. While they put away their lunch dishes that day, the Howard sisters discussed sharing their family information, with Louise doing the honors.

"I don't think I could stand up in front of everyone and speak, even for five or ten minutes," Alice said.

"Of course you could," Jane said, wiping down the counters.

"Don't worry, Alice. I will be happy to do the talking for both of us." Louise put the placemats back in a drawer and then put her hand on Alice's shoulder.

"I think Alice should at least stand at the podium with you," Jane said. "After all, she did half the work."

"I can do that," Alice said, though secretly she knew she would feel just as embarrassed standing up in front of the town.

"I hope it doesn't drag on all night," Jane said. "The Humberts, the Becketts and the Leys will be here for coffee when the assembly is over. Since Martina Beckett is going to sing for Polly, I don't want her to be too tired to give it her best effort."

"Are you going to accompany her, Louise?"

"Yes. She called this morning and said that she would bring her own sheet music."

"What is it?" Jane asked.

"I believe it is a song from *Phantom of the Opera*."

"'All I Ask of You'?" Jane asked. "I hope that's the one. That's what she was singing when I heard her. Her voice was beautiful enough a cappella. I'd love to hear her sing with some accompaniment."

Soon afterward, the latest weekend guests arrived, three families from neighboring states who were meeting for a family reunion in Potterston. Louise informed them that the parlor would be in use that night, but that they were welcome to use the library for their own entertainment. The head of the clan said that they had no plans to stay up late, since they were going to drive to the Gettysburg Battlefield early the next morning and would be gone all day.

"I like having guests," Jane whispered to Alice, while Louise showed the couples to their rooms, "but sometimes I like it best when they only use our home as a place to lay their heads at night."

"Business will slacken off during winter, I'm sure," Alice responded. "We'll have plenty of quiet time for ourselves then."

The sisters were going to walk to town hall, but decided at the last minute to drive the short distance. They piled into Louise's Cadillac, and then headed down Chapel Road.

"*Brrr*." Louise shivered when they got out of the car in the parking lot behind town hall. "There is a definite chill in the air. Autumn is finally here. The nights are getting cooler."

"Look at the crowd," Alice said, marveling at the steady stream of people entering the building. They joined the flow and found teenagers arranging extra seating at the back of the hall.

"Isn't this wonderful?" Lloyd said, directing some youngsters to set up a row of metal folding chairs. "Dee Butorac is seating her students down at the front. We should get started soon."

The sisters found three seats next to Joseph and Rachel Holzmann, the owners of Acorn Hill Antiques. Rachel had on a blue sheath dress with a Mandarin collar, and instead of the Victorian hatpins she normally stuck in her dark, upswept hair, tonight she wore a pair of chopsticks.

"Hello, ladies," Joseph said, nodding. His gold wire-rimmed glasses sparkled from the overhead light. He looked dapper in neatly pressed chinos, a blue button-down shirt, and a tan corduroy jacket.

"How is your store?" Alice asked. "Have you run across any unusual antiques lately?"

"We went to Philadelphia last week and found some well-preserved Civil War medical supplies," Joseph said. "You might be interested in seeing them."

"I might at that. Reading about Clara Barton's Civil War experiences when I was a girl was one of my inspirations to become a nurse." Alice leaned around Joseph. "The chopsticks are lovely, Rachel. Where did you get them?"

She patted her hair and smiled. "Can't tell. I'm saving that for our turn at the podium."

Alice nodded and sat back. Louise and Jane were talking to Dr. Bentley, who had thrust an ancestral chart in front of their faces and seemed to be pontificating about one of his relatives. Louise looked interested, but Jane had a forced half smile on her face that said she would rather be somewhere else.

At that moment, Dee Butorac and Lloyd Tynan took their places at the front of the room. Lloyd tapped on a microphone that had been placed at the podium, and gradually everyone grew quiet.

"If you'll take your seats, we'll get started," Lloyd said. "First off, I want to thank you all for coming. I'm always delighted to see Acorn Hill participate in town projects, and this one has been quite informative. I'm looking forward to hearing from those of you tonight who wish to speak. But first, I'll turn over the stage to Dee Butorac, who started many of us in our first genealogical search."

Everyone applauded. Dee adjusted the microphone and smiled. "I'd also like to thank you all for coming tonight. More importantly, I'd like to thank the parents who stood behind the students in my class while they researched this project. We've already discussed our findings in class, and every one of us realized that we've learned something about not only our families but also about the Revolutionary War period. It's difficult to imagine a life without computers, television, telephones and modern medicine, but we have discovered that our ancestors not only survived, but in many cases, thrived. I think you'll be as interested in their stories as I was."

She smiled broadly. "As for me, I wanted to research my husband's family so that our daughter would know the background of her last name. Her great-grandparents emigrated from Yugoslavia to avoid Serbo-Croatian conflicts, but we can't find any more information older than that. As for my family, we go back to Jamestown on the second or third ship, and my family migrated from that area to Pennsylvania during the War of 1812. And now," she said, pausing to look at the students seated at the front of the audience, "let's hear from my students. Martina Beckett will go first."

Jane, Louise and Alice applauded enthusiastically. Martina blushed as she took the podium. "My dad and I researched my mom's family and discovered that one of her ancestors came to America as an indentured servant. She was living in Massachusetts during the Revolution."

Martina paused and gazed at the crowd. "My father and I got off to a rocky start with this project because we had different ideas about what we were doing but, as Mrs. Butorac said, we learned a lot about our family. Our immediate family, anyway. Mostly we learned that we love each other and that we still love my mom, even though she's not with us. Researching her family made us see that the love we still have for her, and the love she always had for us, will pass down through the years through any kids I might have one day."

Alice wiped a tear at the corner of her eye. The audience had grown silent, and then someone began to clap. Another person picked up the applause, and the room reverberated as Martina headed back to her seat. Her father met her in the aisle, looked at her a long moment, then hugged her. She hugged him back unashamedly.

Dee Butorac had to wait for the applause to die down before she could introduce the next student. He lightened the moment by recounting a few experiences of his Revolutionary era relative, who had been a pig farmer. The audience laughed as he read from a plastic-encased letter that the farmer had written to a relative in France about the ornery characteristics of the porcine nature.

"Who doesn't like a good pig story?" Jane whispered to Alice.

"Clara Horn might not appreciate it," Alice said, referring to a neighbor who had a Vietnamese potbellied pig for a pet.

As the students continued their presentations, Alice was impressed with their research. Many had forebears who had lived in colonial times. One had a relative in Mexico. Still another recounted his family's forced migration as slaves from Africa to America, and they were all reminded of that troubled part of the country's heritage.

After the last student had spoken, Dee Butorac asked them all to stand at the front of the room. The town applauded their efforts, and she turned the floor back over to Lloyd Tynan.

"I'm impressed with these students' hard work," Lloyd

said. "Kudos to you as well, Dee. Now I'll open the floor to anyone who would like to talk about their Revolutionary-era relatives. Keep it to no more than five minutes. I know you genealogy buffs like to detail every aspect of your research, but please cut to the chase. Who would like to go first?"

To Alice's surprise, Rachel and Joseph Holzmann waved their hands wildly. Lloyd invited them to the front of the room. At the podium, Rachel patted the back of her hair, causing the chopsticks to click together. "Some of you may have thought that Joseph poured my dinner over my head."

The audience laughed.

"The truth is that I wanted to honor one branch of my family. It's one of those sixteenth-cousins-four-times-removed situations, but I had a relative who went to China as a missionary long ago and married a woman there. It wasn't as far back as the American Revolution, but I wanted to honor the Chinese family that I'll probably never meet. You see, the missionary never returned to America."

"Many of you know that Rachel and I are both of German descent," Joseph said. "I discovered that one of my relatives was pressed into service as a Hessian soldier during the American Revolution, fighting on the side of the British. After the war, he decided to stay in America."

Lloyd thanked them for their information and next called on Nia Komonos. With great animation, she told about her family in Greece. Lloyd then called on several others, and then he asked Dr. Bentley to come to the podium.

The doctor made a great show of bringing his ancestral charts with him, and Lloyd cautioned him that the speaking limit was only five minutes. Dr. Bentley shot him a dark look and launched into a discussion of a British-soldier relative who had died at Bunker Hill.

Dr. Bentley pointed out that few American history classes taught about the impact of the soldiers' deaths on their families back in England. Everyone was quiet, thinking about the British who had died on American soil during the Revolution.

Lloyd took the podium himself, talked briefly about his Quaker relatives and the patriot who, like the doctor's relative, had also lost his life at Bunker Hill. Lloyd swallowed a couple of times, glanced at Dr. Bentley, and then reminded the audience that there had been many deaths on both sides during the Revolution. He then glanced at his watch, announced that it was late and that they would have time for one more presentation.

Alice began to feel relieved. Perhaps, she thought, she would not have to stand up in front of the town after all. But Louise confidently raised her hand, and Lloyd called her to the podium. With a sinking heart, Alice went with her. She stared nervously at the crowd. She only half listened to Louise's story of Nathaniel Howard and Jeremiah Berry, Tory and patriot, who had crossed paths, and how their families had been joined generations later with the marriage of Madeleine Berry and Daniel Howard.

When Louise finished, the crowd started to applaud, but someone stood up at the back of the assembly room. "Mayor Tynan, may I have a word?"

All eyes turned toward Ada Murdoch, who was sitting by herself in the back row. Alice realized the author must have slipped into the room unnoticed some time after the presentations had begun.

"Would you like to add something to our discussion, Mrs. Murdoch?" Lloyd asked.

Ada nodded. "Ladies, do you mind if I join you up there?"

"Please do," Louise said, and she and Alice stood to the side of the podium.

Ada stepped up to the microphone, looking completely at home. "Mayor Tynan was right," she said. "There were many deaths on both sides during the American Revolution, and each one of them somehow contributed to the freedom we enjoy today. My friends Louise and Alice learned from their research how mercy given from one enemy combatant to another was rewarded over one hundred and fifty years later with the merger of the two families in their parents' marriage."

She smiled out at the crowd. "While I've stayed at Grace Chapel Inn, I've been writing a novel set during the American Revolution in this part of Pennsylvania. I've listened to many of you speak tonight, and it reminds me that this town of yours is like my favorite patchwork quilt. Though the pieces are different colors and shapes and are made from different fabrics, together they make one beautiful work of art. Acorn Hill feels like the best of America to me. Everyone who's spoken tonight has added another lovely dimension to the ongoing history of this town and the people who live here."

Lloyd rose to stand beside her. "How about that? Ada Murdoch, perhaps better known to you as Portia Keyes, is writing about our little area of Pennsylvania. I couldn't have summed up Acorn Hill better myself. Thank you."

The room broke into thunderous applause. Louise and Alice made their way back to Jane, pressing against the crush of the crowd as it surged toward Ada at the front of the room. Standing in a quiet spot by the door, Jane was beaming, her eyes twinkling. "You two were wonderful," she said.

∽

Still excited by the assembly, the Becketts, the Leys and the Humberts all congregated in Grace Chapel Inn's parlor. Jane excused herself to brew coffee and tea in the kitchen. Patsy Ley introduced Martina Beckett and Polly Humbert, while Fred and Vera chatted with Martina's father, Jeff. Alice and Louise ushered Henry Ley to a chair and, not being needed for the moment, sat on either side of him.

"Did you enjoy the assembly?" Louise asked.

"Yes," Henry said. "I enjoyed learning so m-much about the families in Acorn Hill."

Louise noticed that Henry's stutter had become less obvious since he had been doing exercises to correct it. The associate pastor was sometimes called upon to give the sermon in Rev. Thompson's absence, and she knew he wanted to give his best effort for the congregation.

She watched Patsy gesturing between Martina and Polly, her face all smiles. "Has Patsy enjoyed being a wedding consultant?"

"Yes. She has a real t-talent for it," Henry said. "I wish she could help more people in Acorn Hill with her gift, but there j-just aren't that many marriages in our little town."

"Maybe she could branch out to Potterston," Alice suggested.

"Or run some sort of on-line wedding consulting service," Louise added. "It seems like she knows quite a bit about preparing for the event. Polly's wedding was short notice, but Patsy stepped in and got things organized."

"I hope Polly doesn't feel pressured to select this girl as her soloist," Henry said. "P-Patsy went over to the high school to hear her choir practice one day and came home ecstatic."

"Patsy wouldn't overreact," Alice said.

"No, she wouldn't," Henry said. "She knows how important f-finding the right soloist is to Polly."

Patsy came over to the group. "Louise? Are you ready? It's been a long, exciting day. Perhaps we'd better get started."

Martina held out the sheet music, and Louise could see that the accompaniment would not be difficult. She preferred the classics and was not a devotee of show tunes, but she was familiar with the song from *Phantom of the Opera* that

Martina had selected to sing. It turned out that Polly was familiar with the song too, and that she and Alex, her groom-to-be, had once attended a touring performance of *Phantom* in Philadelphia.

"I am delighted to be playing for you," Louise said to Martina. "Jane told us about your gift for singing."

"Thank you," Martina said. "This sheet music is already in D flat, a key I prefer."

Louise smiled and set the music on the piano's stand. "I'll just follow your lead."

Since Martina and Louise were ready, everyone else quickly found seats and quieted. Martina positioned herself, and then nodded. Louise played the opening notes, and Martina took up the song.

The music was written as a duet, but Martina sang it beautifully as a solo. She sang beyond her eighteen years, and even Louise was stunned. She didn't dare look up from the sheet music for fear of spoiling Martina's performance, but Louise sensed that the audience was transfixed.

All too soon, the song was over, and when the last note had faded, the audience rose to its feet with applause. Martina bowed, and then gestured toward Louise to honor her performance as well.

Polly was the first to make her way to the piano, and she impulsively hugged Martina. "That was beautiful. The words describe exactly how Alex and I feel about each other. Will you please sing at my wedding?"

"I'd love to," Martina said. She blew upward at her bangs and was a teenage girl again.

Jeff Beckett hugged her, holding her close. "You were great, Marti. Your mother would be so proud."

Louise noticed that the girl looked up at her father with tears in her eyes. "Thank you, Daddy," she whispered.

Patsy and Henry marveled with Polly over Martina's

talent, and Jane announced, "I'm going to get coffee and tea."

While Alice helped Jane prepare a tray in the kitchen, Louise sat on the bench, exhausted. It had been a long day, yet what a wonderful ending. Seeing Polly so clearly in love with her absent groom brought back gentle memories of Louise's own wedding to Eliot. It had been a long time ago, but she remembered the feelings of a bride.

Vera and Fred Humbert briefly hugged each other, happy about the impending marriage of their daughter. Sweet too, was the tender way Jeff Beckett kept his arm around his only daughter. He was delighted with her.

Alice reentered the parlor just ahead of Jane and helped her serve coffee and tea and the delicious chocolate-tipped orange cookies that Jane had made. Everyone else was still talking about Martina's performance, the upcoming wedding, and even the highlights of the evening's town assembly.

Finished for the moment with hostessing, Jane took a seat beside Louise on the piano bench. She took a sip of coffee and then studied her oldest sister. "What's wrong?"

Louise turned and smiled. "I have been thinking about Father. I think he would be so happy to know how much love is in this home. Especially now, right in this room. A bride, two sets of parents—"

"Don't forget sisters," Jane said, putting an arm around Louise. "I'm pretty proud of both you and Alice tonight."

They watched as Alice poured tea for Vera Humbert, then caught her eye and smiled. She nodded and went back to serving the other guests.

Louise and Jane smiled at each other. "Yes, I think Father would be happy that we have prospered at Grace Chapel Inn," Louise said.

Chapter Fifteen

Much later that evening, Ada Murdoch returned home. The other bed-and-breakfast guests had turned in to get a good night's sleep before their battlefield tour on Saturday. Tired but happy with the evening's events, the sisters had said good night to their company and were putting away the coffee and tea service.

"What are you ladies still doing awake?" Ada said. "I figured you'd have long been asleep."

"We had guests," Louise said, explaining about Martina's performance for Polly's approval.

"Sounds like fun," Ada said, yawning. "*Hoo*, forgive me. It's been a long night."

"Where have you been?" Alice asked. "All those people didn't keep you at the town hall, did they?"

"No." Ada sat at the table and wearily rested her head in one hand and shut her eyes. "Everyone who wanted to talk, and that means at least half the town, moved over to the Coffee Shop."

"But it isn't open that late," Jane said.

Ada yawned. "The owner opened it. She was one of the ones who wanted to talk the most."

"What did everyone want to discuss?" Louise asked.

Ada covered another yawn with her hand. "Everything about the American Revolution," she said. "Once they learned that's what I'm writing about, they wanted to share their family histories. I think they hoped I'd include them in my book."

Alice laughed softly. "No wonder you don't want to tell people what you're writing about before you've finished."

"Does that happen often to you?" Louise asked.

"More than I'd like," Ada said. She straightened, smiling. "Oh, I'm just tired. I like talking to people. They're only trying to be helpful."

"It was nice of you to come to the assembly," Louise said. "What you said about Acorn Hill was very complimentary."

"I call it as I see it," Ada said. "You have a nice town here. Lots of good folks."

"So did you get any good stories from any of them?" Jane asked.

"None that I can use in this book," Ada said, "but I might be able to transfer some of the stories to another book with a different time period. What I'm really interested in is your family story. I have a similar situation in my book, about two soldiers on opposite sides of the Revolution."

"Just like Nathaniel and Jeremiah," Louise said.

Ada nodded. "I always like to have an epilogue in my books, and I'd like to work it into the story that over two hundred years later, the soldiers' descendants marry. Would you ladies mind if I used that aspect of your family history?"

The sisters looked at each other and nodded. "It's fine with us," Jane said.

"Wonderful," Ada said. "And now, if you'll excuse me, I'm going to head upstairs."

"Don't tell me you're going to write that epilogue now," Jane said. "It's nearly midnight."

Ada laughed. "Not tonight. I'm going to bed. After all, I have a book signing tomorrow morning."

"I had nearly forgotten about that," Louise said. "Is Ethel excited?"

"She said she would be there an hour early to set up. She's bringing fresh doughnuts and hot coffee from the Good Apple Bakery." Ada shook her head. "I should hire that woman as my public relations specialist. Good night, ladies."

Alice handed Jane the last cup to stack in the dishwasher. "Do you think Aunt Ethel talked anyone into showing up tomorrow to buy a book?"

Jane shut the dishwasher and grinned. "More importantly, do you think Viola Reed will even open the door?"

The next morning Jane fixed a hearty breakfast of omelets, country ham and biscuits for their inn guests and gave them directions to the Gettysburg Battlefield. She, Louise and Alice were hoping to get to the Nine Lives Bookstore well before ten o'clock so that they could keep Ada and Ethel company. By the time they managed to get out of the house and head into town, it was nearly ten. The morning air was brisk, and the sisters walked quickly to keep warm.

"Remember that this signing is for a good cause," Louise said. "Ada is donating her own books, with all proceeds to go to the local literacy program."

"The signing is also to make Aunt Ethel happy," Alice added.

"Yes," Louise said. "Then are we each going to buy a book?"

"I think we should," Jane said.

Alice nudged her sisters. "I don't think that's going to be necessary. Look."

They had turned in sight of the bookstore. Starting in the open door and stretched out more than a block was a line of people.

"Good grief! Do you think they're all here for Ada Murdoch's book?" Jane asked.

"She must have really impressed them last night," Louise said.

Alice smiled. "Why don't we forgo getting books so that other people can have them?"

"Yes, and that way we can go right on in without waiting," Jane said.

They gently moved through the queue, ignoring good-natured ribbing about being line cutters. Inside, Ada was seated near the front door at a table with a stack of books. More books sat on the floor beside her. She smiled at everyone who approached the table and took a few minutes to chat, while Viola opened the book to the title page for Ada to sign.

Ethel was passing out Styrofoam cups of coffee to those still waiting in line outside in the chilly air. When she came inside for fresh coffee and saw the sisters, she nearly squealed with delight. "Isn't it wonderful? We ran out of doughnuts long ago. I just hope Ada has enough books to sign for you girls."

"We will buy them another time," Alice said. "We want to make sure that everyone in line gets one."

"I imagine we can put aside a copy for the ladies who housed our famous author for nearly a month," Viola said, winking.

Louise's jaw dropped. Was this the same person who had refused to acknowledge that Portia Keyes—Ada Murdoch— was a legitimate writer?

"Here are a few more," Viola said, setting a new stack of books beside Ada's elbow. "May I get you anything? Water? Something to munch on?"

"No, thanks, Viola." Ada flexed her wrist and fingers. "Just keep those books coming." Ada saw the expression on Louise's face and winked. She turned to the next customer and smiled. "Hi there. How would you like me to sign this book?"

Louise, Alice and Jane stepped aside. "I don't understand," Louise murmured. "Viola was dead set against Portia Keyes's books. What do you suppose happened?"

Jane shrugged. "Beats me. But they're certainly selling. Ada's raising a lot of money for the literacy program. Maybe we'd better head over to the Coffee Shop until this thing is over."

"You couldn't budge me from this spot," Louise said. "I have to find out what caused such a transformation in Viola."

"I guess that means I'd better get some coffee from Aunt Ethel then," Jane said, "because it looks like we're going to be here awhile."

The last two people in line were Florence Simpson and Clara Horn, who was pushing a baby carriage. Florence and Clara were friends of Ethel's, and the sisters' aunt made a great show of introducing them to the author.

"This is Portia Keyes," Ethel said, "my very favorite author. Of course, she goes by Ada Murdoch in real life, but she'll always be Portia to me. Ada, this is Florence Simpson and Clara Horn."

Florence picked up a book and studied the author photo on the back. "It doesn't much favor you." She squinted and studied Ada's face. "I'd say it's time to get a newer photo."

"Thanks for the advice," Ada said cheerfully, her pen poised over the title page. "How shall I sign this book?"

"I suppose you'd better make it out to me, F-l-o-r-e-n-c-e," Florence said, "though I'm not sure when I'll have time to read it. Ethel made me check out one of your books from the library, but I kept falling asleep at night before I could read more than two pages."

Ada's smile never wavered as she signed the book and presented it to Florence. Then she turned to Clara and glanced over the table at the baby buggy. "And whom do we have here?"

"Why it's my precious Daisy." Clara reached into the buggy and pulled out her miniature Vietnamese potbellied pig that, as usual, was dressed in baby clothes.

Ada laughed aloud. Clara's lower lip quivered, and she hugged a drowsy Daisy close. "Are you laughing at me or at my Daisy?" she asked.

"I am laughing at myself," Ada said, "because I wasn't expecting such a beautiful pig. Doesn't she look sweet in those clothes?"

Clara beamed. "That's what I think," she said, then sniffed in Florence's direction, "though *some* people don't appreciate my little girl."

"Would it be all right if I autographed the book to Daisy?" Ada asked. "Maybe you could read it to her."

Clara smiled broadly and tucked the pig back into the carriage. "That would be wonderful. I'm sure we'll both love it."

After Florence and Clara left, and the store was empty, Viola declared that they had exactly three copies of the book left. "One for Ethel, one for you Howard sisters, and one for the library," she said. "I promised Nia I'd save one that the town could share. Meanwhile, I'll be ordering more copies of this book, as well as other Portia Keyes titles, for my store."

"Don't forget," Ada said, "that if you send them to me in Florida, I'll autograph each one."

"Thank you, Ada. That would be wonderful," Viola said.

The sisters looked at one another, and Louise could stand the suspense no longer. "Viola, what changed your mind about Ada's books?"

Viola picked up one of the remaining books on the table. "After Ada left these here yesterday, I took one home. I started reading after the assembly last night and didn't finish until three AM. I was enthralled."

"She said my research was impeccable," Ada said. "When I got here this morning, we had time to have a nice chat about all sorts of topics."

"Ada is an avid history buff, and we had a wonderful discussion about Queen Victoria. It seems that we've both read the same obscure biography that discusses her influence on the literature of the day," Viola said.

"We both agree that having a woman on the throne enabled Dickens's work to flourish. The serializations of his novels in magazines were geared toward women." Ada paused. "Some would say that his were the first true cliffhanger novels, since he ended each installment on a suspenseful note to compel the reader to buy the next issue."

"I think your work shows the same ingenuity," Viola said, flipping the end of her bright yellow scarf over her shoulder. "You end each chapter in such a way that the reader wants more, right up until the final page."

"Why, thank you," Ada said. "That's quite a compliment coming from you, Viola."

"I have decided that not *all* popular fiction is bad, especially if it's rooted in good historical research," Viola said. "May I take you to lunch, Ada? Or should I call you Portia?"

She laughed lightly, and Louise smiled. Viola was not the type to say she was wrong, but her actions and speech indicated that she knew she had been.

"I'm Ada to my friends."

"May I take you to lunch . . . Ada?" Viola asked. "You too, Ethel. Ladies?"

Ada smiled. "I think that would be lovely. Can we go to the Coffee Shop? I love to chat with that Hope Collins. She's so down to earth."

The sisters looked at one another for confirmation. "I'm

available for lunch," Alice said. "Our guests have all gone to Gettysburg for the day."

"And the only item on my schedule is to meet Martina at the chapel at three o'clock." Louise said. "We are going to rehearse her solos for Polly's wedding."

Viola stuck the Closed for Lunch sign in the window of Nine Lives, admonished the store cats to behave themselves, and locked the door before they headed toward the Coffee Shop. Jane excused herself from lunch, saying that she needed to do some work for Polly's wedding shower, which was just a week away.

Ethel linked arms with Ada and Viola, chatting nonstop as they walked. Louise and Alice took up the rear. "So Polly did ask you to play at her wedding?" Alice asked.

Louise nodded. "She asked me last night. She apologized for taking so long to make a decision, but once she heard Martina sing, she felt that she wanted both the organ and the piano. She wants the organ for pre-ceremony music, the wedding march and 'The Lord's Prayer,' but she wants piano accompaniment for 'All I Ask of You.'"

"Martina is very talented," Alice said.

Louise nodded. "I am looking forward to accompanying her."

"And I'm looking forward to hearing both of you," Alice said.

After lunch, Louise headed straight for the chapel. She limbered up her fingers on the organ, relishing the sound of the powerful instrument in the stillness of the empty building.

In the middle of a Bach concerto, the old organ suddenly wheezed and snuffled. Louise knew that the air support for the instrument came from a single blower, located in the basement below the pipes. Her best guess for the organ's loss in sound quality was that there was a problem with the blower or the leathers that delivered the air.

Martina raced into the chapel, clutching a stack of sheet music. "I'm sorry I'm late, Mrs. Smith."

"That's all right, Martina," Louise said, getting off the organ bench. "Perhaps it would be better if we moved to the piano to practice 'All I Ask of You.' The organ doesn't want to cooperate right now."

"*Ooh.* Do you think you can play it during the wedding?"

"I don't know. I hope so, but we should be prepared in case I can't. We don't want Polly's musical memories of her wedding to be of that gasping old organ."

Louise and Martina walked up the aisle to the front of the sanctuary. A seldom-used, small upright was positioned to the side of the altar, close to the wall. Like the organ, the piano had seen better days. Although its tonal quality was not as good as that of the baby grand at Grace Chapel Inn, it had been tuned recently.

Louise set the sheet music on the stand. "We would do well to rehearse both of your numbers here at the piano. Which piece would you like to practice first?"

"Let's try 'The Lord's Prayer.'"

"Certainly," Louise said. She spread out the music, a succession of single sheets that she laid across the stand so that she would not have to worry about turning pages.

Martina took the position she would have during her solo. She sang a few arpeggios in ascending keys, and then cleared her throat. "I'm ready."

Louise began and Martina came in. "Our Father, which art in heaven, hallowed be thy name ..."

Once again, Louise was entranced with the young woman's singing. She found herself holding her breath as Martina plunged into the most difficult part of the number, where the words and music built to a crescendo: "For thine is the kingdom and the power and the glory forever. Amen."

Louise played the closing notes, and then smiled at Martina. "That was beautiful," Louise said.

"I didn't quite hold a couple of notes as well as I could," Martina said, with a sigh of discouragement.

Louise rose from the piano and gestured toward the front pew. "Perhaps we should rest for a minute. I've wanted to ask you more about your singing group."

Martina sat beside her. "There's not much to tell. It's a group of twenty people. My choir teacher told me they were holding auditions in Philadelphia, so I tried out in August and got accepted."

"Have you started rehearsals?"

Martina shook her head. "We start in November on weekends, since we are sprinkled all around the Philadelphia area. Then next summer we go on the European tour to major cities. We'll be singing to mostly community groups and churches. In fact, one of the songs we'll be singing is 'The Lord's Prayer.' The director told me that I have a chance to solo."

"Based on what I heard today, I would say you are a good candidate." Louise smiled. "Your father must be very proud of you, Martina."

"Yeah," she said, scuffing a toe against the carpet. "I'm kind of worried about next summer, though."

"Does he not want you to go?"

"Oh no, ma'am. He's okay with the idea, but I think he'll miss me, with Mom gone and everything," Martina said.

"Every parent has to let go of his child eventually," Louise said. "I remember when Cynthia went off to college. My, my, that was quite a while ago, but it seems like only yesterday."

"I bet you were lonely when she left."

Louise smiled. "I'm sure I was, but it has been such a joy watching her grow into the woman she is today that I really don't remember any loneliness or sadness. I imagine that your father will feel the same way."

"Well, he's said that this is an opportunity I shouldn't miss, but I'm still not sure. When I get back from Europe, it will be time for me to go to college."

Louise put a hand on Martina's shoulder. "Your father is right. You have been given a gift. It is something that needs to be nurtured so that it, and you, will grow even lovelier. Your father will be here for you in Acorn Hill, just as my father was."

Martina smiled. "Thanks, Mrs. Smith. You know, this sounds crazy, but I almost look forward to going away just so that I can come back home to Acorn Hill."

Louise smiled at her fondly. "I will always look forward to seeing you, Martina."

Chapter Sixteen

Since Polly was coming home from Penn State the Wednesday before the wedding, the Howard sisters agreed to have the shower that Jane had promised on Thursday evening at Grace Chapel Inn.

Alex and Polly had leased an apartment in State College to live in after the wedding. Of course, he would soon head out for basic training, but Polly would live in the apartment while she finished school. The sisters decided that the shower should have an apartment theme: kitchen, bed and bath items in particular, but anything that would spruce up the couple's first home. According to Vera, the apartment was in a shabby student housing complex, and she hated the thought that their first married dwelling together might be dismal.

"A little paint and the right furnishings can spruce up any place," Jane said cheerfully.

"Yes, Vera," Alice said. "Remember what this home looked like before Jane and Louise moved back here?"

"Then Jane took her creativity, paintbrush and wallpaper to the rooms," Louise said.

"I have a hunch that Polly and Alex can do the same to their apartment," Jane said. "In the meantime, we'll host a shower for them so that all of us who love them can give them a few nice things to start out. Besides," she said, winking, "showers are part of the fun of weddings. It gives us ladies a chance to be silly."

While the sisters were setting up for the party in the parlor Thursday afternoon, Louise took Jane aside. "You're not planning on any silly shower games, are you?"

"Who me?" Jane said innocently. "Now, Louie. What's wrong with a little fun?"

"Fun is one thing. Embarrassment is another."

Jane put her hands on her hips and pretended to look indignant.

They invited everyone who was going to be in the wedding, including Polly's sister, Jean, the maid of honor. They also invited Polly's friends from school who were already in town, and Alex's mother and younger sister. The sisters also included Clarissa Cottrell, Patsy Ley, Sylvia Songer, Clara Horn (they politely asked her to leave Daisy at home) and Ethel. Several other Acorn Hill women had been invited, but could not attend. Ada had also begged off because she was at a crucial point in her book.

Alex's mother, Francie Neal, was a tall, tanned, blonde who looked as though she played a lot of tennis. Her handshake was as sure as her posture was erect, and she walked into Grace Chapel Inn as though headed for a board meeting. She wore a smart navy-blue suit and carried an expensive-looking black leather handbag.

Kimberly Neal, Alex's sister, was a high school senior and one of the bridesmaids. For the shower she wore a pastel pink dress and pulled her long, naturally blond hair back into a ponytail. Jane introduced her to Martina, who was the same age. Martina was dressed in a basic black dress and sported her usual heavy eye makeup. Alice noticed that they eyed each other warily for a moment, but then Jane said something that made them both laugh. After that, they stuck next to each other like old friends.

As each guest arrived, Jane handed her a name tag with a wedding-related term, such as *honeymoon, altar, best man* and *vows.* "You're not allowed to say the word that's on your name tag," she instructed them. "If you do, and someone hears you say the word, she can take your sticker. The person with the most stickers at the end of the shower wins a prize."

She grinned. "And I hope you'll all want it. It's a box of my homemade truffles."

Alice stuck a tag reading *engagement* on her dress. Louise received one that said *Alex,* the groom's name. Louise rolled her eyes, but good-naturedly affixed it to her pastel blue blouse.

When all the guests had arrived and everyone had examined the words on each other's stickers, Jane led them into another game. "Have a seat, ladies," she said. "Let's get started."

Chairs had been arranged in the parlor in a circle, and all the participants looked expectantly at Jane, who stood in the center. "Since we are not all acquainted, let's go around the circle and say our names. But you must also add an adjective about yourself that starts with the same letter as your name. I'll start. My name is Jane and I'm jazzy."

Polly, Martina, Alex's sister Kimberly and several others smiled at the fun. Louise and Francie Neal frowned.

"I'll go next," Alice said hastily, hoping that Jane had not overestimated the enthusiasm of the shower guests. "My name is Alice and I'm awestruck."

Jane laughed. "Leave it to my sister. Louise?" she said, pointing to Alice's left.

"My name is Louise and I'm, um, I'm . . ." She struggled to find an adjective that started with the letter *L.*

"Large?" Francie Neal said. "Lax? Lenient?"

Louise sat up teacher straight as though one of her piano

students had just hit a sour note. Alice racked her brain to offer a more flattering suggestion. Louise would never say anything to Francie Neal, but it was clear she was disturbed by the suggested adjectives. Surely Francie was only trying to be funny.

"How about *likeable?* " Martina said, smiling.

Alice relaxed. So did Louise. "I'll settle for that. Thank you, Martina."

Sitting next to Louise was Vera, who smiled at the group. "I'm Vera, and I started to say *vain* or *vicious*, but those don't fit, so I'll go with *vivacious*."

"That's good. The only thing I could think of was *voracious*," Francie said.

Vera blushed, and the room went silent. Polly shot her mother a stricken look. Alice felt sorry for Vera and for the bride-to-be, and yet she still was not sure that Francie actually had meant what she had said. She could be suffering from nerves—and a bad case of foot-in-mouth disease.

Across the circle and breaking the order, Ethel stood up and sang out, "My name's Ethel, and I'm *elegant*." She struck a pose with one hand on a hip and the other hand behind her head, as though she were wearing a high, feathered headdress. Everyone laughed, and the tension was broken.

Bless you, Aunt Ethel. Bless you. Alice smiled across the seated circle, hoping to catch her aunt's eye.

Now the participants went out of order, according to who dared take the floor next. "I'm Martina, and I'm *magnetic*."

Everyone applauded her unusual adjective. Martina plopped back to the seat, and not to be outdone, Kimberly rose beside her, grinning. "I'm Kimberly, and I'm *kinetic*."

All the women applauded again, chattering among themselves. "Great word," Jane said.

The rest of the guests participated, each one trying to outdo the previous person, until only Francie Neal was left.

Warm with laughter, everyone looked to her to come up with the topper of all adjectives.

She glanced at Vera, then shrugged and said, "I'm Francie and I'm frivolous." She sat back down and said loudly enough for everyone to hear, "I've played this shower game before, and it's always the same adjectives."

Jane quickly rose and stood in the middle of the circle. "Great game, everybody. Now that we all know one another, we're really going to have some fun." She brought out shopping bags and broke the room into groups, excluding Polly. "The object of this game is to see who can design the prettiest bride's dress." She grinned, holding up rolls of white and pink crepe paper, scissors, and plastic tape dispensers. "With only these items."

"*What?* How are we supposed to do that?" The guests chorused their good humored outrage.

Jane laughed. "That's up to you and your group. Pick someone in the group to be your 'bride.' The rest of you have to design the dress on her. Polly, our real bride, will pick her favorite design, and each member of that group will win a prize."

"Goodness. Can you imagine if Alex walked in right now," Louise said nonchalantly.

"Alex! You said *Alex!*" From across the room, Sylvia Songer lunged at Louise. "I get your sticker. I get your sticker."

Alice had to laugh at the normally reserved Sylvia demanding that Louise hand over the name tag. Sylvia pocketed it gleefully.

She saw Alice watching her and shrugged. "I never win contests like this." She patted her skirt pocket. "One down, more to go."

As Sylvia headed back to her seat, Louise leaned toward Alice. "I was afraid no one would hear me," she whispered.

"I'm glad to be rid of that thing. Now I can enjoy the rest of the party in peace."

Alice suppressed a laugh. She would never have guessed that her sister would throw a party game.

"Well done, Sylvia," Jane said, obviously delighted that at least one person was enjoying her activity. "Now, ladies, let's design those wedding dresses."

"Maybe I should sit this game out," Sylvia said, her enthusiasm replaced with worry that her professional expertise might give her an unfair advantage over the others.

"Go ahead and play," Jane said. "I think you'll find that toilet paper fabric is a great equalizer."

Jane put Vera into a group with some of Polly's friends, Martina and herself. Alice's group included Francie, Clara Horn and Polly's maid of honor, Jean Humbert. Like Polly, Jean was sweet-natured and endeared herself to Alice even further when she suggested that Clara Horn be their group's bride.

"Me?" Clara said, clapping her hands together. "How fun! Really? Me?"

Alice wondered if Jean knew that she had picked the right person. Since Clara loved to dress her pig Daisy, it stood to reason that she would love to be dressed up herself, even if it was just with crepe paper and plastic tape.

"This is the silliest thing I've heard of," Francie said to Alice. "Honestly. Grown women dressing up other grown women."

Alice tried to think of a pleasant response. Polly had assured Jane in advance that she wanted to play games, no matter how goofy.

Fortunately, Jean stepped in. "Come on, Mrs. Neal. I bet we can win the prize. This will be fun."

"*Ooh* yes. Make me look pretty," Clara said, holding out her arms. "I want Daisy to see how lovely I can look."

"Daisy?" Francie said.

"I'll tell you later," Alice whispered and then said louder for Clara's benefit, "Jean, as maid of honor, you probably know more about bridal dresses than the rest of us. Where should we start?"

With mock seriousness, Jean critically studied the eager Clara. "Let's use the pink paper for roses to decorate a white gown."

"*Gown!* That's your word!" Sylvia dropped a roll of crepe paper she had been separating and planted herself in front of Jean.

"Wow!" Jean said. "You were way over there by the piano. How did you hear?"

Sylvia shrugged, holding out her hand. Jean peeled off her sticker and handed it to the exuberant seamstress, who marched back to her group in triumph.

"As I was saying," Jean began.

"Yes, yes, white dress, pink roses," Francie said, waving her hand. "Whatever. Let's just get this silly thing started."

The members of the group took turns wrapping swaths of white paper around Clara's arms, then torso, hips and legs. When they stepped back to admire their work, they looked at each other in silent horror. The still-smiling Clara looked more like a mummy than a bride. "Do I look pretty yet?" she asked.

"Well, *er* . . . " Alice began.

"It just needs some roses," Francie said. While the rest of the group had been working, she had pinched off squares of the pink paper to fold into delicate flowerets. She handed these to the others to tape to Clara's dress.

With the addition of the rosettes, the "dress" looked more creative. "These are pretty, Francie," Alice said, sticking a flower to Clara's knee. "Where did you learn this?"

"I'm a school librarian and sometimes I teach origami.

Even the most unruly children stay quiet when they see what they can do with paper."

"Do you think you could make a really large one out of pink for a headpiece?" Jean asked. "The rest of us could make a veil with streamers of the white paper."

"I'll give it a try," Francie said. While she worked on making a large rose, the others continued to attach tiny roses. When they were finished, Francie had fashioned a large beautiful pink rose. They carefully taped it to a white-paper chinstrap and slipped it over Clara's head. Then they attached long white streamers of crepe paper to make a fingertip veil.

"That's the same length as Polly's," Jean said, giggling. "Maybe we should add a blusher veil for the front too."

"Good idea," Alice said. "We could add a few lengths of paper in front of Clara's face to simulate a blusher."

They worked to add chin-length streamers in front of Clara's face, and Francie taped a sprinkle of pink rosettes. She stood back and studied their creation. "Not bad," she pronounced.

Clara, swathed in paper, still had her arms stuck straight out. "Are you finished? I can't see anything," she asked, her voice a bit muffled behind the paper. She paused. "My nose itches."

"Oh no, Clara, don't scratch," Alice pleaded. "You'll break the paper. Jane's bringing Polly around now to judge the creations."

"I really do need to scratch my nose," Clara said.

"They're looking at the next group now," Jean said.

"Yes, hang on, Clara," Alice said. They had worked so hard on the silly dress. Perhaps Francie would feel better if they won. "Just think of how proud Daisy will—"

"*Achoo!* "

Clara jerked forward with the momentum of the sneeze.

The paper dress split, and the veil lay in tatters at her feet. One pink rosette clung to a square of paper at her shoulder. Clara looked sheepishly at the others, who sighed as one.

At that moment, Jane and Polly moved to their group, studying the remnants of their once masterly creation.

"Well," Jane said, "something seems to have gone wrong here. Was it sabotage or an accident?"

Polly lifted a shred of paper from Clara's arm. "Whatever it was, it was effective, I'm afraid." She and Jane moved on to view the last creation.

"All those rosettes," Francie said sadly. "All that work."

Clara looked heartbroken. Alice touched her arm and smiled. "Never mind, Clara. It couldn't be helped."

"It really was a nice dress," Jean agreed. "And it was fun to create." She smiled at Alice and Francie. Alice smiled back, but Francie knelt to gather as many rosettes as she could.

"Polly's picked a winner," Jane announced loudly. "And it's Patsy's group, and modeling their creation, Ethel Buckley."

"Aunt Ethel?" Alice glanced across the room and saw Ethel swathed in pink and white crepe paper. Her group had fitted her with a skirt and a loose streamer shirt. They had even made her a bouquet of looped paper.

"We had such a lovely dress," Jean sighed. "I know we could have won." She and Alice stood shoulder to shoulder, watching as Jane and Polly awarded the team their prize, a box each of sugar cookies shaped like wedding bells that Jane had baked.

"If they're only giving foodstuffs as prizes, I'm just as glad we didn't win," Francie Neal said, sniffing. "I'd be as big as a horse eating all those goodies."

Once again, Alice bit her tongue to keep from replying. Instead, she helped a still-disappointed Clara Horn remove all the stray crepe paper from her clothing. Jean helped them gather all the loose pieces to throw away.

"Would you like to open presents next or have some refreshments?" Jane asked, deferring to the guest of honor.

Polly's eyes gleamed. "Seeing and hearing about all this food has made me hungry. I've been looking forward to your goodies all day."

"Coming right up," Jane said. "Alice, would you help me, please?"

In the safety of the kitchen, Jane took Alice aside. "How are things going with Francie Neal?" she whispered.

Alice shook her head. "Not so good. She seemed to enjoy making that silly wedding dress, but then when it disintegrated, she went back to being unhappy."

Jane uncovered a large bowl of curried chicken salad, and a platter of cookies and teacakes. "I hope Vera is all right."

"She has enough to worry about without Francie making things difficult for her or Polly," Alice said.

"Before we started the party, I heard her nit-picking to Jean about the wedding. It seems like every other sentence out of her mouth was 'Where we're from, we do it this way' or 'I don't know how you feel,' and then she would expound on exactly what she believed without letting poor Jean get a word in edgewise. It didn't matter what they were talking about, whether it was how to celebrate Christmas, conduct a wedding or entertain at a bridal shower. Francie Neal is the authority on everything."

"I'm sure that they perform weddings very much in the same manner as Pastor Ken will perform Polly's on Saturday," Alice said, trying to make light of the situation. "Everything else, decorations, clothing and food, is very much just a matter of personal taste, as you know."

"*Vows!*"

Alice and Jane heard Sylvia's shriek all the way from the

parlor and knew that she had managed to steal another sticker. They grinned at each other. "Wasn't that Francie Neal's name tag?" Alice said.

Jane nodded, then sobered. "I don't mind what that woman thinks about my hostessing abilities. I just hope Francie doesn't start picking on Polly. She and Patsy have worked so hard on this wedding to get so much done in such a short time."

Alice smiled, relieved that her sister had not taken personal offense. Jane and Louise were always her first concern. "I'm sure it will be fine. The ceremony will be beautiful no matter how they perform weddings where the Neals come from."

Jane handed Alice the bowl of chicken salad and followed her into the dining room with a tray of cheese straws. They returned to the kitchen, where Jane opened the freezer and took out a cookie sheet on which lay rounds of frozen fruit salad that she had removed from molds earlier in the day. She quickly transferred the rounds onto an iced platter, which Alice took from her to the dining room. Finally, she withdrew a large punch bowl from the refrigerator, gently stirred the bowl's pale-pink contents and slipped in a ball of ice in which she had frozen a pink rosebud. Lifting it carefully, she carried it toward the dining room. "Back into the fray," she said cheerfully.

After they had eaten, Jane announced that it was time for the presents. Polly tried not to look too eager, but she was having a hard time concealing her emotions. Alice could not blame her. She had seen some of the gifts before they had been wrapped, and any young woman would be pleased to receive them.

Louise and Ethel retrieved the presents from the dining room where they had been placed as the guests arrived. The two women had to make three trips, and each time Polly's eyes grew wider at the stacks of elegantly wrapped packages. Everyone reacted with enthusiasm.

Jane directed Jean, as Polly's maid of honor, to sit beside her and collect all the ribbons and bows from the packages. One of Polly's bridesmaids was pressed into service as a scribe to record all the gifts and names of givers in Polly's bridal book.

The first present Polly opened was from Jean, a beautiful pair of sloping mahogany bookends with brass bases. "These are gorgeous," Polly said, holding them up for everyone to admire.

"I know you and Alex like to read and figured these would be put to good use," Jean said.

Next Polly opened a gift from Louise, Alice and Jane, a rattan-and-bamboo picnic basket with a red-and-white-checked tablecloth, napkins, and compartments for flatware, a cutting board, and a cheese knife.

"There's even a place for a wine bottle and glasses," Jane said, winking at Polly. "When you want a little romance in your picnics."

"You said *romance!*"

Jane peeled the sticker off her shoulder and silently handed it to Sylvia. The seamstress stashed it in her pocket with the others and returned triumphantly to her seat.

The group's attention turned back to the gift opening. The bridesmaid handed Polly another present, which turned out to be a large photo frame. Made of Italian leather in tan, marbled tones, the antique-looking frame was bordered with embossed gold leaf. "I love this," Polly said to Patsy Ley, the gift's giver. "If I don't put one of our wedding photos in here, I'll put a photo of Alex in his army uniform."

At the mention of Alex's impending military service, the room quieted a bit. "Open my gift next," Francie said.

The bridesmaid checked the tags and found the present. Polly glanced at her future mother-in-law, not certain what to expect. "It's heavy," she said, lifting the box to unwrap the paper.

She cautiously lifted the lid, and then brushed aside mounds of tissue paper.

"Better use both hands," Francie warned.

Polly reached in and carefully lifted a large, brass desktop clock. She eased it on the table and read the engraved plate, which included her and Alex's married names and the date of their wedding.

Set in black glass between two brass Grecian columns was the clock's face. Francie rose and pointed, her voice quavering. "See? The bezel is inscribed with the names of the cities of the world, so you can rotate the face to find out the time in foreign time zones."

She sat down and clasped her hands in her lap. "I thought," she began, swallowed, and then tried again. "I thought you might want to keep track of the current time wherever Alex is. In case he's sent overseas."

Alice felt a lump in her throat. Everyone else in the room seemed to be sniffling or coughing as well. Vera patted Francie's arm as if in sympathy. Francie turned, and Alice could see that, though her eyes were filled with tears, she smiled at Vera and returned the pat on the arm.

Polly gave Francie a hug. "Thank you," she whispered.

Francie returned the hug, and then kissed her future daughter-in-law on the cheek. "You'd better open the rest of those presents, dear," she said, smiling weakly.

Polly returned to her spot, made a small joke to get everyone laughing again, and went back to opening presents. As she unwrapped each gift, Jean looped the ribbons over her arm and gathered the bows in a colorful heap.

From time to time, Alice saw Polly glance at the world

time clock and then smile, and she knew that she was thinking of her groom-to-be even in the midst of all the feminine fun.

Soon all the gifts were opened. Besides the picnic basket, clock, frame and bookends, Polly had received several kitchen appliances, a newlywed's cookbook, and a few fancy sets of sheets and bathroom linens.

"I'm going to have the prettiest apartment in State College," Polly said. "I'm . . . I'm overwhelmed."

All smiles, Jean stepped forward and handed her a bouquet fashioned from the ribbons and bows that had been on the gift packages. "This will overwhelm you too. You're supposed to use it at your wedding rehearsal."

Polly accepted it, laughing along with everyone else.

"That's not all," Jean said, winking at her older sister. "Legend says that each ribbon you broke while unwrapping the packages signifies how many children you and Alex will have."

Polly cried out good-naturedly. "I must have broken them all."

"I counted eight," Jean said.

Everyone laughed. The gathering broke up into small conversation groups, and Jane and Alice cleared the empty plates and cups. As the group was beginning to gather sweaters and purses, Jane called them all to sit for one more moment. She brought out a large, bright yellow oval ceramic platter and a black marker. "Each of you please write one line or Bible verse about love, or some wisdom you want to share with Polly and Alex, then sign your name. Polly, when you get home, you can fire this in your oven for thirty minutes and you'll have a reminder of this shower."

They all signed, some taking their time to write a personal note, some writing much-loved Bible verses. Alice thought for a moment and wrote, "Love is patient, love is kind," quoting from I Corinthians 13. The expression seemed simple, and nearly everyone was familiar with the phrase, but Alice believed that so many arguments in life could be resolved by remembering and heeding those six short words.

Sylvia sidled up to Jane and said, "Did I win the truffles?"

Jane laughed. "Of course you did. Here they are, Sylvia. You earned them."

The seamstress beamed.

The party began to break up. When everyone else had left, Vera, Francie and Kimberly loaded Polly's presents into Vera's car. The bride-to-be hugged each of the Howard sisters. "Thank you for a beautiful shower," she said. "I'm so blessed to know you three."

They watched Vera, Polly and Jean drive off in one car, and Francie and her daughter drive off in another. Alice's gaze followed them down the road. "I'm not sure that things are any better between Francie Neal and Vera," she said. "I hope they can stay on good terms, at least through the wedding."

"Francie seemed to soften when Polly opened her gift," Jane said.

"Maybe she had just been feeling out of place," Alice suggested.

Louise sat on the porch swing and set it gently into motion. Musing, she said, "Do you think I will ever see Cynthia get married?"

Jane plopped down beside her and let out a long sigh. "I hope it's not this week. I'm exhausted."

Chapter Seventeen

O n Friday morning Jane began preparing the food for
Saturday's wedding reception. Clarissa had graciously
offered the Good Apple Bakery refrigerators and freezers if
Jane needed them. Craig had volunteered to order the rental
china, glassware, silverware and serving pieces for the
reception.

Fortunately, their latest weekend guests were not due in
until late afternoon. Louise canceled the day's piano lessons
so that she and Martina could rehearse. The teenager seemed
nervous about her first wedding performance, and Louise
wanted to do everything she could to put the talented girl at
ease. She also wanted to practice her own music, particularly
on the organ. Besides Martina's solos, she would be playing
the wedding's prelude and the processional and recessional
music.

Alice volunteered to be a runner for anyone involved in
the wedding preparations, whether it was Louise, Jane,
Clarissa with the wedding cake; Sylvia with the bridal gown
and bridesmaids' dresses; Craig Tracy with the flowers and
rental equipment; or Polly and Patsy with everything else.

Ada came downstairs for a leisurely breakfast, while the
sisters chattered and bustled about with wedding business.

Jane clearly wanted all of them out of her kitchen so that she could get to work, but every time they rose to leave, they would think of something else to discuss. Polly and Patsy had asked Alice to check with everyone periodically during the day, but Alice did not see how she could dart back and forth from all the various locations.

"Why don't you just give everyone involved your cell phone number?" Ada asked, sipping idly from her coffee cup. "If someone needs you, he can just phone. Otherwise, you can stay wherever you're needed most."

"None of us has a cell phone," Alice admitted.

Ada raised her eyebrows. "This is the twenty-first century, girls. You need to modernize."

"I don't know that I'd ever need one," Alice said. "Or that I'd know how to operate it."

"It's simple," Ada said, pulling a cell phone from her pants pocket. "Here, use mine. I have lots of available minutes. When it rings, press this button. If you want to make a call, punch the number buttons, then this one to send."

Alice felt bewildered, but she accepted the phone. It was so small that it fit in the palm of her hand. It felt and looked like a toy.

Ada wrote down the cell phone's number on several slips of paper. "Give one of these to everyone who might need to get in touch with you today," she said. "Starting with Jane and Louise."

"Thanks, Ada," Jane said, pulling food from the refrigerator. "You're the greatest."

"Are you going upstairs to write today, Ada?" Alice asked.

She shook her head. "I think I'll have a stroll around town. Maybe go visit Viola at her store or Nia at the library."

"I was heading to the Good Apple Bakery first, then Sylvia's Buttons, which is close by," Alice said. "May I walk with you into town?"

Loaded down with sheet music, Louise headed for the chapel. That left a relieved Jane alone in her kitchen.

Walking beside Ada down Chapel Road, Alice saw that the leaves of the oak and maple trees were collecting on the ground in colorful profusion.

Ada stooped to pick up an orange leaf. "Autumn is a good time for a wedding," she said. "I know most say that they like a June wedding, but I like all the colors associated with this time of year. They're warm colors that make me feel secure. Brown like the earth, so solid. Orange like a warm fire. Yellow like an Indian summer sun."

"That's lovely, Ada. I've never thought of it that way."

"I think your Polly and Alex picked a wonderful time to be married and start a new branch in their family trees. After all, like the effect of the season's colors, families are all about security."

Alice was sorry that she and Ada had to part company. She enjoyed talking with the writer, but there was much to be done today. "Here's where I turn off toward the bakery," she said. "Thank you for the cell phone."

"I hope it helps. Good luck with your day." Ada whistled as she strolled toward Nine Lives.

At the Good Apple, Alice headed toward the pastry-decorating studio. It was glass so that people could watch her work.

"Hi, Alice," Clarissa said, tying a large white apron over her blue and pink flowered housedress. "I was hoping you'd come by. Look at the layers for Polly's cake. Aren't they luscious?"

"Beautiful," Alice said. "What kind of cake is it?"

"Italian cream. It has coconut and nuts. Do you want to stay and watch me decorate it?"

"I'd love to, but I just stopped by to give you my cell phone number in case you need me for anything. There's no telling where I'll be at any given moment."

Clarissa accepted the slip of paper with the number, her elderly face wrinkling into a frown beneath the net she had gathered around her hair. "I didn't know you had a cell phone."

"It's on loan," Alice said. "I'll be back later to see how the cake's coming. I'd better check on Sylvia and Craig. Call me if you need any help."

At Sylvia's, Alice found Vera Humbert standing on a platform in front of a mirror so that Sylvia could hem her floor-length dress. Her mouth full of pins, Sylvia waved at Alice and went right back to hemming.

"Hi, Alice." Since she could not turn around, Vera smiled at Alice in the mirror.

Alice walked beside her, studying her dress. It was a mauve crepe sheath with a matching jacket. "It's beautiful, Vera. Is Sylvia finished with Polly's dress?"

Crouched on her knees, Sylvia mumbled something around the pins in her mouth. Alice, however, could not understand her.

"She says it's finished," Vera said, translating. "I saw it hanging in a garment bag in Polly's room, and it's gorgeous."

"I'm sure Polly looks lovely in it too," Alice. "If everything's under control here, I'll just leave the phone number where I can be reached today."

Vera took the piece of paper that Alice offered. "Did you and your sisters break down and buy a cell phone?"

Alice felt exasperated. Does everyone think they are technologically backward? "Not yet," she said, making an effort to sound cheerful. "This one is just on loan for the day."

A chirping noise sounded in her pocket. Startled, she dug out the phone and pressed the button Ada had indicated. "Hello?" she said tentatively.

"Polly and Patsy are looking for you over at the Humberts' house. Don't they have the cell phone number?" Jane asked impatiently. Alice could hear her working while talking, and she understood her younger sister's irritation. Jane did not like to be interrupted when she was cooking.

"I'm at Sylvia's right now, but I'll head straight over there," Alice said.

Jane hung up without a good-bye, and Alice knew she was definitely busy. "I'm headed over to your house," she said to Vera. "Apparently Polly and Patsy need me."

"Is anything wrong?" Vera looked alarmed. She peered at the seamstress at her feet. "How are you coming, Sylvia?"

"*Mmph fmmph,*" Sylvia said, moving to Vera's opposite side to continue pinning.

"I'd better go, Vera. Good luck with the dress. Sylvia, it looks beautiful," Alice said, then bustled out the door to the Humberts' house.

She had barely raised her hand to knock when the door opened and Patsy Ley pulled her inside. "We have a small crisis," she said without preamble. Polly was seated on the sofa, pressing a tissue to her eyes.

Patsy looked like she wanted to cry too. She bit her lip. "This is just terrible."

"Oh no. What's wrong?"

"We ordered all the decorations for the chapel and the reception, but I neglected to think of one thing: Who's going to decorate?"

Alice felt a wave of relief wash over her. This was a minor problem. "I'm sure we can think of someone," Alice said.

"Who?" Patsy asked. "Everyone will be busy doing something for the wedding."

"I'm not," Alice said.

"You can't do it alone," Patsy said. "Who will help you?"

Alice thought for a minute. "Perhaps the ANGELs can help. The decorations aren't too involved, are they?"

Polly sat up straight, her sniffles quieting. "No," Patsy said, looking hopeful again as well. "The chapel is so elegant in its simplicity that we decided not to do much there. You can't improve on the beauty of those stained glass windows. We're hanging white satin bows at the end of the pews and scattering rose petals down the aisle. Of course, Craig is making a rose floral arrangement for the altar."

"With my direction, the ANGELs could hang those bows," Alice said. "How about the reception?"

"We have tablecloths and rose topiaries for the tables, and we plan to move the altar floral arrangement to the head table. We've also rented white lattice screens for the backdrop behind the buffet table. Craig is going to twine ivy and fairy lights on them."

Alice smiled. "The ANGELs and I can help with that too. What time is Craig delivering the rented items to the church?"

"Eleven o'clock. He'll bring the flowers later."

"Somebody will be there at eleven to decorate," Alice promised. "Meanwhile, give me all the other decorations and I'll go ahead and take them to the chapel. Then they'll be there for tomorrow."

Patsy loaded her down with several large shopping bags. "Thank you, Alice. I don't know what we'd do without you."

"Yes, thank you," Polly said, her eyes shining.

Alice headed back to Grace Chapel Inn to contact some ANGELs members to help with the decorating. Jane was still working in the kitchen. Alice stuck her head in the door just long enough to say hello. Then she backed out and headed for the phone at the reception area.

She drummed her fingers on the reception desk. It was not quite lunchtime. She hated to wait until school was out late in the afternoon to contact the ANGELs. She decided to call their mothers instead. To her relief, all four of the mothers that she called were sure that their daughters were free the next day and would love to help.

Louise returned from the chapel around lunchtime. Jane set out a loaf of bread and cold cuts on the dining room table. "I'm sorry, but the kitchen is off limits for eating until I'm finished with the reception food. I have so much spread out, there isn't room to eat."

"Does anyone know if Ada is back from town?" Alice asked.

Neither Louise nor Jane did, so Alice headed for the stairs. "I'll see if she is. Maybe she would like to join us for lunch. I need to return her phone to her."

To her surprise, she met Ada coming down the stairs, suitcase and laptop in her hands. "You're going?" Alice asked.

Ada smiled. "It's time for me to leave, my dear."

Louise and Jane appeared at the bottom of the staircase. "She's leaving," Alice said simply, somewhat stunned. Ada was like one of the family.

Ada smiled at Louise, Jane and Alice. "You ladies have made me feel so at home. I've never had finer care or service. As much as I hate to leave you, I'm looking forward to seeing my daughter and her family," she said.

"We understand," Louise said. "And we know you have worked very hard. It is time for a break."

"Did you finish your book?" Alice asked.

Ada nodded. "I wrote the epilogue this morning. Oh, I'll do some editing and tinkering while I'm at my daughter's this winter, but the book is ninety percent complete."

Jane sighed. "Writing a book must be incredibly hard work," she said. "And you've done it a hundred times. That's amazing."

Ada shrugged. "Writing is what I'm gifted at, just as you're gifted as a chef, Jane. And Louise is a musician, and Alice has the gift of nurturing."

She looked at each one of them in turn. "My name, or

rather my pen name, goes on the cover of each one of my books, but everybody who believes in God and uses his talents for His glory has his own name written in the book of life." Ada smiled. "And that's what it's all about, isn't it?" She winked at the sisters. "Maybe next time I'll come for a real vacation, and you won't have to think of me as the crazy lady hiding up in her room."

"You're hardly that," Alice said. "Thank you for lending me your cell phone today," she said, handing it back. "It certainly came in handy."

"I was delighted to help," Ada said, as she tucked the phone into her purse.

"What about Ethel?" Louise asked. "Does she know you're leaving?"

"I said good-bye to her this morning, as well as to Viola and to Nia."

"Is that why you wanted to walk into town?" Alice asked.

Ada nodded. "You had your mind on this wedding, so I didn't want to say anything." She started toward the door. "Well, girls, it's time to say *sayonara* so that we can all get on to the next chapters in our lives."

The sisters helped Ada carry her belongings out to her SUV. Ada put her laptop into the passenger front seat, then turned. "That's it." She sucked in a deep breath of air, and then rubbed her arms from the chill. "*Brrr*. I can't wait to feel that Florida sunshine."

"We'll miss you," Louise said. "Please come back to visit any time."

"Yes," Alice said, echoed by Jane.

Ada grinned. "I may just do that. You ladies have a fine setup for yourselves here, and you run a great inn. Oh, I left a little something for that teenager you have got cleaning rooms. She did a wonderful job for me. Kept things clean and tidy but never disturbed my work. There's an envelope on my dresser for her."

"Thank you, Ada," Alice said. "I'm sure Martina will thank you too."

"I hope the wedding tomorrow goes well," she said. "I know you have a lot to do, so I'll skedaddle. You ladies take care, all right? Keep digging into that family history. You never know what else you might find."

She pulled a surprised Louise into a hug, then Jane and, last of all, Alice. She stepped back and grinned at each one in turn, her last gaze resting on Alice as if they shared a special secret. "May you each experience a little romance in your lives."

Before Alice could reply, Ada got into the SUV and started it up. The sisters stood back so that she could pull away safely. She honked, waved a final time and then drove out of sight.

Martina came over later that afternoon for another rehearsal with Louise, and the sisters told her to check the Garden Room's dresser upstairs for a gift from Ada. Martina practically ran back down, a white envelope in her hands.

"Listen to this note," Martina said. "'May your singing always bring you and others great joy.' Isn't that wonderful? And look at this."

She opened the envelope wide so that the sisters could take a peek. Inside was a crisp fifty-dollar bill. Martina beamed.

"You can save it for your trip to Europe," Alice said.

Martina laughed. "I certainly will. I always enjoy the company of Ulysses S. Grant."

Soon after, Louise and Martina headed to the chapel to rehearse. Alice, now without Ada's cell phone, had to rely on the phone in Grace Chapel Inn's reception area. Sure enough, it was not long before Patsy and Polly called with an urgent request for help, and she went back into town.

Jane was alone at the inn in the kitchen, wrapping scallops with bacon for the reception. She had already parboiled a mountain of vegetables to serve with dip, and had made dozens of miniature pastry puffs that she would fill with creamed chicken. The scallops were proving tricky to wrap, however. She did not usually lose her confidence in the kitchen, but she was beginning to question the wisdom of adding this particular item to the menu.

"Hello?"

She thought she heard someone talking in the foyer, but she shrugged it off. *These scallops are making me hear things.*

"Hello!"

The voice sounded more insistent. Suddenly she remembered that their weekend guests were schedule to arrive in the late afternoon.

"Coming!" she yelled, then set down the scallop so that she could wash her hands. She did not want their guests' first impression of their inn hostess to be one inspired by *eau de fish*.

She was still drying her hands on a dishtowel when she entered the foyer. "I'm so sorry I didn't hear you. I was in the kitchen."

A middle-aged couple and three teenagers stood in the foyer, luggage stacked at their feet. The man smiled. "That's all right. We didn't know what the protocol was. We weren't sure whether to ring the bell or just walk on in."

Jane forced a smile, even though her mind was still on the slippery scallops in the kitchen. "You must be . . ."

"Ray Roswell," he said, extending a hand. "This is my wife, Debra, and these are our kids, Jerry, Tony and Connie."

"How do you do?" Jane said, shaking his hand. She turned to Debra, who was smiling as broadly as her husband was. The teenagers seemed unusually cheerful too, and Jane shook each one of their hands as well. "We're so glad that you chose Grace Chapel Inn."

"We found your Web site through the online bed-and-breakfast directory," Connie said.

"We'll be traveling in the area this weekend checking out colleges for Connie," Debra said. "Connie's a junior in high school."

Ray laughed. "We're hoping that she'll choose a college that's fairly near home. We're a close-knit family." He smiled at his wife. "I'm a music minister at a small church in Virginia and the rest of the family sings in the choir."

"How lovely," Jane said. "If your travels don't interfere, we'd love to have you worship with us at Grace Chapel, just across the way. Grace Chapel Inn is run by my sisters and me, and our father used to be the pastor at the chapel until he passed away recently."

"I'm sorry," Debra said.

Jane smiled. "The silver lining was that it brought my sisters and me back together here, and that's when we decided to open our family home as a bed-and-breakfast."

Ray filled out the registration, and Jane escorted the Roswells to the second floor to let them pick out their rooms. Ada's room had not been cleaned yet, so she showed them the other three. Jerry and Tony chose the Sunrise Room, Ray and Debra the Sunset Room, and Connie the Symphony. After she had explained the details of Grace Chapel Inn, Jane excused herself. "One of the young women from town is getting married tomorrow, and my sisters and I are helping with the wedding. I'm catering the food for the reception, and I have to get back to the kitchen. If you need anything, you can find me there."

The Roswells seemed to understand, so Jane headed back to the scallops and bacon, determined to wrap the slippery seafood once and for all.

Chapter Eighteen

That evening, Alex's parents hosted the rehearsal dinner at Zachary's supper club for the members of the wedding party. Louise, Alice and Jane were so exhausted from the day's activities that they were happy that they had not been invited. Saturday would be another busy day followed, of course, by the wedding in the evening.

Jane finished her catering preparations, with everything ready for the reception and stored in either Grace Chapel Inn's refrigerator or the one at the Good Apple Bakery. She had already arranged with the ANGELs to help with moving the food to the church.

Alice had volunteered to cook dinner that night for an exhausted Jane. Since they were all so weary, she made a simple meal of grilled cheese sandwiches and canned soup.

"This reminds me of when I was a little girl," Jane said, biting into her sandwich while they sat at the kitchen table. "You and Louise used to make me this meal for lunch."

"It reminds me of Mother too," Louise said. "She taught Alice and me how to grill the sandwiches and heat a can of soup when we were quite young."

"This was also one of Father's favorite lunches," Alice said. "I cannot remember how many times I would bring a tray to him in the library while he prepared his weekly sermon or read the latest theological journal."

"Sometimes simple meals can be the most satisfying," Jane said.

"This wedding was supposed to be simple, but it has turned into quite a to-do," Louise observed.

"Any wedding, no matter how small, can certainly be a lot of work," Jane said. "And it definitely involves a lot of details."

The phone rang. The sisters looked at one another, each too tired to answer. "You cooked, Alice. I'll go," Louise finally said.

"I'm closest," Alice said.

Jane smiled. "We're quite a bunch of slugs if it has come to this."

Alice lifted the receiver to the kitchen's extension and voiced her greetings. She was met with an immediate half sob, half wail, which she could barely discern as belonging to Vera Humbert.

"Slow down," she said. "What's wrong, Vera?"

The sobbing intensified, and Alice had to hold the receiver away from her ear. Louise and Jane glanced at each other in bewilderment.

Alice held the phone closer again. "Now take a deep breath and tell me what's wrong."

Louise and Jane watched as Alice's expression changed to something like horror, then sympathy. "I'm sure that it will be fine, Vera. Everyone is under a lot of stress, that's all. I know that you want Polly to have a beautiful day tomorrow. We will all do our best to maintain our kindest, most loving nature, all right? Get a good night's sleep, and I'll see you in the morning."

She hung up and Jane nearly pounced on her. "What was that all about?"

Alice sighed as she sank back into her chair. "Apparently Alex's mother took several swipes at Vera again tonight at the rehearsal dinner."

"I'll be glad when that woman's out of Acorn Hill," Jane said. "I hope she doesn't cause trouble for Polly later on."

"She didn't seem to have any disagreement with Polly," Louise noted. "Just Vera."

"She's probably just nervous about tomorrow, as we all are," Alice said. "Goodness knows, I am glad we're not in the regular wedding business. It's hard on the emotions."

"Not to mention the body," Jane said, stifling a yawn. "Let's clean up, then take Alice's advice and get a good night's sleep ourselves. Tomorrow will be downright frantic."

Jane's prediction came true, and more than once Alice had to remind herself to be thankful that weddings were scarce in Acorn Hill. She loved the visual pageantry of the pretty dresses and, of course, the solemnity of the ceremony, but she didn't think she could endure it on a regular basis. Especially when it seemed that so much conspired to go wrong that day.

Alice woke just before dawn to the sound of rain. "Oh no," she murmured. Normally she would have gone back to sleep, but she was so upset at the thought of Polly and Alex's day ruined that she put on her robe and headed for the kitchen.

To her surprise, Jane and Louise were already there, sipping coffee, also clad in their bathrobes. "Don't tell me you couldn't sleep either," Jane said.

"I heard the rain," Alice said, slipping into a chair.

"Me too," Louise said. "I am worried about Polly's wedding day being spoiled by the rain, but I'm also worried about the organ. It doesn't seem to play as well when the weather is poor."

"And I am worried about my chicken puffs," Jane said.

"Surely we can protect them long enough to carry them from our oven to the Assembly Room," Alice said.

Jane shook her head. "I'm worried about the moisture in the air affecting them. I don't want them to be soggy."

She handed a cup of tea to Alice, who sipped on it thoughtfully. Louise set down her own cup. "I am too agitated to sit here. I'm going to get dressed and go to the chapel to check on the organ."

"Would you like some company?" Alice asked.

"No, thank you," Louise said, grim-faced, now heading upstairs.

Jane made a simple breakfast of English muffins and jam for herself and Alice. Then they prepared a fancier breakfast for their guests. Still the rain came down.

The phone rang, and Alice answered it, certain that her help was needed somewhere. Vera was on the phone, and before she could begin wailing about the weather, Alice cut in. "Now, Vera, I'm sure that everything will be fine."

"What? You mean the rain?" Vera said. "I'm not worried about that."

"You're not?" Alice was stunned.

"Heavens, no. Fred woke up and said that his arthritis was not bothering him in the least, so he knew that it would be just a short rain. He says that it will end soon and the sun will come out and dry up the puddles."

Alice knew that Fred did seem to possess a talent for weather prognostication, and she hoped that this was not the time that he was proved wrong. "I hope so, Vera. Meanwhile, is there anything I can do for you or Polly?"

"No, thank you," Vera said cheerfully. "I just called to ask you to pray for us today and for the wedding tonight."

"Are things better between you and Francie Neal?" Alice could not help asking, though she doubted that the two women had seen each other since the rehearsal dinner. They could not have found time to patch their differences. Still, Vera sounded unusually happy.

"Nothing's new," she said. "I just decided to take your advice and pray for a beautiful day for my daughter and future son-in-law. And that God would bless Francie too. Somehow, that has made all the difference in my attitude. No matter what she says to me, I'm not going to let her spoil the day. I have never heard her say an unkind word to Polly, so I will focus on that."

"Good for you," Alice said. "If you need me, please call the inn. Otherwise, I will be at the chapel when you and the wedding party arrive, in case you need last-minute errands there."

"Thank you." Vera paused. "You've been such a help to me during this emotional time. I don't know how I would have made it without you, Alice. Either during all this wedding planning or throughout all the years we've known each other, for that matter."

Alice smiled. Vera was her dearest friend. It was easy to follow the Bible's admonition for a friend to love at all times. "I am always happy to help in any way I can," she said. "But especially today. Polly will have a beautiful wedding."

"Yes, she will," Vera said, then said good-bye.

Once again, Alice was amazed by the calm confidence in her friend's voice.

Louise found the chapel organ to be in the condition that she had feared. When she tried to play, the old pipe organ wheezed and gasped like an emphysema patient, worse than it had ever sounded before. It would be impossible to play for the wedding.

She curled her hands into fists over the keys. Why did this have to happen today? Polly would be so disappointed.

Louise determined not to dwell on the negative. This was a day of joy.

"Lord, nothing happens without Your permission," she whispered. "So I have to trust that You have a plan in this. All I ask is that this not spoil the wedding today."

Feeling better for having prayed, Louise rose. She touched the organ briefly as if it were a sick friend, then moved to the piano. She would rehearse there. Polly and Alex would have her best talent and music on their wedding day, even if it was not performed on Grace Chapel's best instrument.

When she returned to the inn, the Roswells were finishing their breakfast in the dining room. When she stopped to say hello, Ray Roswell frowned. "Is something wrong?"

"You do look down," Debra said.

Louise was taken aback that these virtual strangers could read her so well. She *was* still disheartened about the organ. She briefly explained about the pipe organ.

Debra and Ray smiled at each other. "You know, I play the organ," Ray said.

"I know that you are a music minister, but I didn't know that you played."

"I grew up playing the organ, and one of my hobbies is pipe organs. I have a friend who rebuilds and sells them as well."

"I wish he were here," Louise said. "Perhaps he would have some advice."

"I've learned a thing or two from him over the years. Would you mind if I took a look at it?"

"Not at all, but I do not want to interrupt your plans for the day."

"The kids and I can make ourselves comfy here," Debra said. "We've finished our breakfast and weren't planning to leave for a while, anyway. Let Ray have a look."

"Very well," Louise said, reminding herself not to get her hopes up. "The chapel is right across the way."

⚭

Alice waited all morning for Vera or Polly to call, but the phone was silent. Feeling nervous about the arrangements, she made a final check with her ANGELs about decorating the chapel and the Assembly Room and delivering the food to the reception. Sarah Roberts' father had a delivery van, and he agreed to pick up the food, with two other parents riding along to make sure the platters and boxes did not topple over on the trip to the chapel. They would also arrange the food in the reception area while the ceremony was in progress upstairs.

Alice met the ANGELs at the chapel at eleven o'clock. She knew that Louise and Ray Roswell had left for the chapel some time before to check on the organ, but when she got there, they were gone. She shook her head sadly, concluding that they had been unable to make repairs.

Along with the arriving ANGELs, Alice found Craig Tracy unloading the supplies that he had arranged to rent for Polly and Alex's ceremony and reception.

In the sanctuary, the girls looked through what he had brought. "Where are the flowers?" Ashley Moore asked.

"Yeah, I want to see the bride's bouquet," Jenny Snyder said.

Alice smiled. She knew that each one of the preteens was dreaming about her own wedding day, and along with a wedding dress, the bride's bouquet was a top attraction for these girls.

Craig Tracy winked at them, as if he understood their feelings too. "I'll bring the flowers over later. I want them to stay as fresh as possible. Take a look at this unity candle, though," he said, holding it up for the girls.

They clustered around the round white candle, personalized with the day's date, a cross with two superimposed wedding rings, and Polly and Alex's names.

Jenny wrinkled her nose. "What do they use this for?"

"It goes here, see?" Craig showed them a silver floor stand for three candles. The larger round candle fit in the middle and a white taper fit on either side. "The bride and groom each light an individual candle on the side, and then with the flame from those, together they light the larger one."

"It symbolizes the unity of their marriage," Alice said. "They are two people joining together as one."

The girls sighed, and all thoughts of the flowers seemed temporarily forgotten. "Do you have anything else that's as romantic?" Ashley asked, her eyes dreamy.

Craig smiled. "I'm afraid not. What I do have is a bunch of large white bows that I understand you ladies are going to attach to the end of the pews. And this aisle runner."

The girls studied the heavy white cloth roll, imagining it unfurled the length of the chapel for the wedding procession. "Ooh, that looks like something for a princess," one of the girls said.

"Or a queen," another added.

"Let's place it on the floor last," Alice said, "just in case we may still have a bit of mud from the rain on our feet. We can start on the bows."

Craig arranged the unity candle, tapers and stand beside the altar. "I'll take the reception stuff downstairs," he said, "and when you're ready to work there, it'll be right at hand."

"Thank you," Alice said. "I'm sure these bows will keep us busy for a while."

As they worked, the girls began to chatter about the large white satin bows that they affixed to the ends of the pews. When they were finished, they stood back to admire their work.

"They didn't seem like much when Mr. Tracy showed them to us," Ashley said, "but I think they look nice now."

"Polly said that she didn't want many decorations in here," Alice said. "She didn't want to ruin the beauty of the chapel's simplicity, especially the stained glass windows."

Ashley glanced at the windows as Alice spoke, and then squealed. "Miss Howard, it's stopped raining."

Alice turned. Sunlight streamed through the stained glass, warming the colors and the inside of the chapel. She smiled, marveling at the accuracy of Fred's prediction.

"It's beautiful," she said, her heart lifting with joy. "Let's put down this aisle runner. It should cover the length of the chapel's usual red one, all the way from the steps at the altar to the back of the church. Two of you hold the runner here at the altar, and two of you carefully unroll it down the aisle to the back of the church. I'll help out by moving from the outer aisles between the pews to straighten."

They all took off their shoes to make sure they didn't leave any prints. When the cloth was in place, they met back at the altar. "And now, for a finishing touch, here's what we need to do," Alice said, knowing her girls would enjoy this decoration. "We have to sprinkle these rose petals mixed with tissue paper confetti up the length of the aisle."

"Shouldn't a flower girl do that?" Ashley piped up. "I thought she always did it just before the wedding party comes out."

Alice shook her head. "Polly said she wanted everybody to walk on these for her wedding day. She wants everyone she loves to be honored."

Again, the girls sighed, and they eagerly set to work.

Louise and Ray heard Alice and the girls decorating in the chapel, but they were in the basement examining the blower to the organ. "The leathers from the blower are quite dry and brittle, as you can see," Louise said.

"Yes." Ray said, concentrating as he examined them. "I can see several holes." He reached up and touched them gently, then turned to Louise. "Do you have any duct tape in the church?"

"I think there is a tool kit down here somewhere," Louise said. "Perhaps there is some in there."

She rummaged around and found a kit that Rev. Thompson used to make minor repairs in the church. Opening the lid, she was delighted to find a nearly full roll of duct tape.

"Ah, the repairman's best friend," Ray said, taking it from her hands. He smiled. "Perhaps this will do the trick. At least to get you through the wedding and maybe even longer, if we're lucky."

"You mean you're going to use that tape to fix the holes?"

"I intend to try." Ray smiled, and then went to work. He measured out lengths of tape, and Louise cut them with scissors she found in the kit. While they worked, Ray talked about some of the organs he and his friend had helped restore or replace.

"I'll give you my card before my family and I leave," Ray said. "If you ever want my friend to do a thorough evaluation and recommendation, you can contact me."

He stepped back. "There. That's the best I can do. Let's go upstairs and see if this beauty still has a little life in her."

The sanctuary looked beautiful with the decorations Alice and her girls had added. But Louise took little notice of the bows and confetti-sprinkled white aisle runner. She headed straight for the back toward the organ and sat down, holding her breath.

She played a full chord in her favorite key, E flat. The organ did not sound as majestic as it had in bygone days, but the sound was a vast improvement over its normal gasping of late. She launched into Mozart and found that the tonal quality held.

Louise turned to Ray, who stood beaming at her side. "You are an answer to prayer," she said.

"I'm glad that I was," he said. "And now I will leave you to your rehearsing. I must get back to my family so that we can begin our college visits."

Louise thanked him. After he left, she pulled one organ draw knob after another, and then pressed the keys to make a joyful noise to the Lord.

All too soon, the bridal party arrived at the chapel with their dresses carefully covered in garment bags. Alice showed them to the vesting room, where they would change. Patsy Ley took charge of making sure that every girl looked perfect.

It had been a long time since Alice had been around a group of college girls. She delighted in hearing them giggle with happiness as they dressed, fixed their hair and put on makeup.

Vera stood to the side, watching Polly and her maid of honor, Jean, with pride. Jean helped her older sister apply makeup, since Polly declared her hands were shaking too much to apply eyeliner and mascara.

Alice slipped an arm around Vera and watched the girls with her. "I remember when they used to play in the sandbox together. One of them would get mad at the other and throw sand. Then they would both run home crying."

Vera nodded, her eyes wet. "They are both so beautiful, and I don't think I could be any happier."

"I'm not surprised," said a voice behind them.

Alice and Vera turned to see Francie Neal. She was lovely and dignified in a pearl gray silk suit, looking exceptionally trim next to the more matronly Vera in her mauve dress.

"Excuse me?" Vera said. "Did you say something, Francie?"

Francie studied the Humbert sisters primping at the mirror. "I only said that I'm not surprised that you're so happy. You're not losing your daughter the way that I'm losing my son."

Alice felt a slow warmth creep into her cheeks. What a thoughtless thing to say.

Vera, however, remained calm. "Why, what do you mean, Francie?"

She shrugged. "You know the old expression. 'A son's a son till he gains a wife, but a daughter's a daughter for all of her life.'" Her lips quivered, and she looked as though she were trying hard not to cry.

Suddenly Alice understood. Francie Neal was not angry with Vera; she was worried about losing her son to marriage. Perhaps she felt she would never see him again or that he would not pay attention to his own family now that he was marrying into a new one. Alice felt her annoyance with Francie melt into compassion.

Vera put her arm around Francie. "Polly is so lucky to be marrying Alex," she said in a soft voice. "He is a wonderful man because you have raised him to be one. She has told me often about how much he respects and admires you, and she feels the same way."

"Really?" Francie said.

Vera nodded. "Fred and I couldn't be happier with Alex. You have raised a wonderful son."

Francie burst into tears and embraced Vera. "I'm happy he's marrying Polly too, but it's difficult to let him go. I used to hold his hand while we crossed the street and I used to tie his shoes . . . I know this is silly. He's been an adult for a long time, but it's hit home hard lately, with him marrying *and* joining the Army. We don't know whether he's going to be sent overseas or . . ."

"I know," Vera said, patting her gently. "Fred and I have been praying regularly for Alex. We've been praying since both our girls were little for the future husbands we knew they would one day marry."

Francie stepped back and wiped her eyes with a handkerchief. "That is so comforting, Vera. We're happy that Alex is marrying into your family too. I know I haven't been the nicest person lately. I'm so sorry that I've been rude."

"I understand," Vera said, "and it's all right, Francie. Let's start off new, okay?"

Francie nodded, then gave Vera another hug.

Alice smiled. Weddings were meant to be beginnings of new unions, and they also bring reconciliation.

Soon Fred knocked on the vesting room door to announce that they were ready to begin, and Alice headed for the chapel. An usher escorted her to the pew where Jane sat, while Louise played prelude music on the organ. Alice looked at Jane in astonishment. "I thought the organ wouldn't play," she whispered.

"Our guest Ray Roswell apparently knows a thing or two about pipe organs," Jane whispered back.

Alice nudged Jane, nodding toward the chapel's door. An usher was seating Vera, which signified that the wedding was about to begin. Rev. Thompson took his place at the altar, and Alex stood beaming not far from him.

Alice turned toward the chapel door. The bridesmaids were lined up to proceed, with Kimberly Neal at the front and Jean, the maid of honor, at the back. Behind them all was Polly in her beautiful bridal dress, her hand on Fred Humbert's arm. Fred looked dignified, if a bit nervous, in his tuxedo.

Louise segued into Clarke's "Trumpet Voluntary," and each usher paired with a bridesmaid to walk down the aisle to the altar. The dresses sewn by Sylvia were beautiful; each one had a floor-length velvet skirt, with each top made of satin in a different pastel color.

When Jean and her escort reached the altar, Vera rose and turned toward the door. The guests also stood, and Louise began the traditional wedding march.

Polly and Fred proceeded down the white runner sprinkled with rose petals and confetti. At the altar, Polly turned and faced Alex, their faces lighting with love for each other.

Alice had tears in her eyes. Jane glanced over at her and silently handed her a tissue. Alice dabbed her eyes with it several times during the ceremony, especially during the solos. Martina was dressed in pale blue chiffon, her hair curled and arranged with a matching pale blue ribbon. Her eyes were minus their usual heavy black makeup, and she looked beautiful. She sang "The Lord's Prayer" perfectly. When again she soloed on "All I Ask of You," Alice had to stop herself from applauding.

The ceremony was beautiful. Rev. Thompson smiled as he asked Polly and Alex to say their vows and to light the unity candle. Then Alex gently folded back the blusher veil and kissed his wife.

Before Alice knew it, Jane whispered to her, "Come help me downstairs in the assembly room. Carlene will keep them busy with wedding photos, and we can make sure everything is ready to go for the reception."

Jane had checked on the delivery of the food and punch before she went to the ceremony, but she wanted to make certain there were no last-minute surprises. The buffet had been arranged prettily on a long table, and the wedding cake sat on its own table, looking like a beautiful sculpture.

Alice was overwhelmed with the lovely display. She had last seen the room when she and the ANGELs decorated, but that was before the parents brought over and arranged Jane's culinary offerings.

"Everything looks perfect, Jane," she said. "What are in all these warming dishes?"

"Sesame chicken, mini Maryland crab cakes, artichokes stuffed with Boursin cheese, and my favorite, scallops wrapped in bacon," Jane said proudly. "The chicken puffs are on that heated tray." Jane looked around again. "You and your girls did a wonderful job. The lattices transform the room, and Craig's rose topiaries are lovely."

They heard voices in the doorway, and Jane quickly donned an apron, ready to replenish the food and sparkling fruit punch as needed. Alice went to look for Louise. When she found her, she said over the growing din of laughter and conversation, "What happened with the organ?"

"Ray Roswell fixed it with duct tape," Louise said, smiling. "It is only a temporary fix, but it worked beautifully." She patted Alice on the arm. "There's Martina. I must congratulate her."

Alice and Louise headed toward the young woman, but her father reached her first. "Marti," he said, tears in his eyes. "Your singing was wonderful. That was the best, honey."

"I love you, Daddy," she whispered, then spontaneously hugged him. Alice and Louise backed away, unwilling to interrupt the tender moment.

The beaming, newly married couple cut the wedding cake, and then, all too soon, it was time for them to leave for their honeymoon. Polly, having changed into a rose wool traveling suit, stood at one end of the room. "I'm going to throw my bouquet," she said. "Every unmarried woman must come over here."

All the young unmarried women—including Nia Komonos, Jean, the bridesmaids and Martina—bunched in close and pretended to jostle each other to get the best position for catching the bouquet. Polly turned her back and tossed it over her shoulder. Amid whoops and hollers, Martina caught it, glanced at it in surprise, and then tossed it back into the crowd of young women. Nia Komonos leaped up like a basketball player, snagged it, and held it close. "Sorry, ladies, if Martina doesn't want it, it's mine," she said smiling.

Everyone laughed.

The crowd broke up and Alice found herself next to Martina. "Didn't you want the bouquet?" she asked.

Martina shook her head. "I'm too young to think of marriage. Besides, Dad didn't look too happy when I caught it. He's not crazy about my even having boyfriends."

Alice smiled. "You have lots of time, Martina. I hope you will keep in touch with my sisters and me after you stop working for us."

"Oh, I will, Miss Howard," Martina said. "I definitely will."

Outside, everyone tossed birdseed at Alex and Polly as they headed into a limousine that was to take them to the Philadelphia airport. The Howard sisters stayed to chat with the stragglers, but it was clear that everyone was tired. The reception wound to a quick close, and after helping Jane pack up the leftover food, the Howard sisters headed home themselves.

They gathered in the library for a moment to recap the wedding. "It was a beautiful wedding," Alice said, "and I'm proud of you both for your creativity, talent and hard work."

Jane sank into a chair. "The same goes for you. You and the ANGELs saved the day." She sighed. "I know I'll have to rinse all those chafing dishes and plates before the rental company comes for them on Monday, but right now I'm relaxing." She slipped out of her high heels and rubbed her arches. "*Ahhh.*"

"I think I'll take a warm bath and head for bed," Louise said. She glanced guiltily at Alice. "Do you have that Portia Keyes book we got at the book signing?"

"Louie!" Jane said, pretending shock. "Don't tell me you want to read fiction."

"Ada Murdoch was one of our guests," Louise said, raising an eyebrow. "That is the least I owe her."

"I think you'll enjoy it very much," Alice said. "I was going to read it myself, but you can have it first."

Jane sniffed. "I told you romance novels were good."

Alice slipped off her own shoes and leaned back in her chair, yawning. "Who would have thought that there was the making of a romance novel in our family?"

"Do you mean Father and Mother?" Louise asked.

Alice shook her head. "No, I mean the Berrys and the Howards knowing each other all those years, and then their families joining nearly a hundred years later."

"Bringing them together truly was a blessing from God," Louise said.

"And now He has blessed Polly and Alex," Alice said.

Jane reached out and took her sisters' hands. "And He has blessed us."

Louise smiled. "Indeed."

Chocolate Dipped Orange Cookies
YIELD THREE DOZEN

½ cup butter (softened)
½ cup sugar
1 large egg yolk
2 tablespoons frozen orange juice
    concentrate, thawed
2 teaspoons orange peel, grated
1½ cups flour
½ teaspoon baking powder
4 ounces semisweet chocolate, melted

Beat butter and sugar until creamy. Mix in egg yolk, orange juice concentrate and orange peel. Mix in flour and baking powder, and beat well. Place dough on plastic wrap and shape into rectangle about ¾ inch thick. Wrap and chill until firm. Set oven at 350 degrees. Cut dough into ¾-inch strips and roll into rods about the width of a finger. Cut these into two-inch lengths and place about two inches apart on greased cookie sheet. Bake for about ten minutes until golden brown. Cool on wire racks. Melt the chocolate and dip tip of each cooled cookie into the chocolate. Place on waxed paper and chill until chocolate sets.

About the Author

The late Jane Orcutt is the best-selling author of thirteen novels, including *All the Tea in China*. She has been nominated for the RITA award twice. A proud wife and mother of two sons, she lived in Fort Worth, Texas.